THE RENEGADE

Chris Robinson was born in 1956, in Northwich, Cheshire. He grew up on a council estate and graduated in 1988 from Crewe and Alsager College of Higher Education with a degree in Creative Arts / Combined Studies. In between these years, he was a trainee reporter and photographer, and moved to Germany when Margaret Thatcher came to power, finding employment with a US military community newspaper. He has three older brothers, a younger sister, and is the son of factory worker parents. He co-authored the book *The Road to Recovery* (2011) with Alan Boden, and wrote *Can't Pay, Won't Pay* (2023). *The Renegade* is his first novel.

'The world is in flames, and the Russians are at the gate. Not the 2020s, but the 1940s – at a time when Britain and the USSR were supposedly on the same side, much to the dismay of some within the hierarchy who would prefer to do business with Hitler. Meanwhile those in the firing line face a desperate battle to survive. From the frozen Steppes of Stalingrad to the treacherous clubs of Mayfair, Major Nikolai Solov encounters danger at every turn – and finds himself questioning both the nature of his enemy, and his own political idealism. Chris Robinson's epic and powerful novel is a timely reminder that cynicism and deception are nothing new – particularly in a time of war.'

Mark Piggott, author of *Fire Horses*

'Fast-paced, unpretentious and exciting. This reads like a Tarantino pulp fiction of the Eastern Front! One can imagine Pavel having his own screwed up copy in his satchel. Great stuff!'

Lee Garratt, author of *Where the Skylark Sings*

'A story about spiritual exile - Solov having no home or state to return to, but finding solace and contentment among fellow misfits. The underlying message is that belonging isn't a place or a flag, but the people we stand beside. Chris Robinson shows us real unity.'

Martin Mellett, author of *The North Star*

'Set at the height of the Second World War, *The Renegade* is a fast-moving thriller that draws you into a world of advanced guerrilla training, Russian sleeper agents, and the conflicts between ideology and truth at a time of conflict. At the centre of the novel is Major Nikolai Solov, a character that seems to jump out of the pages of a Graham Greene or John le Carré story: courageous and possessed of a joie de vivre and yet also vulnerable and easily betrayed. *The Renegade* is not just a story of action and bravery at a time of global conflict but, on a smaller, individual level, a redemptive, timeless story of one man's search for justice and love.'

David Stephens, author of *The Disappeared*

'This book hit like a shot in the dark - sudden, sharp and impossible to ignore. *The Renegade* drags you through the wreckage of war, betrayal and identity with unrelenting force. It's not just a story about survival - it's a story about what you lose in order to keep breathing. Brutal and brilliant.'

Tony Tak, ex-London market maker

'The line "They only know how to laugh and kill." What was once a derogatory statement concerning rogue elements in an army has become the standard among US mercenaries and the IDF in Israel / Palestine. What a pitiful state we're in, but at least Nikolai Solov, a 20th century Russian, displays some of that old, seemingly long-lost nobility and virtue.'

Jeff Weston, author of *Mutler*

'I stopped and thought of the human character in different situations when I read "You're either bragging or whining." Robinson takes us to the centre of war – its smell, its discourse, its pointless exploitation of men.'

Ade Kolade, ex-researcher at The University of Manchester

'We all have back stories. We all have pain inside us which knows it cannot partake in the daily ritual of life without upsetting or disturbing the perfunctory status quo. Robinson, thank god, shows us the tinges, the hues, the subtly-altered aftermath of cruel engagement.'

Andrew Routledge, a man with a big brain

'"They were stuffy and choking with privilege." Robinson consistently fills our heads with great narrative and barnstorming dialogue. He is a pleasure to read. In some ways he's the Oliver Anthony of fiction.'

Matthew Mason, the most forthright bloke in Britain

'*The Renegade* offers an escape from life, but also the deep, muddy, confusion of war and its perilous testing of men.'

Jessica F, album Peachy, *youtube.com/@JessicaFMusic*

Chris Robinson

THE

RENEGADE

THINKWELL BOOKS

Edited by Jeff Weston.

Cover design by Alejandro Baigorri

Interior formatting by Rachel Bostwick.

Published by Thinkwell Books, U.K.

First printing edition 2025.

For Leon Trotsky

(1879 – 1940)

- a true revolutionary

"They picked up a file and wondered:

'Who's been a naughty boy?' Then looked

under 'S' and found me."

- Nikolai Solov

TABLE OF CONTENTS

ONE

S talingrad. January 28, 1943. Hell frozen over. Across the hard-packed, ice-bound fields, avoiding the more treacherous roads, Pavel rode his motorcycle.

On every trip, he ran an invisible gauntlet. He never knew whether a German counterattack would engulf him or not. He kept his rifle strapped across his back for reassurance. He feared the image of the films he had seen back in Voronezh, what the fascists had done to prisoners of war. The way they were starved to the point they needed no guards but were pointed in the direction of the nearest field kitchen. He'd even heard talk of prisoners eating their dead comrades to stay alive, but that was only talk.

He pulled his machine to a halt at the next hill, rear wheel skidding under him. There were no Germans waiting for him, only a few trees next to vehicle tracks that had churned the ice. He knew the field post he was looking for was there, and a possible hot mug of tea and, if he was lucky, a shot of vodka.

Pavel came to a halt on the edge of the first group of tents housed beneath a sprawling, white tarpaulin stretched amongst the trees. The post was a distance from the river Volga and it formed a link in the communications for the troop movements that now surrounded the city. It was part of a rifle division. Pavel saw food being prepared but no fires were allowed yet, in daylight. The communications tent buzzed with the static of radio talk. Soldiers sat around talking or silently cleaning their weapons. A sergeant wiped his hands on an oily rag while he worked under the bonnet of a truck. Pavel propped up his motorbike, nodded at the sergeant who shook his head at the engine. An officer stood at the entrance to the first tent and Pavel snapped to, then grabbed the two canvas satchels that were strapped to his pillion.

"Peaceful trip, comrade?" asked the officer.

"Yes, sir," Pavel said. "Getting better by the day. Pretty quiet around here?"

"That'll change in about forty minutes from now. The next barrages are due." He smiled.

"Ours or theirs, sir?"

"Ours, of course. You don't seriously think the fascists in there have anything heavy to throw at us, do you? They'll be running out of earth to dig into." The officer smiled again as he took the satchels.

Pavel followed him into the tent where all eyes briefly looked up at him then got on with their work. The officer emptied the first then the second satchel into a large basket by a desk where the despatches would be registered.

Pavel took a letter from inside his tunic: "Sir, could this be registered first? It's a 'deliver by hand'." The officer frowned and looked at the envelope.

"Major N. Solov. Fine." He laid it on the desk, franked it and quickly handed it back without looking up.

"Do you know where I might find the comrade Major, sir?" Pavel said, eyeing a steaming mug of tea on the officer's desk.

"He's at sector HQ, last I heard. That place is a madhouse. Down the road, head for the riverbank, you can ask the way there. It's easy."

Pavel stuffed the letter back, buttoned his tunic, looked again at the tea and saluted the officer. On his motorbike again, he regained the road. Ahead, he saw what he thought was a dark sky, but it was black smoke. He began to make out the crumbled skyline of the Stalingrad suburbs. The road's right turn was guarded by some infantry. Trucks were filing off from where several launches were unloading wounded troops from across the east bank of the Volga. Curving away to the right, shrouded in mist and smoke, was the rubble of the city that looked like nothing on earth. The trucks were cutting up the ice and snow, near the riverbank, as they struggled to find the road.

"Comrade?" Pavel pulled up to a corporal who was directing traffic. "Where's the command post?"

The corporal looked at him.

"There's only one direction. Follow the trucks." He gestured with a gloved hand.

Five minutes down the road, alongside the river, Pavel weaved carefully between the trucks that snaked along, almost bumper to bumper. Some of them carried troops, sullenly staring at him. They were from the east, Tartars or Mongols. Some of them managed a wave and a smile.

Pavel passed by four checkpoints that waved him through. He was glad to get away from the convoy. It slowed him down. He pulled up again near an artillery unit dug in deep away from the road, under camouflage nets. He counted around five guns or so. A sergeant told him sector HQ was right here, behind them. He dismounted. The sergeant asked him for a cigarette and looked disappointed and puzzled when the despatch rider told him he didn't smoke.

"Old enough to shave but you don't smoke?"

Pavel followed him through the battery toward a half-destroyed farmhouse invisible from the road. The half of the building that was destroyed had more netting over it and served as the entrance. Again, there were more banks of radios, tables with maps spread across them. Pavel was ushered inside where another officer looked at the letter, then at him.

"Major Solov is across the river in the city, not far. He's due to return...soon, I think," he said, looking at a pocket watch. Helpfully, he looked at one of the maps. "He's on the edge. You'll see an old tram station as you follow the road when you hit the east bank. You'll come past a main crossroads. There'll be men there. Ask them."

Pavel could see the city now or, at least, what was left of it and could hear the distant rattle of gunfire. Riding carefully downhill, toward the bank where the launches were already beginning to load up supplies to take across, he had to negotiate with one of the crewmen to get a ride over. The crewman helped him to push his motorbike aboard. As soon as the launch was loaded up, they set out.

It was just as chaotic on the east bank when they landed, but Pavel managed to make his way into the first of the battered city. There stood the remains of the tram station. One of the trams had been pulled into the middle of the street, filled with bricks, twisted girders and masonry. Ripped electric cables sprouted out of the shell craters in the street. He passed some soldiers as they walked alongside him, troops from the east again, used to the Siberian winter. One of them laughed, raised his rifle in the air, and shouted: "Stalin!" His fellow soldiers laughed with him. Further along, by the doorway of a shattered garage, Pavel spotted two white Russian soldiers.

"Never mind them, comrade, they only know how to laugh and kill."

"They know how to die too," said the other.

"Got any post for us?"

"Sorry, no," Pavel said. "You know where I can find Major Solov?"

"Solov? Sure. He's about a hundred metres ahead of us. He should be back shortly. See those three apartments with no roof? He's somewhere across the street, on the other side."

"Thanks. I'll go see."

"Wait, soldier. You better wait. We've got another salvo in a few minutes."

"Comrade," Pavel said. "I just need to deliver a letter to him, then I'm out of this shithole."

"Oh, here it comes…" and the rest of the man's words were drowned in the deadly scream of artillery, let loose behind them and Pavel steered quickly into the garage with the others. Behind him, the other troops had already left the street and taken cover in the tram station. The ground shook as dust fell in streams from the ceiling, bits of masonry tumbled down. His motorcycle fell on its side, its front wheel turning. The explosions began to move away towards the city centre where the fascist pockets of resistance were receiving their latest pounding. In the darkness of the garage, Pavel could hear cursing in between the explosions.

"Someone should tell those fucking gunners to stop using our own men for target practice!"

Outside, the troops were back on the street, dusting themselves down, calling to each other. Nobody was hurt.

"If you want to find Solov, you'd better go now."

Another explosion sounded not too far away.

"That's a mine! Someone's stepped on a fucking booby trap," said one of the soldiers in the garage. He grabbed a pair of binoculars from his companion. Pavel struggled to pick up his heavy machine.

"It's Major Solov's party. I think he's got trouble. Let's get over there. You can come too, son," he said to Pavel. "Leave your bike, it'll never make it over the rubble."

Pavel let his motorbike fall again, reluctantly. He followed the soldiers out of the garage and saw the Eastern troops follow them while pausing to slide his rifle from his back and fumbled with it as he ran in a crouch behind the others. Pavel wasn't used to this. He'd relied on his bike for too long, so the others left him behind. They reached the shelled-out apartment block and made their way to the front windows that faced the street on the other side. They saw four men standing in the middle of the roadway. A short distance from them was the crumpled body of a soldier in the middle of the street, his uniform still smoking, the one who had stepped on the mine.

"Major Solov!" someone yelled.

"Stay back!" came the order. "Stay where you are! We've lost one man already."

"That's Major Solov," one of the soldiers from the garage told Pavel. Solov was a metre or so from their side of the street.

Behind him, his three men were on the other side. The dead soldier lay between them.

Solov called to them: "I'll retrace my steps, stay still." Solov turned, placed a foot on his last footprints and made his way toward his men. He unstrapped his steel helmet, revealing a clean-shaven head. He leaned forward and gently threw the helmet somewhere between them into the street.

"You do the same so you'll have some stepping stones," said Solov. As the other men's helmets hit the ground, they all faced away expecting an explosion, but none came.

"Alright, Litinov," said Solov, "you first. Use your comrade's body. He won't mind."

The nervous soldier crept forward and stepped onto the helmets - one, two, three - onto the dead soldier, and grabbed Solov's hand to safety, then followed Solov's steps to the apartment block. The next soldier advanced confidently. He stepped onto the helmets, almost lost his balance on his comrade's body, but landed onto Solov's footprints as his major grabbed his hand…just in time to meet a sniper's bullet that tore into his back and exited his chest.

Solov held his arm to stop him from falling backwards.

"Hold on!" Solov yelled.

The soldier's legs buckled. Solov fell backwards as the soldier hit the ground. No explosion came. His dead body now formed a better bridge with the other. It was useless to try and locate the sniper. They all knew that.

"Covering fire!" someone yelled and a volley peppered approximately where the shot came from as the third soldier skipped across the helmets, his dead comrades' bodies, and ran to the apartment block with Solov. They made their way back toward the tram station.

Pavel approached Solov with the letter. "Major Nikolai Solov, sir?"

Solov glanced down at Pavel, then the letter.

"I know this isn't a good time, sir, but…"

"In this place, no time is a good time," he said.

TWO

Back at sector HQ that night, Nikolai Solov entered the relative warmth of the bivouac he shared with his friend and comrade, Captain Leonid Vatutin. He was greeted by the offer of a Turkish cigarette from his fellow intelligence/ reconnaissance officer who he had known since the summer the war began. Vatutin was younger than Solov, though his raven hair was greying at the sides. The right sleeve of his tunic was pinned across his chest. He had lost his arm at the beginning of the Polish campaign in '39. Nevertheless, this had not prevented him from being in the thick of the fighting when the Germans invaded two years later.

He had been a staff officer and one of the tens of thousands of troops left behind and cut off once the Nazi blitzkrieg had thrust forward across the steppes and encircled whole army groups. Like so many others, like Solov himself, he had regrouped with other soldiers who had also wandered around the countryside for weeks and came together, independently, to harass the German lines of communication as best they could. This was how they met. Solov had enormous respect for this one-armed man whose example had inspired so many.

Eventually, as these partisan bands had been organised more effectively, valuable officers like Vatutin and Solov had been pulled back to the defence of Moscow in the winter of '41 – '42. After being promoted, they were sent back as reinforcements to the retreating armies of the south to Stalingrad when Hitler diverted his armies toward the Caucasus and the promise of capturing the Baku oilfields his war machine so badly needed. They saw more action there together throughout the murderous battle of Stalingrad, taking part in much of the desperate street-fighting.

Now, as that struggle was nearing its end, they could relax more often, as now, in a few snatched moments in their shelter, and take stock, as they had so many times before.

"Things are looking up, Niko." Vatutin lit his cigarette for him with a small twig from the cast iron stove he had rescued. "Who knows? Soon, we could be smoking decent cigarettes instead of this dried camel shit and, maybe, when things quieten down, the farm girls will come out of hiding again."

Solov forced a smile: "Yeah, things are bound to get better, aren't they?" He looked down at the letter in his hands, the smoke from the cigarette curling up around it.

"News from home?" Vatutin noticed his pensive demeanour.

Solov handed him the sheet of blue army paper. Vatutin held it toward the light from the stove. It was from Army HQ in Moscow, on behalf of the Party.

"I smell trouble," Solov said, blowing a trail of the foul tobacco.

"Niko, they probably want to give you another medal or something."

"You know as well as I do, if that was the case they'd say so, if it was only for the propaganda value. No, they probably have more time on their hands these days, now the war's starting to go our way. They're not so busy so they pick up a file and wonder who's been a naughty boy? They've looked under 'S' and found me. You watch, it'll be some shitty desk job in Murmansk."

Vatutin laughed at Solov's black mood, in doing so, trying to beat back his own mood. He handed the letter back and pulled out a bottle of vodka from beneath his makeshift cot, along with two beakers.

"I don't think they'd treat one of the 'Soviet Union's finest war heroes' as bad as that. I'm more likely to wind up in Murmansk. Shit, they've probably just realised I've only got one arm after all this time." He poured and replaced the cork in the bottle he held between his thighs.

Solov smiled and took the vodka. "You can't call me a hero. I'm just a soldier and nothing else."

"Maybe that's been the trouble, Niko." He tapped his beaker against Solov's. "You've never bent over backwards to be a Party man's man, that's for sure."

"Leon, you know I can't play politics."

"The army will forgive you that, but the Party? Well…maybe they'll rap your knuckles to keep you in line? I mean, you say you're a soldier yet sometimes, my friend, you cut it fine…remember the guy from State Security?"

Solov remembered. The man was called Vosik or Vesik, some kind of big cheese political commissar touring the lines last July. Morale had been low. Food and drink had been scarce, arms and ammo, even decent clothing. Despite the man's status, he had been a weedy rat of a bureaucrat with thick lenses in his glasses. Dressed in a black leather raincoat, he'd stuck out amongst Solov and his bearded, filthy men.

He'd spouted party slogans, the latest being 'Not One Step Back'.

He'd talked about the threat of infiltrators, spies, deserters. Solov and his men had looked on, numb. The little man had backed his speech up with: "Remember! Keep secure, keep safe!" Unfortunately for him, he slipped over in the mud to the delight of everyone. As his entourage had scurried to pick him up and wipe his megaphone down, Solov had called to him: "Not too many steps back!" to the further pleasure of the troops and the embarrassment of the official, who made a point of remembering his name.

"It's all probably been lost in the fighting, Niko," Vatutin assured him.

Solov wasn't anti-communist, but he hated some of the pompous Party hacks he met. Especially the ones he spoke to who always tried to get him interested in politics. He didn't need politicising. He was politicised enough, maybe too much, that's why he didn't allow himself to be drawn into the internal battles that had taken place over the years when Trotsky was still around and the Left Opposition was still a force to be reckoned with. He knew when to keep quiet, especially after the Trials and the purges of the general staff.

"Remember that story you told me about Minsk?" said Vatutin, refilling his beaker. "When was it?"

"1940."

Solov smiled as he recalled the military awards ceremony. Officers and men were invited to attend a party along with generals, commissars and their wives. A State Commissioner had spotted Solov's 'Order of the Red Banner' he'd won in Finland and asked about his political background.

"And you said…" Vatutin encouraged him.

"Commissar, the Party, to me, is like having a wife…"

"And then you said…'I like her because she's the only one I've got'. Oh, shit, Niko, you really know how to make a splash." Vatutin laughed. "Y'know, some have got ten years in a labour camp for less than that."

"Lucky the guy had a sense of humour."

"No doubt it was remembered."

"That's what I'm worried about." He looked at the letter again, folded it up and slugged back the vodka. "I'd better get some rest. It's a long train ride to Moscow. If I don't see you in the morning, it's been nice knowing you, comrade."

Vatutin shook his head, slowly. "Silly bastard. They can't tie you to a desk, you're too stupid."

"Thanks, friend."

"Hey, bring me back some decent cigarettes."

THREE

Trains always took Solov away, not just in the physical sense. He had spent a lot of his younger days around them. The railroads had been the arteries of the old Russia, the time of the Tsar, and the lifelines of the Revolution.

In the 1880s, before he was born, massive foreign investments, especially from Britain and France, had underwritten the expansion of railways, mines and industry. His family had moved from their peasant commune to the grandiose city of St Petersberg - Petrograd, now Leningrad - in 1883. The men and women of the family found work in the grim factories and steelworks. His father, Giorgio, became a fireman on the trains, shovelling the black fuel into the gaping mouths of the engines. His uncle worked in the sprawling Putilov steelworks where thousands of other peasants became industrial workers, the new working class, the proletariat. His aunts worked in cotton mills and bakeries. All of them exchanged the backwardness of agricultural labour, for the empty promise of wage labour. Giorgio had been relatively lucky to work on the trains. Although the work was hard and the hours long, he had the pleasure of travelling the lines from Petrograd as far as Moscow or even Kiev in the Ukraine, bringing back truckloads of grain, or to the primitive Ural Mountains for the coal or iron ore.

Mother Russia changed drastically in these years, a lot faster than the rulers wanted her to, to be sure. But the changes were irresistible.

His father told how he saw the glaring contrasts and contradictions of a feudal state painfully entering a cruel modern world of industry, a harsher, more concentrated cruelty. The whip hands of the landowners were exchanged for the lash of factory owners. Giorgio could see the poverty, the backwardness of the wide, endless steppes and returned to the dark pools of the cities. Where the peasantry was scattered, god-fearing and tied to the seasons on the land, the new class of industrial workers were enclosed together in the rat runs of damp tenement buildings on the edge of the cities, experiencing the same deprivations together.

While Giorgio later became a train driver, his brothers and sisters were trapped in the cycle of sixteen-hour days amongst machines and dirt. They could be fined their wages, be laid off, even beaten for showing disrespect. But soon they would find a way of fighting back as an explosion of anger was channelled, but not into the usual old peasant ways of revolt and riot. Many a peasant uprising was crushed by the Tsar's troops or the Cossacks mounted on horses, waving their flashing sabres. In the towns and cities, the workers formed new organisations called unions, and they wielded their new weapons - strikes, sit-ins, factory occupations.

Nikolai was born in 1900, in June, during the turn of a new century and the establishment of a new class preparing to fight back against the dead hand of Tsarism that struggled to hold progress in check. Socialism was on the agenda. His father Giorgio helped to lead a strike, with other workers, around Petrograd. The trains only moved on the say so of the workers and the machines lay idle. His father was absent from his birth as he attended political meetings around the city. His mother, Lara, took the baby Nikolai, a few days old, to his first strike committee meeting.

Nikolai's earliest memories were of waving his uncle Piotr away to war at Finland Station as he made the short trip to join his battleship at Kronstadt. They'd been at war with Japan and they didn't even know where it was. Piotr was a sailor because he couldn't find work. He was father's youngest brother and wanted adventure too. He looked good in his naval uniform. Nikolai remembered the crowds, the music, the flags. His father had picked him up, looking solemn, as he held back the tears as his moustache tickled Nikolai's face.

"I beg you," said his father to the little boy in his arms who couldn't understand why he was so upset. "Never wear the uniform for the Tsar."

"I promise, Papa."

To his shame, Nikolai was to break that promise, twelve years later, but not of his own free will. Another train had taken him away to another war.

Piotr, his youngest uncle, only nineteen, was killed by the Japanese at Port Arthur, at the other end of the world.

Nikolai was jolted awake as the train's whistle blew and the carriages ground to a halt. The heavy engine was getting its breath back.

"They're stopping for water again," said one of the heavily bandaged troops. He pulled a window down and looked down the track.

"Close it, it's freezing enough in here," said the soldier's comrade sat next to the window.

Outside, there was nothing but a blanket of snow and ice, nothingness, flat nothingness.

"Major?" The trooper offered a flask of vodka to Solov, his bandaged hand encrusted with black, dried blood.

"No, thanks, comrade." Solov felt the haziness of a few hours ago was still with him. He wanted food before he drank more alcohol. The crowded carriage smelled of sweat and infected wounds. The wooden seats were not good places to try and sleep, or even to sit, for endless hours.

"Where are we?" he asked no one in particular.

"Nowhere," the trooper said, screwing the top back on his flask.

"We've just come from Nowhere - it's called Stalingrad," his comrade said.

"I need some air," Solov said, rising, stepping carefully over the legs of soldiers who were trying to sleep. The corridor was also packed with bodies crouched or laid down under blankets. He pushed past to the nearest door, opened it and stepped down onto the hard ice of what looked like a platform. A hundred or so metres away, a group of workers shovelled fuel onto the train from a coal wagon. Three military police were walking amongst other soldiers who had the same idea as him, to stretch their legs. One of the MPs was a lieutenant, a cloak draped around his shoulders.

"Major?" The lieutenant nodded at him.

Solov grimaced. "How far from Moscow, Lieutenant?"

"We're about ten hours, but you might want to multiply that by three with this weather."

"Shit. Cigarette?"

"Thank you, sir." The lieutenant took one. The two MPs with him looked on.

"Take one each," Solov urged. They thanked him, eagerly.

"Good news from Stalingrad, eh, sir?" one of them blew smoke away from him.

"Excellent news."

"The fascists finally threw it in."

"It was only a matter of time," said Solov. "Their goose was cooked before December."

"You boys did a great job," said the lieutenant.

"Yes, we did. The German high command didn't do too much to help the sorry bastards. They were counting on supplies and ammo getting through, getting dropped by air, what did they get? Black pepper and condoms."

The MPs laughed. The train hissed along with them.

"Pepper and condoms," they laughed.

"Bet that spiced up their sex lives," said the lieutenant.

Solov stamped his feet: "Goering really fucked up there," he said. He climbed back onto the train and waved to them.

"What's the weather like in Moscow?"

"They say it's colder up there."

Solov made his way back into the relative warmth of the carriage to try and get some sleep. He had lost his place by the window so wedged himself between two sleeping soldiers and pulled his greatcoat around him. When he woke again, it was dark, though he could see the snow outside. He turned uncomfortably on his side, yearning to get back to his dreams, thinking of Piotr, in his sailor's uniform, the music and the flags, to get his mind away from the image of Piotr's body sinking in the sea near Port Arthur. Piotr's face took the place of the soldier killed by the sniper's bullet in the ruins of Stalingrad as he caught his hand again and pulled him toward him. Piotr's smile turned to pain as the bullet struck him in the back and punched a hole through his chest, splattering blood in his face until he sank in a sea of blood around Port Arthur again and Solov woke up, sweating in the dark, rattling carriage.

By daylight, Solov was woken up again by the sounds of the train and the lively voices of the soldiers in the carriage. They were having what sounded like a lively debate.

"…if this is progress, you can shove it," it went.

"Look," ran another argument. "If we didn't have progress how could we have resisted the Nazis this far? We would have no planes, no tanks, no guns. They would have kicked our arses all the way back to Vladivostok." The last speaker was a thickset man with a Ukrainian accent.

"That's fresh coming from you," said the soldier with the bandaged hand by the window. He noticed Solov was awake and offered him his flask again. Again, Solov waved it away, but accepted a cigarette. The soldier was trying to recruit him to his side in the discussion.

"That right, Major?"

"What?"

"Our Ukrainian friend saying the Nazis would have kicked our arses when his people welcomed them, back in '41."

"Hold on, you saying I'm a fascist-lover or something?" the Ukrainian said.

"Isn't that right though? Ukrainians welcomed the Nazis when they first invaded?"

"Bullshit. No, we hate them worse than Stalin," said the Ukrainian.

"Careful, soldier," said Solov.

"Sorry, sir, I didn't mean to…"

"Don't worry about me, son," said Solov. "Just be careful who might be listening."

"If Stalin hadn't industrialised the economy," the soldier with the bandage said, "then we would have been finished. I don't doubt that. But look at the 'Five Year Plan', all that hard work in the 30s. Alright, apart from being able to defend ourselves, if there hadn't been a war, how did we benefit, I mean, ordinary workers were no better off with so-called progress."

"We got rid of the Tsar, didn't we? said the Ukrainian. "Isn't that progress in itself?"

"Yeah."

"Well, what you talking about?"

"You know as well as I do the only difference now is, instead of freezing our arses off in the communes, we're freezing our arses off in the factories. Instead of a hoe in our hands, we've got a hammer. Take these fucking trains. Here we are going around and around in circles, just to end up where we came from in the first place. Just for the privilege of making them run, millions of men are scraping around underground for coal."

"You're full of shit, comrade," said the Ukrainian. "And just for your information, if you want to go scratching around in a wheat field for the rest of your life, there's plenty for you back in my beloved Ukraine. Me? I'll take a train ride any time."

"And just for anyone's information," Solov found himself saying, "Yes, some of the Ukrainians did welcome the fascists as liberators because they hated us after Stalin forced the famine on them. Remember how he sent the army in to seize the grain, and shoot the livestock? But I can tell you, from personal experience, I fought with a lot of Ukrainian partisans in '41 and '42 and they contributed heroically – and I mean heroically. They delayed the Germans' advance. I know because I fought alongside them."

"Yeah, but…"

"And as for progress, soldier…" Solov hoped he didn't sound like he was pulling rank now, or didn't sound like one of the Party's political commissars he so detested. "…Progress, in the form of our trains, helped to save our revolution from being crushed by the foreign armies of intervention. We were surrounded remember? These trains you so despise gave us the advantage of rushing troops from one front to the other to stop us collapsing. When you've got all kinds of armies from America, Britain, France, Poland, Japan, even Czechs, surrounding us, not to mention the old Tsarist forces, you can only imagine what they had in store for us if they'd have won. It wouldn't have been progress, quite its opposite." Solov tapped the window. "That snow out there would have been pretty pink with the blood of us all, and our families, make no mistake. That's progress. And who organised that? The workers and soldiers of the Soviet Union. And who organised them, who organised the Red Army?"

Nobody answered, just the sounds of the train filled the void. It was one thing to deride Stalin, dangerous even. Very dangerous. But to praise his nemesis, quite another. Especially since he had been murdered in Mexico by a Stalinist agent a couple of years ago. The dead were meant to stay buried.

"Comrade Leon Trotsky," said the Ukrainian for him.

"I'll take that drink now, soldier," said Solov.

"You a Trotskyist, Major?" asked the Ukrainian.

"I'm a soldier," he said. "And my father was a train driver. Is that not enough progress for everyone?"

Twenty-four hours later, Nikolai Solov was being driven through the streets of Moscow towards army central HQ. Civilians shuffled through the streets that were being turned to slush by the traffic - trucks, buses, trams, horses and carts. Most of the civilians were old people and children, most workers were in the factories or in the forces. The great city squares were criss-crossed with people going about their business, some of them pulling sledges full of bread and blankets, or with the infirm. A company of soldiers marched across an intersection and the car stopped to let them pass.

"How were things in Stalingrad, sir?" asked the driver. She liked Solov. He sat up in the front with her and didn't treat her like a taxi-driver.

"Tough, but tougher for the fascists. It's not over yet. We've liberated a lot of rubble and the Germans are pulling back, but we haven't seen the last of them. There's a lot more to do."

The driver knew better than to ask too many questions such as - 'If there's a lot more to do, what are you doing here?'

"We've got a good chance of turning things around now," Solov said.

A loudspeaker attached to a lamp post spluttered into action with some Tchaikovsky before a female voice announced something about daily bread rations and soup kitchens, then went into reports about the front.

The driver looked at Solov and nodded at the speaker: "Kills the art of conversation but helps keep up the spirits." She stood on her brakes. "Hey, you kids, out of the way, you want to get killed?"

A group of children playing war with frightening precision

crossed the street. One child pulled his friend out of the way and looked defiantly at the driver. The car moved away and eventually pulled up at the steps of a grand baroque building with gothic pillars leading to a pair of ornate doors. The driver couldn't park properly as other cars were in the way. Solov's nerves, all the way from the station, had been jagged. He looked at the steps he would have to climb and where they would lead him. He saluted the driver and wanted to get back into the car with her, or at least, just to ride a few more times around the block. He climbed the steps which had been kept ice free. At the top, he offered his ID to one of the two soldiers by the door while the other opened the way for him. Once inside the cavernous, marble-floored hallway, he stood a few moments to take in the high-domed ceiling, the marble pillars, the sumptuous stairway curving upwards where he could see five doors evenly spaced apart on the second floor. From the ceiling hung four crystal chandeliers. Straight ahead, a reception desk, he showed the female sergeant there his ID and the letter that had summoned him here. She nodded and picked up the receiver from the phone on her desk.

"Major Solov, sir," she said. She waved him towards the staircase and said: "Number three, just go in and report to the reception desk there." Solov smiled and took himself upstairs, two at a time. He slowed near the top. Why was he in so much of a hurry? He walked to the third door, tapped and walked in. He entered another large space, decorated with tapestries and paintings of dukes and priests and a large incongruent red banner on either side of a massive portrait of Stalin, in profile, looking out benignly, that enigmatic smirk on his face. It had always irritated him as to why the Party surrounded themselves with feudal and religious icons considering Marxists were supposed to be atheists. But he figured that was exactly his father's point about Stalin. He was no Marxist. He had even allowed the churches to be re-opened, 'the opium of the masses'. He found it offensive having saints peering over their shoulders, like Stalin needed some form of insurance, just in case there was a god, after all.

Another desk and another door beyond that, another

secretary, armed with a typewriter, phone and intercom, announced his arrival. At the end of the room, a cluster of desks with more secretaries and typists sat near a telex machine.

"You can go through, Major," one of the women said. Solov tucked away his letter and ID, tugged at the bottom of his tunic and walked in through the door. This was a more welcoming room. To his left, three desks formed a horse- shoe together beneath another portrait of Stalin, this time showing him as the latest in a line of - from left to right - Marx, Engels, Lenin. Ahead of him, two doors, above them the red banner again. To his right, three armchairs and a leather couch arranged around a huge fireplace with burning logs. On the large mantel was a wrought iron hammer and sickle screwed to the wall. There were three men sat drinking and smoking. One of them stood up to greet him as Solov removed his cap and tucked it under his left arm and saluted.

The man came toward him with his hand outstretched, smiling. He introduced himself as Colonel Bosck.

"Major, you can dispense with the military stuff here. We're all comrades under the skin. Come and have a drink."

Colonel Bosck led Solov across to the others where the cigarette smoke was the thickest. Beside the fire was a small silver table with a drinks tray.

"Please, sit yourself down," Bosck indicated the couch. Bosck looked to be in his early fifties, balding and bespectacled.

"Drink?" Bosck jerked a thumb at the tray.

"Coffee, perhaps, comrade Colonel," Solov said, seating himself on the couch opposite them.

Bosck walked over to the desks and used an intercom: "Coffee for our guest." When he returned he sat in the vacant armchair in the middle. To his left, he introduced a Colonel Mitsuenko of army intelligence, a fat man with bushy eyebrows like the villains in Chaplin films. On Bosck's right was Colonel Lavenko, of foreign affairs intelligence section. His head, like

Solov's, was clean- shaven. His fingers, Solov noticed, were heavily nicotine-stained, on his lap, a leather-bound file. Mitsuenko got up and poured himself a drink.

"Sure you wouldn't prefer a real drink, Major?" he said. "Whiskey, brandy, cognac? Or a cigar?"

"Thank you, sir, I'll stick to cigarettes and coffee."

Mitsuenko poured a double brandy. The others already had drinks balanced on the arms of their chairs.

"Firstly, Major," said Mitsuenko. "What fantastic news from Stalingrad. I'm sure you've already celebrated. Nevertheless, what a fantastic victory in what was, no doubt, a titanic struggle." The others raised their glasses and Solov nodded.

Bosck cleared his throat: "Obviously, I have no need to stress that the following discussion is not to be repeated in any way outside this room. Utmost secrecy."

"Of course, comrade Colonel."

"Our branches of intelligence and foreign affairs are working closely together on this one..."

Solov lit a cigarette as they were interrupted by the arrival of his coffee. He was grateful for this pause as he felt relief ease his body. He realised this discussion had nothing to do with disciplining him at all. It sounded like a new assignment. After all, he thought, as he was handed the coffee, stirred in the sugar, and slowly unbuttoned the three top buttons of his tunic - the heat from the fire was a dash of paradise - why would they drag him all the way to Moscow just to put a bullet in his head? Leon Vatutin had been right. Once the secretary placed the coffee pot on a small table next to Solov and left the room, Bosck continued.

"For some time now, we've been keeping a careful watch on your activities and your character, Major..."

Solov slumped a little, maybe not, he thought...

"We can inform you that…we like what we see…"

"Thank you. Thank you very much."

"We are especially interested in your time spent training and fighting behind the lines with the partisans. We find your written reports most…exciting. Indeed, sometimes, you read like an American thriller."

Mitsuenko laughed out loud, showing perfect teeth: "An American thriller, that's a good one."

"It's true. Even Comrade Khrushchev agrees. You know he likes a good tale."

Solov raised his eyebrows. He was surprised to find he impressed somebody high up in Stalingrad.

"However," said Lavenko, speaking for the first time, "we shall overlook, for the time being, this small matter of your political attitude…"

"Sir, I must stress, I am a soldier, whatever remarks I have made have been in an unthinking, spur of the moment manner. I confess that I lack tact, but tact has never been a part of my make-up…"

Bosck looked up: "You're a bit of a renegade, aren't you, Major Solov?"

"Perhaps. But I'm a socialist too, comrade Colonel. Socialists, by nature, are renegades, nonetheless, sir…"

Bosck laughed. "The 'Red Renegade'. I like it. Yes. 'Renegade'. You've got some balls, Solov. I'll give you that. I knew you'd be the right man for the job. Why, that can be your code name: 'Renegade'. Yes, we'll pass that down the pipeline to your controller in London."

Solov couldn't help but think 'Renegade' would not only pass as a code name to mark him down as an operative but, maybe, as a marked man for some time in the future, when some bureaucrat, somewhere, might pull out his file again.

"Sir…? Did you say London, sir? I…" Solov began.

"Yes. Of course, we understand your dilemma." Bosck waved his hand. "We know that, whatever you lack as a politician, you more than make up for it as a soldier. In times of war, we need soldiers rather than more politicians. You have a distinguished career, Major. You were a fine athlete, distinguished in unarmed combat, marksmanship, explosives. You have studied languages, 1927 – 1930? Very good grades in English, German, Spanish and French. His file, Colonel Lavenko?"

Lavenko placed his drink on the carpet and opened the file on his lap.

"Good combat experience, almost unequalled - the civil war in 1919 to 1921, in Spain in 1936 to 39. Poland in 1939. Finland that same year to 1940 and, as we've already mentioned, you worked with the partisans and lately in Stalingrad."

"Thank you, sir."

"Your work in Stalingrad," Lavenko continued. "Excellent standards in intelligence and reconnaissance and you personally took part in active duty behind the German lines, although you were attached as a staff officer there?"

"Yes, I feel it does a lot for morale when officers get their hands a little dirty…"

"Indeed," said Lavenko. "And this provides good relations with our troops in a very demanding situation, in a war that calls for a lot of sacrifice. However, we are also impressed by your talents in information-gathering and we agree that you could be an excellent investment for after the war."

"What Colonel Lavenko means is," said Mitsuenko, "you have a big future ahead of you."

"Sir?"

"Let Colonel Lavenko explain."

Lavenko downed his drink in one and gave his glass to Bosck who got up and poured him a fresh one. Lavenko took it from him and lit another cigar.

"For more than a year," he began, "our government has called on Britain and America to open a second front in Europe. A second front, as you know, would take the pressure off the Soviet Union considerably. Even now the Allies insist they are not yet ready. But we know otherwise. We know the Americans are content to wait so the fascists can bleed us dry. The last thing they want is for us to move into central Europe because they fear us spreading the revolution there. They think that, if they make excuses about preparations, they can stall and we will be in a weaker position, materially, when they do invade. They also think that we will drain the best Nazi resources and make their task all the more easy for them when they eventually re-enter Europe. For the moment, they are content to chase desert foxes around North Africa."

"Britain's half-hearted attempt at invasion at Dieppe last summer," snorted Bosck. "A fiasco. Churchill bungled it, trying to go it alone then the Americans have to pull them out of the fire again."

"Meanwhile, the Americans are content to sit it out and send us a few supplies to keep us ticking over. The British have a big force in Iran but refused to send them over the border to help us at Stalingrad when it was touch and go. What Churchill was hoping for was a German victory and only then he would have sent his troops from Iran to take control of our oilfields at Baku."

"And let's not forget," continued Lavenko, "what our friend Reichsmarshall Goering said: 'The British entered the war to stop the Germans going into the east but not to let the east come over to the Atlantic.' Even now, our agents inform us of a plot amongst the German general staff of some sort of military coup against Hitler and then to invite the Allies to join them against the USSR. We spill our blood, we scorch our earth to buy the Allies time, we even - and this is top, top secret - we are even beginning to negotiate the winding up of the Communist International and renouncing world revolution later this year to encourage the Allies to help us defeat fascism, to show that we are no threat to them. Yet they have the audacity to say we never give them anything in return! Well, now we are going to send them something."

"Major," said Colonel Bosck. "We are sending them you."

"Me, sir?"

"Yes, sir, you, sir!" Mitsuenko slapped his thigh and roared. "Look at his face! He's in shock!"

Solov shook his head and smiled. He shook his head again and said: "Can I have that drink now?"

Mitsuenko laughed some more and obliged.

"Cognac?"

"Fine."

Lavenko continued: "We are sending you to Britain as a 'special military liaison training officer'. You are part of a new initiative between our governments. We want you to oversee a training programme of a commando force in partisan warfare. The British commandos have met with some success in their brief raids but are real beginners in partisan warfare. Even their Chindit force in Burma has had mixed results against the Japanese. We need a continuous partisan war which triggers and underpins widespread revolts linking up with the French resistance and the general French population. We need a partisan war which is lacking in western Europe, which will help tie up several divisions of Nazi troops. It would be a minor second front. If they won't create one, we have to do it ourselves. Of course, you are only to train the troops, not participate yourself. But, if enough terrorist attacks take place, then the Germans will take reprisals which could serve as a recruiting sergeant to a partisan war, like Tito in Yugoslavia, or even a mass revolt."

Solov was stunned. He never, for a moment, guessed an operation like this would come up.

Mitsuenko picked up the thread now: "You'll be working somewhere in southern England and will receive instructions from our people in our embassy in London. Following your tasks with the commando training, you'll be attached to the embassy staff thereafter. We intend that you will be based there permanently where you will receive further instructions. We will eventually expect you to assimilate in British society and melt away. You'll be what we call a 'sleeper'"

Mitsuenko finished there and stretched back in his chair as if the effort had exhausted him. Colonel Bosck leaned forward to speak again.

"I think we've just about covered everything. We will give you more detailed instructions before you leave for Britain. First, we want you to rest for a few weeks before you go. Any questions you have will then be considered."

"Could I ask you a question now, sir?"

"Yes."

"Won't I be watched closely while training the commandos?"

"Training them will consist largely of lectures and some fieldwork. You will follow instructions the British give you. Your real work begins when you return to London."

"Right, sir."

"Well, that's all, Major," said Bosck. "I think we've got the best man for the job. It will be largely a good public relations operation, to be training British troops. Hopefully, they'll then stir up a mess in France until we get our second front proper, then we'll have you well placed in London for further work. There'll be an officer outside to take you to your room for the night. Tomorrow, he'll take you to your place of rest and recreation.

Goodbye, Major, and good luck."

They shook hands with Solov. Solov picked up his cap and left. Colonel Bosck said: "We've got a good man there."

The others said nothing.

FOUR

Before Nikolai Solov was ready to go to Britain, his few weeks rest and recuperation included several weeks attendance at a Moscow espionage school. He re-tooled some of his military skills, and learned new techniques in areas such as assassination, photography, signalling, learning an array of complex messenger codes and re-visiting the English language. He also attended endless sessions on British politics, culture, history, geography and economics.

Solov initially dreaded going back to school having been exhausted on active service. Since the summer of '41, he had only known the relentless fear and shock of fighting Nazis in the field after the invasion, but he soon relaxed, the tensions of constant combat readiness leaving him.

Two weeks leave were granted, purely to rest and do what he wanted. That was the worst time. He didn't know what to do with himself, where to start. He stayed at an army department block outside Moscow, to the east. Other soldiers there were the same as him. Some showed signs of physical and mental damage, or were just drained, burnt out. That first weekend, he had mostly stayed in his room with the blinds down, a supply of vodka and that was his therapy. He drank, wept, and drank some more, until there were no tears left to shed.

It was only halfway through the second week that he ventured out and, only then, roamed around the gardens at the rear for an hour or so. Some of the men played football or walked around in pairs, talking, reminiscing, probably spewing memories of war and horror. Some had visitors from wives, lovers, families. Solov spoke only when he had to - orderlies, other officers billeted on the same floor as him as they passed by in the corridor or in the mess. More usually, he took his meal tray to his room. By the second weekend, his bad dreams subsided. He cleared up the clutter of his room and bagged and binned the empty vodka bottles, bathed and shaved his face and head. He put on his dress uniform.

He walked into the nearby town. It was still cold but the sun made short, welcome appearances now, the ice beginning to loosen its grip. In a few weeks, the thaw would come, the end of the bloodiest of winters. In these weeks, he also thought about his family. He would have liked to have visited his mother's grave. But this was out of the question. She was buried in the little cemetery at the village commune where she had been born. The commune lay about forty kilometres south west of Leningrad, well behind enemy lines. He could only think of the picture of her face on her gravestone, dark hair, young, not quite beautiful, but his father had loved her. She'd died in late 1938, when he was a 'military advisor' in Spain helping the Republican government fight Franco and the fascists. She'd been buried back in the countryside at her own request. All the years she'd spent in her small apartment in the Vyborg district of Leningrad had been in the hope that, one day, his father Giorgio would be allowed to return. And if he was, he would know where to find her. But he never returned. Giorgio had been an old Bolshevik. He'd joined the party during the 1905 revolution in the wake of the Russo-Japanese War that had carried away his brother Piotr, but mainly because he'd been active for years in the railway union. He was a supporter of Lenin to the hilt. Much later, when Nikolai had been forced to wear the Tsar's uniform, his father had been saddened Nikolai had been conscripted in late 1916, a boy still. But his father was proud when, in the early weeks of the 1917 revolution, he and several of his fellow soldiers turned up to join in the mass meetings and strikes. Giorgio had his faith restored in him. Nikolai had taken his advice: "Soon, if you must go, agitate among the soldiers, join the party, agitate, form soldiers' soviets. The soldiers of Russia and Germany have more in common with each other than they do their own generals."

Nikolai had again gone away to fight by 1919, in the so-called Civil War, having joined the Red Army. Giorgio still remained politically active in his union and the local soviet. When Nikolai was a student, catching up on his neglected education, by 1927, he learned that his father had been sent to a labour camp in

Siberia because of his support for Trotsky and the Left Opposition. Soon after, Trotsky himself had been sent into exile, eventually to an island off the coast of Turkey.

Nikolai never saw his father again. Lenin had long ago died and Stalin and his bureaucratic cronies, piece by piece, began to strangle the democracy out of the socialist revolution. Nikolai had been numbed by fear and the shame of not having followed his father's path. He felt a brave soldier, yet cowardly in his convictions. Should he follow and perish? Live to fight another day? That's how he'd operated as a partisan in this war. He painfully justified his survival to himself now during his walks to the nearby town. When the enemy is stronger, you hit and run, disappear and wait to strike back again. Why, even Trotsky defended the gains of the revolution like that, his voice, pen and ideas were his weapons. But he himself had kept quiet, apart from his own thinly- disguised disdain for the bureaucrats, the Party men, the commissars. Enough to salve the conscience, but not enough to be drawn into bloodthirsty purges of the military in the late '30s.

He'd kept his head down and soldiered, gone to Spain, kept quiet. Survived by defending the gains of the revolution, waiting and watching. He'd wanted a clean war, not the dirt that Stalin provided, he who made a pact with Hitler; he who had stabbed Poland in the back and bullied little Finland. In the end, when the Nazis hit Russia hard, Nikolai had welcomed it almost. It was a chance to cleanse ourselves, he thought. Revenge for the purges, for Trotsky's murder in Mexico, for Giorgio, for his mother. His bravery in war would drown his cowardice in peace.

Espionage school took his mind off things, so he soon began to warm to it. It helped mend the deep hole of inactivity and focused him on the job at hand rather than dwelling on the past. A new task breathed life into him. It was more than a new assignment, it would almost be a new life. He was to go to Britain and, for the next few years, even beyond the duration of the war, assimilate into another country. In effect, he was being sent into a kind of exile, like his father, but they would make use of him. He knew they, the army, the government, felt his skills were still of some use to them, and this probably saved his life. The families of 'Trotskyists', even those politically inactive, were often sent to labour camps, or just shot. He'd been saved because he could serve a purpose. He felt like a collaborator, saving his skin, like a partisan, hiding in the woods, waiting for the chance to strike back. That's how he'd always survived.

Now, it seemed, he was training for another war, more subtle, against enemies in the future, for a secret war, in the peace to come. He didn't understand everything yet but his soldier's instinct told him that if that's what they wanted, that's what they'd get.

So, he threw himself into his school training. He shared experiences with the other students. They were a mixed bag of serious party members, war veterans and a few international comrades from Spain, China, even America. His English tutor was a Cambridge graduate in literature, a born-again Party man called Watkin. He got his students to perform role plays drawn from 'ordinary life'. Another tutor had worked with Stanislavsky in the Moscow Art Theatre and took them through exercises in memory recall and motivation. It gave a few light-hearted moments in a serious business but, all the while, Solov waited as the weeks drew on.

He received news from Colonel Bosck's office that there were delays due to negotiations with the British who were dragging their feet around the idea that the Colonel had referred to as 'opening a mini-second front'. How was this to take shape? What kind of specific requirements were needed? What kind of personnel? How many troops could be spared? What time frame? Bosck's office couldn't even decide which route to Britain to send him - via Leningrad through the Baltic, which was hazardous due to the naval blockade. By diplomatic plane to neutral Sweden then on from there? Then, as March turned to April, the ice- free port of Murmansk was mooted. Yes. Solov was to leave on a

British destroyer escorting a convoy around Norway and across the North Sea.

From then, events moved quickly, within a few days, Solov found himself in a small cabin on a freezing ship. It was a long, boring trip broken by only a few sightings of Stuka bombers crossing over from Stavanger which were seen off by heavy fire from the destroyer and other escort ships. Solov also tried to warm up his English by wandering into the ship's galley and speaking to the cooks, even helping out, peeling vegetables with them. Once across the North Sea, Solov's destroyer peeled off from the convoy, along with three others, and headed south until they came in at Hull where he disembarked with the rest of the crew. There, he was met near the quayside by a Russian embassy staff car, its hammer and sickle pennants fluttering on its wings. The car sped him along unmarked roads down to the darkened city of London.

Solov slept on the rear seat. At the embassy, that night, he was shown to a luxurious room, following a few formalities and a tray of food. He collapsed on the double bed, still in his uniform and slept…slept…

For a bureaucrat, if that's all he was, Nikolai Solov found Stefan Sevoska a good companion.

He'd been a muscular man, but now he'd gone to seed, years of the diplomatic lifestyle had seen to that. He was talkative and often stroked his trim, black beard. He had a gleam in his eyes and his hair combed vainly in a parting across his head.

This evening, he was contained in a tuxedo but he still retained that down-to-earth manner Solov could cope with - no graces. He was like an old uncle. He was obviously well-known among the round of surviving cocktail drinkers of Belgravia and a familiar sight in the drinking dens of Fleet Street he liked to frequent, where he'd generously introduced Solov in the preceding few days. It was the earthiness and general zest he had that the British seemed to be drawn to in Sevoska. He was not the stereotypical Russian, Soviet sourpuss portrayed by the Hollywood films or the Fleet Street caricatures.

He was a wily, well-educated man who had grown up in Rostov and had served as a cavalry officer in the Tsar's army in the first war. He'd been at the fearful battle of Tannenberg in 1914 where he'd been wounded and eventually invalided back to Moscow. The shortages in medical supplies, food and the general hardship of the population contrasted sharply to what he'd observed of the lavish lifestyles of the higher officer class and he'd taken a long time to recover from his wounds. When he did, he was in time to join the mass uprisings of early 1917, joining the Menshevik Party that kept the country at war and saw little change in the people's living conditions. Sevoska crossed over to the winning side when the Bolsheviks took over that October. He was to use what were to flower into his diplomatic skills to try and hold together the uneasy soviets in his area in the heady late summer before the October revolution, but he knew which side to cross over to. He wasn't particularly political, and was content to work behind the scenes when he was needed. He never involved himself in the finer points of the political struggles and just went with the flow and ebb of the historical tide. He moved with the masses. Lenin or Kerensky, he preferred to back the winner. As Stalin's star rose, he could live with that too and stayed away from the faction fights between the left, right and centre.

By 1920, he'd left the army at the age of thirty to study at Minsk. He took several courses in politics, economics and languages. He spent his free time drinking and avoiding the upheavals of the civil war and famine. He became well-known among his fellow students, most of them younger than himself. He gained notoriety for sleeping with the wives of two tutors, he told him. Entering the foreign affairs department didn't restrict his social habits and the work there came easy to him.

As the Soviet Union gradually became less of a pariah state and received growing international recognition, he worked in a variety of consuls and embassies abroad, first in Weimar

Germany's Berlin, in Warsaw, Ankara, Paris in 1933 then, by 1936, he was posted to London where he was an assistant under-secretary.

"It's just a high-sounding title for a busybody and general layabout." He grinned at Solov. "The last seven years have been the best. Paris wasn't too bad, but the French ladies have such expensive tastes. I know I shouldn't say it but the British are so…democratic. They share everything with you, especially their dear wives. Honestly, there are times when I just don't know how I do it. I think they like big Russian bears like me."

"They must like the peasant in you."

They entered the banquet hall of a house in Mayfair, where they were guests for an official reception to commemorate the victory of Stalingrad.

"Another excuse to break open His Majesty's government's spirits reservoir and forget the war for a few hours," said Sevoska.

Solov wore his dress uniform for the occasion and had removed his cap bearing his trademark clean-shaven head. The room was bustling with high- ranking British, American and Russian army, air force and naval officers, a number of lower staff officers, civil servants, diplomats and their assorted female escorts, wives and guests. Sevoska ordered two double whiskeys with ice in a perfect English accent from a passing, white-jacketed waiter.

"Next time," said Solov, "let me get the drinks, just to practise my English. Do these people know why I'm here?"

"No, most of them are here most nights. They've turned this place into a private club. Its owner won't be needing it. He's a guest of the Japanese. Got snapped up in Singapore last year. No, these people are just part of the scenery to fill the gaps in conversation…y'know, 'Oh, I say, old boy, how's dear old Moscow?' You'll get used to it."

Solov hoped he didn't have to. He was bored already. He

despised them. They were stuffy and choking with privilege. Their conversations were filled with glories past and good old Queen Victoria. He had respect for British soldiers, what he'd read about them in the history books.

Sevoska lit a cigar: "This fellow coming towards us with the white hair. Foreign office. A sort of liaison for us. Drinks like a fish. Ah, hello, Sir William, how are you?"

The Englishman shook hands and dabbed at his forehead with a silk handkerchief as he was introduced to Solov.

"Awfully pleased to meet you, Major Solov. I trust you're enjoying yourself?"

"A little early to say but so far so good," replied Solov.

"Nice trip? Destroyer, wasn't it? Awful sea travel at this time of year. I'll just catch myself a drink."

Sevoska glanced at Solov: "You'll get the hang of it. Ah, here's our men."

Two men in dark suits politely moved through the crowd and stood before them awkwardly.

"May I introduce Colonel Lawler?" said Sevoska, "He's in charge of your project. And this," continued Sevoska, indicating the younger man, "is Captain Decker. You'll be working closely with him at the Special Training Centre."

They shook hands and murmured welcomes. Decker gripped Solov's hand, manfully.

"Technically," said Colonel Lawler, smoothing the edges of his moustache with a finger, "I'll be your commanding officer, but it'll be you who will be running the show in conjunction with Captain Decker. I'll be on hand to help in any way I can."

"Pleased to meet you, Major," said Decker, fixing his gaze. Solov felt Decker was searching his face for evidence that he was a better soldier than him.

"Hope you'll be ready to leave on Monday, Major, you'll be meeting the troops. Nice countryside. They're a good bunch of men. Decker will vouch for that, eh, John?" said Lawler.

"I'd say they are some of the best men I have worked with, sir. A few rough edges to iron out but we welcome your advice and instructions, Major," said Decker.

"I'll do my best, Captain. I'll show them what 'blood, sweat and tears' really means," said Solov.

Solov thought the Churchill reference would break the ice but there was a stiff silence.

"Good show," said Lawler, "Shall we get another drink?"

"Oh, I think they already have a good idea about that, Major," said Decker. "We know how to give the Jerries a bloody nose."

"We'll try and put that to some good use then," said Solov.

Decker followed Lawler to get another drink. Sevoska turned to Solov with a grin.

"Nikolai, promise me you'll never apply to join the diplomatic service."

"Just trying to break the ice," he said.

"More like melt the polar cap."

Solov admitted to himself he was trying too hard but the news he'd received about this operation had not been good. What had been talked about as opening a minor second front, vital to the war effort, over the preceding weeks, had been pared down to what would amount to nothing more than a desperate commando raid extended only by the hopes of linking up with units of the French resistance. Although he knew his own role in this was more of a public relations exercise to help the thaw between east and west in a small way that provided cover for his real mission in Britain, it still annoyed him. From a projected battalion of commandos, the British Combined

Operations Executive had scaled things down to a mere squad of not more than a dozen men. He didn't think it was going to set Europe ablaze. Sevoska told him this news when he'd briefed him about their upcoming meeting with Lawler and Decker this evening. It wasn't a good start.

"So, John, what do you think?" asked Lawler, on the other side of the room, dropping ice into his drink.

"Arrogant communist type," sneered Decker.

"By all accounts, he's something of a guerrilla warfare expert, organised partisan bands in the defence of Moscow and Stalingrad. And I know he's a commie but they are our allies."

"I used to think the German army was the only thing that stood between us and the Reds. Do you ever think we may have chosen the wrong side to fight on, sir?"

"Yes, but I prefer to deal with things as they are, not how we'd like them to be."

"Yes. If Hitler hadn't got too big for his jackboots…"

John Decker felt at home around the high society of Mayfair. If only his father could see him now, rubbing shoulders with the upper crust, the 'old money'.

His father, Thomas Decker, was a self-made man who had made his fortune in engineering. He owned two factories in the Midlands. With his wealth, he'd bought a small estate in the country, kept horses, went shooting. He actually held shooting parties and invited the local landed gentry, but they weren't impressed. Thomas was 'new money'. That was vulgar, industry was dirty money and he had the 'wrong accent'. The gentry made fun of him behind his back. Decker remembered how his mother had gone to great pains organising a soiree. Only his father's business associates came, and the nearest local aristocracy, the Egertons.

He could hear his father's voice: "I spent a small fortune on all that claptrap but we're not good enough for 'em," he'd cursed later. "To hell with 'em, if my money stinks then I'll leave a nasty smell behind they won't forget." His father was beside himself with the humiliation.

John was to be one of the symbols of his father's social mobility. He was sent to prep school, then to Eton and on to Oxford University by the time he was nineteen. He'd felt a fearful self-consciousness initially but, at each stage of his education, he'd managed to overcome his trepidation. There were other boys like him from the mobile middle class and, together, they could negotiate the chasm between the 'nouveaux riches' and the sons of the aristocracy. As the years bore on, John acquired the accent and mannerisms, but inside he knew the gap could never be bridged no matter how much he took on the lifestyle. He took on the social and political outlook of the upper class but always felt the outsider, unaccepted, an impostor.

In 1926, he joined other students who helped to break the general strike of that year, crossing picket lines to help deliver the mail. Often, he and his friends clashed with workers, many of them communist party members. This is where he gained the acceptance of many of his fellow students from the upper crust. When it came down to it, he demonstrated which side of the barricades he was on, and he began to cross the line.

Back home, his older brother, also called Thomas, was his father's boy, his heir to the land, the house, the business. John was going to be a manager if he wanted the job. If he wanted the job!

John had bigger plans. He was moving away from his family. He wanted to serve in the military. His heroes were nothing to do with commerce or business, and not some idle estate manager. No, he wanted to be Lawrence of Arabia. He'd read about T.E. Lawrence's exploits in the first war where he had gone out amongst the natives and roused them to inflame the Middle East against the Turks. All down the ages, he had heroes from the history books, myths and actual, Hereward the Wake, Robin Hood, General Wolfe, Nelson and Wellington, The Charge of the Light Brigade, Rourke's Drift, together with the more recent

Lawrence. That's how he was going to break through the class barrier, not by sucking up to upper class snobs who never got their hands dirty.

He'd gone from Oxford to Sandhurst and been posted to the cavalry, but the cavalry was to be mechanised in time. The process was slow, as was promotion in a peacetime army. No, there were to be no valiant cavalry charges on the North-West Frontier for him.

His parents had, initially, frowned upon his military ambitions, but gradually came around to the added prestige this brought, or so they thought. After all, the local gentry had long lines of military exploits in their families and his parents welcomed him making appearances in his dress uniform at functions where the sons of others were paraded.

"Whether that lot like it or not," his father would splutter, "the 'nouveaux riches' are here to stay." 'That lot' being the old families. "They've got the land and the lineage, but we've got the money."

"To the victory at Stalingrad," said Lawler, returning with Decker in tow.

"Stalingrad!" they all said.

"So what exactly will you be teaching us, Major, that we don't know already?" said Decker.

Despite himself, Solov thought Decker had a point.

"You must appreciate, Captain..." Solov began.

"Call me John."

Solov guessed that maybe Lawler had had a quiet word with him in the same way Sevoska had urged him to try and form a working relationship.

"John. You must appreciate the Germans invaded us and took a large area of our country under their control, including a vast amount of manpower that was uprooted, scattered, left behind in the confusion in '41. We hit on the hardly original idea of giving support to the many small bands of troops behind enemy lines, co-ordinated them, forming effective units of partisans. They proved very successful in tying down several divisions of the Wehrmacht and hindered its lines of communications and supply. They contributed to the victory at Stalingrad. Any reprisals the Nazis took out on the civilian population only drove more recruits into our ranks and we trained them too. The Russian people are used to hardship. We suffered for centuries at the hands of the Tsars."

Solov surprised himself. He was openly talking politics again.

"The British are also no strangers to hardship, Major Solov," said Decker.

"Please call me Nikolai. Yes, but a different kind of hardship. Russians have fought on their home ground many times, requiring a different standard of toughness. Take, for example, that old famous British saying 'a man's best friend is his dog'. Very true. It should apply to all animals. I love dogs. They taste very nice when you're crawling on your belly in some bombed out factory in Stalingrad. While you pamper your dogs in Britain, we used to train ours to eat under tractors. They got used to it. We then strapped mines to them and sent them out to look for food under panzers and...you get the picture?"

"I see," said Decker.

"You may think it's cruel. We don't delight in it, but when survival is a necessity for our way of life, we fight with all the means at our disposal, and that's hard. I'm for another drink. Stefan?"

Sevoska nodded as Solov took his glass away. He turned to the two British officers.

"I'm sure he'll be fine once he's garrotted a few more Germans."

FIVE

"Y ou're going to receive a visitor, an officer and a gentleman from abroad, no less. He's going to talk to you and teach you things. Things, they say, that neither I nor Sergeant Miller here can teach you. What's so special about him? I don't know. But he's a guest of His Majesty's government and I want him treated accordingly. Any questions?"

"Sar-Major?" A man called from the middle of the rank. He was shorter than most of the others. He shouted at the top of his voice in parody of the sergeant-major's parade ground manner. The other men around him suppressed a smirk.

"Yes, Mason, what is it?"

"You said an officer and a gentleman, Sar-Major, does that mean we've got two visitors?"

"You think you're so funny, don't you, Mason, lad? One of these days I'm going to scrape you off the toe end of my fucking boot."

Sergeant-Major Redfearn turned to Miller: "Sergeant, see to it that your men are kitted out and ready to receive the CO and guest within the hour!"

"Okay, Sar-Major. You heard what the man said, go to it," said Miller. The men dispersed, sloppily. Most of them shuffling away, a few lighting up cigarettes.

"Miller, a word with you," snapped Redfearn.

Miller sighed and shook his head slowly as he followed Redfearn to a safe distance out of earshot. Redfearn spun around and faced him, his face tight with anger.

"I think you and your men are slobs, Miller. Especially that Mason prick. A more certain candidate for a penal battalion I've yet to meet. He's the ringleader in that undisciplined rabble disguised as soldiers and, by God, I'll see him in the fucking glasshouse if his habits don't improve, understand?"

"I think you should understand, Sar-Major, these men aren't ordinary soldiers. They're trained for work not normally demanded of your frontline soldier…"

"I know what a commando is, Sergeant, don't bloody patronise me. I don't need an education on the subject, but they're still in the army, and that doesn't exempt them from discipline…"

Miller waited for Redfearn to finish. "I'll talk to them," he said.

"You'll talk to them?"

"Alright then, I'll shout at them for a while. They're soldiers, Sar-Major, with respect…"

"Respect? Miller, you don't know the meaning of the word…"

"With the greatest respect, Sar-Major, if you're not happy, take it up with the CO when he gets back. These men are fighting soldiers not square-bashers."

Redfearn glared at him. Miller knew he was a twenty-five year man who had never seen action, too young for the first war and now side-lined forever into one backwater after another.

"Make sure they get ready, Miller," he growled, then stamped away.

Miller watched him recede across the square to the admin block. Redfearn, the eternal NCO of the old school, all bully beef and spud-bashing. If it moves salute it, if it doesn't, paint it. Miller had earned his stripes in action not by long service.

Inside his squad's billet, Miller made sure his men were getting ready. He could hear some of them singing in the showers. Others were sorting out battle dress and webbing on their cots or in the middle of the floor. Mason sat on his cot, struggling to pull on his boots. He looked up at Miller.

"Did he give you a bollocking, Ray?"

"He was ready to castrate you, Mace."

"Balls."

"Exactly."

"Better watch what you say, Mace, he might give us all guard duty, or something," said Barrow, a Midlander hoisting a tangled mess of webbing off the floor.

"He knows he can't give us stuff like that," said Mason, lighting a cigarette before continuing with his boots. Miller took the cigarette from Mason's mouth and pulled on it.

"You just be careful with him. Where there's a will, there's a way. He'll be looking up regulations as we speak."

Mason snorted.

"I'm serious, Mace. Cut him some slack."

"I'll give him some fucking slack, so I will," boomed a voice from the entrance to the shower room. The big Irishman was dripping all over the floor as he towelled himself down. It was Malone.

"You'll show him, Sterl," said Mason.

Sterling Malone walked forward, his bare feet padding across the floorboards.

"So who's this foreign feller they're bringing, Ray?" Malone asked.

"They said he was some kind of expert in his field." Miller shrugged.

"I'd rather stay in our own field," said Mason.

"Mace, y'know, the Sar-Major's right. You're really fucking funny. As far as I know, Sterl, he's a Russkie."

"A Russian? Well, well, well," said Malone.

"Is he one of them Cossacks with a sword and riding a horse?" said Barrow.

"Wonder if he's got any vodka, and those black Russian fags, strong as hell they are," said Mason.

"He'll probably be one of those stiff commies who'll bore the arses off us," said Miller.

"I don't like Russians. They put the willies up me," said Armstrong, coming out of the showers, dabbing a towel at the eagle tattooed across his chest. "They're as bad as the Germans. I don't like any of 'em. We came into this war to help Poland and what d'you know? While Hitler's attacking them on one side, the Russkies were attacking them on the other. They're as bad as the Germans. Now they've been getting their arses kicked, they want to be our friends."

"Thank you, Neville Chamberlain," said Mason.

"I think he's right, y'know," said Barrow. "Didn't they sign a treaty with Hitler?"

"They did," said Miller. "But now we're all fighting the Jerries together."

"We can have some fun with this one. Take him out to the Horse and get him pissed." Mason grinned.

"What can he teach us?" said Armstrong. "Bet that ponce Decker and Lawler have dreamt this one up between 'em."

"Nah," said Miller. "This stinks of some bastard in Whitehall with nothing better to do."

John Decker slowed the staff car to a stop at the third and final checkpoint at the Special Training Centre. Decker and Lawler showed their IDs to the MPs who greeted them with a warm familiarity. Solov showed them his typewritten pass from Combined Operations. The barrier was raised and they drove on.

Solov was relieved to finally be there at the end of a tedious journey, having endured the shallow conversation of the Colonel and the stony silence of Captain Decker. The car had made its way with Solov studying the map from London to the east of Brighton, along the coast road for approximately twenty miles. The training centre was in the form of a rectangle, with various green-painted buildings and huts around the centre linked by gravelled pathways. It was unremarkable, nothing to recommend itself, the word 'special' seemed redundant. It was merely to house soldiers and nothing else. Two garages housed a few trucks, and an American jeep. In the centre, a flagpole without a flag. Solov assumed correctly that all the training was done out in the fields, forests, hills, moors and cliffs that overlooked the Channel. Decker stopped the car outside one of the huts marked 'Admin'. A soldier descended the verandah steps to open Solov's door but the Russian opened it first, climbed out, returned the man's salute and followed Lawler and Decker. The soldier stood and stared at Solov then climbed into the car and drove it away.

Inside, Lawler introduced Solov to his staff.

"This is my adjutant, Lieutenant Carter, his number two, Sergeant Walker. They're in charge of admin and ordinance. Anything in the way of logistics etc. They're your men, Major."

Solov smiled a greeting. Rain suddenly spattered against the windows, breaking the silence.

"Just in the nick of," said Lawler. "Shall we rustle up some hot tea, Walker?"

"Yes, sir."

There was a knock on the door and Sergeant-Major Redfearn walked in. He saluted and announced: "The men are ready for inspection, sir." He threw a glance at Solov and puffed his chest out further.

"Oh, hell, I forgot," said Lawler, and turned to Solov. "I'm afraid I forgot Sar-Major arranged for you to inspect the men.

Would you mind? You can get your first look at them."

"Of course," said Solov. He followed Redfearn out into the pouring rain. He caught up with him as he rounded the corner where nearly a hundred men stood erect in the now torrential downpour, divided neatly into their sections and squads, and in full battle dress.

"Parade, present...arms!" bellowed Redfearn, stamping to attention.

"Thank you, men, for the welcome, but there's no need for you to get unnecessarily soaked on my account. You can dismiss them, please," he turned to Redfearn.

The NCO walked over to Solov.

"Sir, it's just military courtesy to inspect them..."

"It's pouring with rain, now dismiss them. Men! I'm sure we'll meet in good time. I really don't want you getting wet. I'm going to have tea. I suggest you all do the same. Thank you."

With that, the men fell out and Solov returned to admin, leaving a fuming Redfearn trailing behind him. Inside the office, Solov turned to face him.

"Sergeant-Major, I respect your seniority, you must have a distinguished career?"

"Thank you, sir."

"But I can't imagine why you want to get the men soaking wet just so I can take a look at them."

"Just a gesture of military courtesy, sir."

"Courtesy? Is it courteous to let them get soaked? I'm going to help train them. I want their respect, otherwise we won't work well together. Surely, it would have been better to wait until it stopped raining?"

Redfearn looked to his CO, who didn't offer any help.

"I know you probably meant well but, if you look after your men, they'll look after you, and in war that is so important."

"Yes, sir. Is that all, sir?"

"Yes, Sergeant-Major." Redfearn saluted, spun around, and marched out into the rain.

"Was that really necessary, Major?" Decker asked. "Making a fool of him in front of the men?"

"He's a big boy. He can take it. Old soldiers like him find it hard to let go. This is a new type of war. We can do away with all that pointless shouting here."

"Point taken, Major," said Lawler, interrupting them. "Redfearn does pile it on a little, John. He does tend to forget that, primarily, he is in charge of security. Mind you, Major, be mindful not to override his authority, especially in front of the men. It just isn't done here, and I'm sure it isn't done in the Russian army," Lawler added, diplomatically. "Sergeant Walker?"

"Sir?"

"If you would arrange Major Solov's room, collect his things from the back of my car?"

"Sir."

"Gentlemen, if you could follow me into my office. Glenn," Lawler turned to Lieutenant Carter. "Could you do the honours once the kettle's boiled?"

"No problem, sir."

Lawler led Decker and Solov into his office.

"The men looked well turned out anyway, Colonel," said Solov, seating himself, watching the rain through the window.

"Yes," said Lawler. "They're what's left of what used to be two hundred and fifty."

"What happened?"

"Mainly Dieppe, last year," Decker said, offering him a cigarette. Lawler stayed with his pipe.

"From this unit we lost seventy-eight killed, thirty or so captured, another dozen or so seriously injured," said Decker.

"Yes, bit of a mess, really," said Lawler, filling his pipe.

"Then we had a few returned to their units, and the rest have been dispersed mostly to the Med, North Africa," said Decker. "Some of them went to India to join up with General Wingate's Chindits."

"I've heard of the Chindits," said Solov, turning as Carter came in with a tray of drinks. "Ah, the famous British cup of tea." Solov smiled, taking a cup.

"1st Squad leader Sergeant Ray Miller, sir." Miller introduced himself as they were all assembled in their hut, later, to meet Solov. Decker, Lawler and Carter sat off on chairs at the front and to the side.

"This is Corporal Harry Tobey," Miller continued. Tobey was a tall, thin man with a broken nose and slanted smile... "and the rest, sir...Private Philip Armstrong..." He rose and looked straight through Solov... "Private Joe Anderson..." a tough-looking youth... "Private Ed Barrow...Privates Sterling Malone...Frank Mason, Antony Scalleni..." another young man, cheerful, Italian probably, thought Solov, judging by his looks and name... "Robert Thornton..." another big man, nearly as big as Malone... "Ed Wheeler," serious-looking with a bad scar above the left eye.

Colonel Lawler tapped his pipe into the palm of his hand and stood up.

"Men, you are about to undergo more training. This time in advanced guerrilla warfare techniques, sabotage and harassment within the enemy's territory. We have with us a visiting officer of the Soviet Union, our ally, who is an expert in this field and will be working closely with you and Captain Decker over the coming few weeks. He's only been in our country a few days, but his English is excellent, as long as you don't bamboozle him - confuse him..." (Lawler smiled at Decker) "...with too much slang. He is eager to tell you about himself and his profession. I'll let the Major take over from here. Major?"

There wasn't a murmur in the room as Solov took the floor. He stood silently for a few moments, his eyes meeting each of theirs. Most of them met his. One or two looked away. One of them, Mason, smiled back at him.

In an even tone, he began: "Thank you, Colonel. You're a fine-looking band of soldiers. Most of you have seen a lot of action. You are accomplished in your work. What then, you might be thinking, is a Russian doing here? Our governments, yours and mine, in their infinite wisdom, seem to think I can teach you a few things."

Mason interrupted: "Question, sir?"

"Yes?"

"Will we all have to have our heads shaved?"

Laughter broke out.

"A man with a sense of humour." Solov smiled.

"In answer to your question," Solov said to Mason. "No, you will not. Nor will you be having much chance to shave at all, or wash, or eat hot meals, or sleep in beds while we are training. By the time we are finished, you won't have the strength to lift a razor."

The room was silent again.

"Now what happened to that sense of humour?"

They laughed, this time directed at the sheepish-looking Mason. The squad now paid close attention. Solov felt he'd broken some of the ice between them, and felt less apprehensive now, much more at home in his role of lecturer.

"During the next few weeks, I hope to be able to teach you some of things I learned while fighting the Germans in my homeland. When the Germans invaded the USSR in June, 1941, you'll remember they covered tremendous distances in the first few weeks. Many prisoners were taken - 300,000 at Minsk, 200,000 at Smolensk and more than twice that amount at Kiev. More than a million men, besides all the civilians they rounded up. They were given no food and all the Germans had to do was point them in the direction of the nearest field kitchen, they didn't need guards!

"A lot of those men, the more resourceful ones, managed to escape, which was not difficult. They formed small bands at first, for self-defence. They made raids for food, ammunition and weapons. Little pinpricks. They stole trucks from convoys for supplies and used the trucks as transport. As they became stronger, they attacked larger convoys. The German troops sent out to track them down were themselves ambushed by men who knew the terrain. Help was provided by the local civilian population who gave shelter and protection. Gradually, a small army was built up and specially trained officers were dropped behind German lines to lead them. As a result, several divisions of the Wehrmacht were constantly tied up and enemy resources were diverted from the front. The partisans attacked, hit hard, then disappeared. Any abandoned field guns, tanks or transport were repaired and used in the struggle, so we were an army in the enemy's rear where there was no army before. If food was scarce, the partisans would eat what they could, roots, dead horses, dogs. The key words in the partisans' vocabulary were 'survive', 'harass' and 'kill'. You must remember these words, live by them, die by them, if necessary."

Solov finished and sat down. Colonel Lawler took the floor.

"Thank you, Major. Men, I can assure you, the Major experienced all he has been talking about at first hand. He was one of the 300,000 men captured at Minsk. You will begin work tomorrow. And if you only have half as hard a time the Major had when he learned the hard way, then consider yourselves very lucky."

They applauded. The Colonel pulled Solov aside and said: "I think they like you."

~ ~ ~

"Get them out here! Now! Get all the children out!" There were cries, women were pleading, even one of the old men was on his knees praying to a god long banished, though Stalin had allowed some churches to re-open after the invasion.

"Get them out!" called Solov.

They stood in a semi-circle at the front of the commune. Three of his men ran into the building. He could hear more screams, this time from children.

"Please, comrade, please not the children, I beg you!" The old man was on his knees before him. Solov ignored him, tried to look away. He pointed his Schmeisser in the air and fired a short burst.

"Out now!"

His men dragged five children out of the first house, they were crying. Seven of his men had been killed and crates of valuable arms had been recaptured by the Nazis because children had stumbled upon them in the marshlands and told what they saw. The Waffen SS troops had come and his men had put up a valiant fight to the last.

"Against the wall!" he yelled.

One of the young mothers, or a sister, maybe, ran to embrace two of the crying children.

"Get her away from them!" he ordered.

"Sir, do we have to?" said his right hand man, Karel.

"We have to. It's an example to others. We can't afford not to. Move that woman!"

By now, she was holding tight to the children but was being prised away from them. She was strong in her fear.

"Fuck!" growled Solov. "Leave it!"

His men dropped her legs onto the ground. Solov levelled his machine pistol and fired...fired...long and hard...

Solov sat upright in his cot for a few seconds and swung his feet to the floor. He stood and opened the curtains, looking out onto the small parade ground. He couldn't get rid of the nasty taste in his mouth. At least, it wasn't raining. He walked back to the cot and threw the blanket over it, covering the pillow. He had to get moving. He pulled a kitbag from under the cot and began to get dressed in the rough British Army khaki uniform. It had been issued to him yesterday. If he was going out and about with the troops, he had to wear whatever they wore, no insignia, no rank, no badge on the beret. He was just another soldier. Only the clean-shaven head gave any clue there was something about him. He wanted to retain something of his identity.

He'd been assigned a small room next to the adjutant's office, and given his own phone so he could give verbal reports to Sevoska. Already, he could hear the clatter of a typewriter. He would have liked to have sat on the bed a little longer, just to smoke a cigarette, but he remembered he couldn't make a hot drink in the room and he was thirsty.

Sergeant Walker made up his mind for him when he tapped on the door and entered, balancing a tray with a cup and saucer on it, and smiled: "Thought you might like a quick cuppa before you turned out for breakfast in the mess, sir? It gets a little crowded in there and it is your first morning with us..."

"Thank you, Sergeant, I'll have it here," he said, indicating the small bedside table. Solov took a swig.

"Sergeant, is that all you English drink, tea?"

"No, sir, but if you'd like…"

Solov raised a friendly hand: "No, I didn't mean it like that. This will be fine. Thank you."

Solov waited until he was alone then poured the tea through the window. He didn't like tea with milk, especially that powdered milk, and he didn't like to be mothered. He pulled on his tunic and made his way to the officers' mess. He could hear the sound of conversation and cutlery. There was one long table draped with a white cloth. The officers turned their heads or looked up when he entered. Conversation turned down. There were seven officers there. One stood up, a napkin wiping his mouth, Lieutenant Carter,

"There you are, Major. Sorry you had to find your own way over here. Thought it best not to disturb after you travelled all that way from London yesterday."

"That's alright. I was awake anyway."

"Then you must be famished, sir."

Solov followed Carter around the table to an empty seat next to Carter's own. The rest of the officers nodded greetings. He nodded to Decker who looked down at his meal.

"Listen, chaps, Major Solov will be here for a few weeks," said Carter, "working with John's outfit. Sir, may I introduce…" he worked round the table left to right: "Lieutenants Wood, Spencer-Williams, Troy, you already know John, Evans and Captain Ferry, security."

Ferry looked warm, friendly even. His greying hair gave Solov the impression he'd been a captain for thirty years or more.

"I'm very pleased to meet you, Major," Ferry said. "It's not often we get visitors from afar…unless you include the Yanks. Oh, and Canadians, got quite a few Canadians in our team." He shook Solov's hand. Solov smiled in return.

Carter continued: "I don't think I've left anyone out," he said, sitting next to Solov.

Breakfast continued in a stilted silence. A soldier served Solov with eggs, bacon, sausage and mushrooms. Captain Ferry grinned from across the table: "Someone managed to acquire real eggs. I know a certain farmer, y'see." He winked.

"Which is why the Captain is in security," said Solov, smiling.

"Where does the Major hail from in the USSR?" asked Lieutenant Wood.

"I was born near Leningrad. Have you been to Russia?" Solov tasted the bacon. It was delicious.

"Yes, as a matter of fact, I have," replied Wood. "Leningrad, your hometown, summer of '37. I was with a university trip. It was only cold if you stopped moving. Lovely ice cream, I remember, and the ladies, something to behold. Not what I expected."

"Did you think all Russian women have moustaches, old boy?" said Spencer-Williams. The others laughed, even Solov smiled.

"Only in winter," he said, "helps keep them warm."

They were served with hot coffee, much to the relief of Solov. Some of the officers drifted away, including Decker. Carter rose and excused himself.

"I'm afraid some of us have work to do, gentlemen."

Solov found himself alone with Captain Ferry who gave him a cigarette while an orderly gathered up the plates.

"He hates the sight of you," said Ferry. Solov knew who he meant.

"Decker? I think you may be right. And thank you for being so frank."

"You only have to look at him to know that. Queer sort of fellow."

"Why?"

Ferry shrugged: "He's a strange one. Solitary chap. He's seen plenty of action - Norway, St. Nazaire, a short spell in Egypt with the long range desert groups, then Dieppe last year. He's a good soldier, but nobody knows him well. He hates the krauts though. I don't suppose there's anything wrong with that since we're at war with the buggers. That's all he seems to think about…going back in at them."

"I admire dedication," said Solov, blowing smoke at the ceiling.

"Just thought I'd better let you know," said Ferry. "So you'll know what you're up against, old chap."

"I have no feelings either way on the matter. I'm like Decker. I have a job to do. We all have. Then we can all go home when it's done, but thank you. Now, if you'll excuse me…"

He dropped his napkin onto his plate and left Ferry smoking on his own.

There's nothing like stumbling into a private club, thought Solov, and finding you're not a member.

SIX

L aid up in the long grass in a meadow, eight miles or so from the training centre, Ed Barrow listened to Frank Mason telling him how they were going to desert from the army.

They'd paired off for an 'initiative test'. Since six that morning, they'd been running around the muddy tracks of the countryside, startling farmers and heaving the weight of their knapsacks while Sergeant Miller had led them up every hill, down every slope, across every cold, deep stream they happened to find.

Miller had let them rest for ten minutes, then split them up. They were to find an old farmhouse and meet up there.

Mason and Barrow had been among the first to set out. Barrow had let Mason talk him into laying low and latching on behind another pair at a discreet distance and let them do all the brainwork of finding the rendezvous point. With Mason persistently talking, they'd lost the other two and, worse still, lost their compass. They'd wandered around until, exhausted, frustrated, they found the meadow to rest in.

"Deserting's easy if you go about it in the right way," Mason said.

"Yeah, and if they catch you, it's twenty years hard in the glasshouse," Barrow said.

"Well, I wouldn't get caught, would I?"

"That's what they all say."

"Not me. Hitch-hike to Bristol or Holyhead, get a fishing boat to Ireland. They're neutral, y'know."

"I don't trust neutrals. Anyway, what would you do in Ireland? It's just spuds, bogs and Guinness."

"Just get a job or something."

"You wouldn't get as far as Bristol."

"Bollocks."

"You wouldn't, mate."

"Not with you moaning and groaning."

"Why did you volunteer for this outfit?"

"Well, that's the army for you, innit? I was in the infantry, this horrible sergeant, worse than Redfearn, kept riling me, so I asked for a transfer."

"And?"

"There was nothing going, the company commander said. Except they needed volunteers for a special unit. I think he was taking the piss. He said there was no square-bashing, none of that spit and polish stuff. He said it was an irregular force. He said if I just wanted to have a go at the krauts and be a hero the commandos were the people for me. So, here I am, on a whim…"

"You don't really want to desert, do you, Mace? Deserters get shot."

"So do fucking heroes."

Three miles away, on the crest of a hill, Phil Armstrong and Joe Anderson were pleased with themselves as they'd already found the old, stone grey farmhouse, spotted from a distance.

"Home and dry," said Armstrong. "Now, wait till I see that little fucker Mason. Trying to tag along with us, the bastard."

"He's shit. He can't find his arse with both hands," said Anderson.

"Don't believe a word he says," said Armstrong. "He's an arsehole. Just my luck to be in the same outfit as a creepy toe rag like him, and that fucking Eyetie kid. Now, to crown it all, we've got to take orders off a fucking Russkie."

"He's not what I expected a Russkie to be," said Anderson.

"That's what he wants you to think, mate. Showing us the tricks of the trade? Teaching us to suck eggs, more like. It's a cheap propaganda stunt. Fucking hell, those communist bastards helped the krauts take Poland in '39. They forget all that. Give me Miller's stripes, I'd give this squad a kick up the arse."

Anderson knew Armstrong pretty well by now. He'd once been a sergeant but had lost his rank. He was still full of resentment. Nevertheless, he gave him his cue to start his usual rant.

"How did you lose your stripes again? Over a woman?"

Armstrong spat in the grass. He didn't need much encouragement. "I was with the Coldstream Guards. Just got back from Dunkirk…"

"Yeah? Hard fuckers them Guards…"

"Yeah. I was fighting on the perimeter of Dunkirk near to the end. Hand to hand combat, mate. It doesn't get tougher than that."

"Anyway…"

"Yeah, anyway, there was this girl, see." He rolled up his sleeve and revealed a small gallery of tattoos. "It's a good likeness."

"Looks like that Betty Grable."

"I thought so too. The face on this one." He rolled his other sleeve up, "Doesn't do her justice though."

"Smart. Nice colours, aren't they?"

"Anyway, I was going steady with her but I got stuck on duty. By the time I got off and went to the pub I caught her with another bloke. Did I leather him good and proper? Decked her as well. Got really pissed, started wrecking the next pub. The landlord called the Redcaps and I took them on too. Bang go my stripes.

Then I really blew. Belted my CO, didn't I? Got a court martial but I was given a choice, a penal battalion in Egypt or, because of my good service record, I could volunteer for special services. That's how I got into the commandos. Apart from putting up with pricks like Mason, I'm doing alright. And I didn't want to wind up in Africa with all those black bastards out there…"

Anderson interrupted him and pointed to the farmhouse down the hill. "There's some of our lot now."

"Yeah. Don't matter. No prizes for getting there first." He spat into the grass again. "Let's go."

"What do you make of the Russian feller, Harry?" said Ray Miller, as he sat on a low wall outside the farmhouse.

"Bet he's got a cold head in this weather," said Tobey.

"That was fucking funny at the welcome parade when he dismissed us. Redfearn's face."

"Good on him," Harry Tobey said. "All that rain. Redfearn was way out of order."

"He knows enough English to put Mason in his place too. And he doesn't fit in with the other officers. You can sort of tell."

"Don't forget, Ray. He's a communist. Our brass are all public school guys."

Miller walked over to an old, rotted bench beneath a broken window. He looked through into the dark interior, a table lay on its side, one of its legs missing. How it must have looked in better days: a blazing fire in the grate, a family around the table, children scolded by a harassed mother as the father comes in from the fields. Maybe a dog used to doze on a rug by the fire, a shotgun might have hung on the wooden beam above the door. Tobey came and stood next to him.

"This place gives me the creeps," he said

"Scared of ghosts, Harry?"

"Looks kinda haunted, doesn't it?" He grinned back at Miller and accepted a cigarette from him. Miller struck a match on the wall.

"There's no ghosts here, Corporal. They've all had their call-up papers."

"Alright, hande hoch, schnell!" They turned around. Miller laughed.

"It's a German with an Irish accent," he said. The tall Irishman, Sterling Malone, grinned back then vaulted the wall.

"There's no scaring you Brits, is there?" Malone said. Behind him, Wheeler followed.

"Brits?" said Tobey.

"Alright, one Brit and one colonial Canadian," said Malone, "Saw you a mile off. Thought we'd surprise you, right, Eddie?" Wheeler nodded.

"Here's two more," said Tobey, nodding at the hill.

"Looks like Scalleni and Thornton," said Malone. "And look here, will you? Isn't that taking initiative too far?"

A jeep was speeding around the hill. On the back of it they could make out Mason waving at them.

"Bastard's hitched a lift," said Miller.

Decker was driving with Solov sitting next to him. Behind them were Barrow, Mason, Armstrong and Anderson. When the jeep skidded to a halt, everyone dismounted except Decker. Miller called on his men to keep quiet after the first few rowdy greetings.

"Sergeant," said Decker. "The Major will accompany you back to base. He may take a few detours."

"Yes, sir. Welcome aboard, Major."

"I'll see you all later," said Decker. "Enjoy yourself, Major." He reversed away from them, turned and sped away as quickly as he'd arrived. Solov stood beside the men as they watched the jeep disappear. He was dressed in his British Army uniform, complete with a knapsack on his back and a Sten gun over his shoulder. He gripped a beret in his hand.

"Better put your hat on, Major. Gets pretty chilly out here," said Mason.

The Russian smiled and pulled his beret on.

"There you are, sir," said Mason, "You're one of us now."

"Very well, Sergeant Miller," said Solov, "where to now?"

"Double time back to base, sir?" said Miller.

"Take the lead, I'll follow."

The squad fell in according to Miller's orders, in their pairs. At Miller's command, they began their gruelling hike.

"Home, James, and don't spare the horses," Mason called out. Tobey ran alongside Solov and glanced at the rain running down his stubbly head as he tried to re-fit the beret. He felt he was beginning to develop a liking for this Russian guy. What officer, whether he was Russian, English or Outer Mongolian, would choose to share this with the Other Ranks? Or was the man a nut? Maybe they all were?

After a few miles, Solov called them to a halt and told Miller to take his place in the group. He would lead for the rest of the way.

Solov stepped up the pace as the rain began to pound harder at them, stinging their faces. He called a halt a few times, not to rest, but to run them through spirit-breaking push-ups, getting down in the mud with them, counting out loud, goading them to do one more…one more…just one more…

To their relief, they approached the woods where the

training centre lay. Their boots squelched through the gates. On the small parade ground, Solov called them to attention.

"Men, you did well. That's just an introduction to what is to come. Miller, send each man to come and see me in my office. I'll take him first in five minutes," he said, indicating Barrow. "The rest of you are dismissed until it's your turn."

Solov spent around fifteen minutes with each man in turn, taking notes scribbled in his own language on a notepad. He liked to know something of the background and character of these men he was to work with, their skills and experience.

Most of them were from the regular army and had volunteered for the commandos either for adventure, like Thornton, or as an alternative to punishment for some misdemeanour, like Armstrong. Some were young, Antony Scalleni was only twenty-two. His first action was last year in the Dieppe raid. He was a second generation Italian whose family had moved to London in 1925. His father had been a trade unionist who couldn't live under Mussolini's fascist regime after serving a year in jail. Harry Tobey was a Canadian who had seen service in North Africa and had been wounded in the early desert campaign. He'd also been evacuated from Greece in '41. Back in England, he'd joined the commandos in time for the Dieppe raid.

Armstrong didn't speak much, or meet his eye. He was sullen. Solov knew about his record and how he'd disgraced himself, but he was an experienced soldier.

"Maybe you can win your stripes back?" said Solov. Armstrong grunted something.

"Your anger may be useful in a pub brawl but in combat, it can cloud your judgement, Armstrong," he said.

"Will that be all, sir?"

Solov was impressed with the big Irishman, Sterling Malone. "Why is an Irishman fighting England's battles, Malone?"

"It's not just England's fight, sir. It's an international war against fascism."

He told Solov his father had been at the post office battle in Dublin, during the famous 'Easter Rebellion' of 1916.

"My father fought alongside James Connolly. He saw how they treated the great man. Kicked him when he lay wounded, sir."

Solov knew of Connolly, the Scottish socialist who had helped organise workers in Ireland. The uprising had proved premature, a year before the Russian Revolution, two years before revolutionary movements had swept across Europe and ended the war.

"Connolly was a comrade of your great leader, Trotsky," said Malone. "Trotsky was a fine man and he didn't deserve to die with an ice pick stuck in his head, sir."

Solov nodded. It was refreshing to speak of Trotsky so openly, dangerous in the Soviet Union. He remembered the photographs with Trotsky's images carefully airbrushed out.

"Stalin and his cronies have a lot to answer for," Solov heard himself saying.

"Yes, sir. That man has more blood on his hands than Hitler."

"We've got to take care of Hitler first, Malone. Maybe Stalin later."

"Yes, sir. That's what I mean, it's an international fight against fascism. That's why I went to Spain in 1936 with the International Brigade..."

"I was there too."

"Did you take part in...?"

"Killing Spanish socialists? No, I did not. That was a betrayal. I was at the front," Solov said.

Solov knew Malone was referring to the Stalinist-led purge against the left in Spain that undermined the Republican struggle and helped Franco to victory.

"We must find time to discuss that, Malone, as two old class warriors, eh?"

"Yes, sir."

Solov was also impressed with Miller. He had a good war record - at Dunkirk where he'd helped defend the beaches from Stuka dive-bombers from the back of a truck with an old Lewis machine gun. He'd joined the commandos from the beginning. He'd been in operations in Norway, Holland, France and at Dieppe. In all, Solov knew he had a good group. His only concern was their officer, Captain Decker, the unknown entity.

~ ~ ~

"Gentlemen, you'll excuse my son. He'll be late for his own funeral. He's very much an unknown entity."

"Apologies, dear father and guests."

"Non-entity, rather."

"Oh, do be quiet, Tom," John groaned. His older brother never missed an opportunity to snipe at him in his way of siding with his father, even if it was meant to be good-natured. He'd learned, over the years, to fend him off. John Decker had always found family gatherings and dinner parties thrown by his father quite a social ordeal. The longer he'd been absent from home - at prep school, at Eton, at university and at officer training at Sandhurst - the wider the gulf yawned between him, his father and his brother, Thomas the Younger, as he liked to call him.

"You've missed a beautiful meal, but you're still in time for brandy and cigars," said Thomas, his father. John could tell he was annoyed but was hiding it well. He wasn't going to say anything untoward in front of the visitors.

"Went the meal well?" said Decker, turning on his charm to his father's guests. There was Bernard Wise, his father's solicitor, a grey-haired man with a pretentious pince-nez. Next to him was George Silas, owner of a fleet of lorries that distributed his father's goods. Standing near the window were Andrew Forster, his father's bank manager, turning from his conversation with father's guest of honour, a man called Meyer from Germany, dressed in a pinstripe suit, dark hair turning grey and a pencil-thin moustache. John's mother, he knew, would be off somewhere with the womenfolk, probably showing off her ornamental garden so the men could indulge in - well - men's talk.

As expected of him, John wore his second lieutenant's dress uniform. He complied with his father's wishes as a way of making up for being late for dinner. He knew the evening was important for his father's business and Thomas Decker wanted the prestige of his uniform there to impress.

"This is our chance to expand our horizons, John," his father had written to him. "The Deckers are going international." John had foregone the trains from his base at Salisbury and had decided to come on his beloved Triumph motorcycle with his friend and fellow officer, Richard Gregory, riding pillion. They'd stopped at some of the pleasant inns along the way and arrived a little under the influence, holding in their laughter. They'd been ushered upstairs by his mother, lightly scolding him out of earshot of his father. John left Richard asleep on his bed, the cool evening air sweeping over him from the window he opened. He bathed and changed into his uniform and joined the men in his father's library.

"You must be proud of your sons," said Meyer. "One in business, and the other a dashing young officer."

"Yes, I am," said Thomas Decker. "I suppose they're the twin pillars of the Empire, commerce and military service."

John took a glass of brandy from his father, avoiding his look of reproach.

"That's right," John said. "Thomas the Younger makes the bullets and I fire them."

"To be pedantic, dear brother, I make the parts for the thingamajigs."

Young Tom offered him a cigar which John waved away.

"Thingamajigs? Pedantic?" John rolled his eyes.

"So, how long have you been one of His Majesty's officers?" said Meyer.

"Finished Sandhurst nearly a year now. Waiting for an overseas posting."

"And where would you like to be posted?"

"Somewhere hot and dusty where the flies bite," Tom interjected.

"You see, Mr Meyer, wherever I'm posted, Tom will know he'll be safe with chaps like me guarding him while he's tucked up in bed."

Meyer laughed, which seemed to give everyone else permission to follow suit.

"I don't really mind where I go. India, Malaya, maybe Egypt or somewhere else in the Middle East. Palestine looks quite busy with all the bother between the Arabs and Jews."

"Ah," said Mr Meyer, "the Promised Land."

"John just wants to get away from the dreary British weather, don't you, John?" his father said. "You might end up in Scotland. Now there's some fine country up there. Do you know the Highlands in Scotland at all, Joachim?" His father was trying to steer Mr Meyer's attention away from John. Meyer was undeterred.

"What would you do in Palestine?"

"About the Arabs and Jews squabbling over land? I'd keep

them apart from each other if they can't co-exist. Divide the land up equally, according to the size of population. Stop immigration there. I don't know why people can't decide where they want to be."

"Sometimes, people don't have a choice. Some people are subjected to persecution…"

John could see his father raise a hand behind Meyer, trying to communicate something to him. But Meyer was interested in this young man.

"Do you believe in the Jewish people having their own homeland, John?"

"Yes, but home is where the heart is, wherever you hang your hat. Jews have lived all over the place since, well, since time immemorial, the diaspora and all that. I mean, in this country and in your country, Mr Meyer. It's very political."

"Yes," said Meyer, his eyes searching his. "Your Mr Balfour spoke for a homeland in Palestine and if Herr Hitler gets to power, next year, he's made his position clear what he thinks of the Jewish people."

"Hitler's a politician," John said, "He wants to rebuild Germany. We need a strong Germany again as a buffer against the communists, stop them spreading their poison. I mean, whoever gets to power, we need Germany to re-arm and we need to keep them on side. The bigger threat is from the Bolsheviks…"

"I know that only too well, my boy," said Meyer, "I had to bring my family from Russia after the revolution. Not because we are Jewish, because we are capitalists. Lord knows, the Tsar gave our people a bad enough time during the pogroms…"

"You're Jewish, Mr Meyer?"

"Yes. Formerly Mannsky of Minsk. The Soviets took over my factories, that's why I left. Not because I'm a Jew. I mean, Trotsky is a Jew. Why, Karl Marx himself was a Jew. I am a businessman, like your father, an unashamed capitalist. We live in worrying times. Yes, I believe, like you, in a strong Germany, but what kind of Germany? If Herr Hitler comes to power next year, will there be a place for people like us? Or must I wear sandals in Palestine?" Meyer laughed.

"Hitler speaks sense when he speaks of the enemy in the east," said John's father. "But he uses the Jewish question as a means of winning votes. On the one hand, he talks about 'Jewish Bolshevism', then, on the other, he says that capitalism is a Jewish world conspiracy, I ask you. He's a politician and he'll say anything to get elected, depending on which audience he's talking to. Once he's elected…

"If he's elected," said the younger Thomas.

"If he's elected, he'll forget all that nonsense and it'll be business as usual, mark my words."

"Let us wait and see," said Meyer.

"Shall we go and join the ladies on the patio?" said the older Decker, he didn't like to mix politics with business, not politics as sensitive as this. As their father led his guests out toward the French windows onto the patio, John blocked his brother Thomas.

"So, we're doing business with the Yids now?"

"You Mosleyite. Business takes precedence over politics."

"Idiot. Business is politics! Why do you think we spent all that time commie-bashing in the General Strike? Oh, excuse me, all that time I spent commie-bashing while you were too busy passing the brandy and cigars in your boardroom meetings."

"Grow up, Johnny. You've got to learn the difference between a Bolshevik Jew and a capitalist Jew."

"A Jew is a Jew! You've changed your tune," whispered John, harshly. "What about the union-busting I helped with when father had the pickets on his gates in '26?"

"What's that got to do with Mr Meyer and the Jews? I think Oswald Mosley's gone to your head. Have you joined his new party then?"

"You're so colloquial. You can't see beyond those factory gates. If Mosley has half the success Hitler's having in Germany, you'll have more money than you can shake a stick at. A fascist British Empire standing by Nazi Germany, bye-bye Stalin, commies and unions."

"You really are taking all this anti-Semitism to heart. It's just a political battering ram to cause division, to form a focal point. Christ, even I can see that, and I never even went to university..."

"Boys?" It was their father at the open French windows. "Would you care to join us?" His sons held each other's stare for a few moments more and adjusted themselves for their father's guests outside.

"We can debate all this later if you like, brother." Tom smiled. "But not right now."

"Fine," said John, and followed him outside.

"Wine anyone?" their father called. On the patio a large round table was set with two carafes of white and red wine. The wives were seated, talking. Sitting on one of the stone balustrades at the top of the steps that led down to the gardens was a young woman in a pretty, flowing white dress. She looked about eighteen.

"Oh, yes, please." She gave her mother, Mrs Meyer, a quick look. She nodded her consent.

"But only one, Ruth. You know how it makes you giggle."

"Oh, mama," said Ruth, embarrassed at having that pointed out, especially in front of the younger men. "What's wine for if you can't have a giggle?"

"Very pretty," noted John to his brother, quietly.

"Meyer's youngest daughter. You haven't seen Isadora yet."

"Isadora?"

"The older one."

"Where's she?"

Tom nodded diplomatically towards the steps. John nonchalantly made his way to the table and helped himself to a glass of white, ignoring the conversations. At the top of the steps, he looked down into the gardens, sitting on the edge of the fountain with one hand playing with the water and a glass of wine in the other, he saw her. He took a sip from the glass and made his way down. As he approached, she looked up. Blinded by the sun behind him, she lifted a hand to shield her eyes.

"Hello," she said. "You must be John, the soldier?"

"Not John the Baptist. Sorry. Lame joke."

"That's no matter. I'm not religious. Far from it. I'm Jewish by race, not by religion."

John was flustered. "I didn't mean…"

She smiled without parting her lips and gave him a look. John saw big, round eyes, dark. They were set in a chiselled face surrounded by thick, black curls that rested on the collar of her satin jacket. Her legs were crossed in a pair of tight brown jodhpurs tucked into riding boots.

"Do you ride?"

"Does she ride? Dressed like that, does she ride? You idiot," laughed Tom, from the top of the steps. Their father joined him and called down to his youngest son.

"Why don't you take her out for a quick canter around the estate?"

John smiled at her: "Would you be interested?"

"I'd be delighted," said Isadora, and gulped back the wine in one, handed him the glass and stood up.

"Give me ten minutes to change into something more comfortable," John said. She followed him up the steps. At the top, she linked arms with him and announced to the party: "I'm joining the cavalry," to laughter. When the sun was out of his eyes, John glanced up at the window he'd left open upstairs. He noticed the bare-chested figure of his companion, Richard, obviously now awake, but he stepped back quickly out of view.

"Won't be long," John announced.

He stepped smartly through the doorway and made his way upstairs, two steps at a time. He entered the bedroom and there was Richard under the covers of the bed, a cigarette in hand.

"You shouldn't smoke in bed. It's bad for your health," John said, as he began to gather up suitable riding gear, trousers, shirt, jersey. "I'm going for a ride."

"So I heard," said Richard, pulling back the cover revealing the clear white sheet, he rubbed his hand up and down it, invitingly.

"I haven't time for that," said John, and went into the en suite bathroom to change. He discarded his uniform. As he was down to his underwear, he gasped as he felt a hand grab him from behind, hard. Richard's other arm turned him around and thrust him against the wall. Richard was completely naked, his face close-up to his, his eyes searching his face. Suddenly, Richard began to kiss him full on the mouth, passionately, violently. His hand went down below again, this time more gently. John's hands came up and pushed him back.

"I told you, I haven't time for that."

"For that, or for me? So, you'd rather go riding with that bitch?"

"Just a ride. I'll be back before you know it."

"This is Melissa all over again, or Julia."

Cutting a pathetic figure, Richard stood in the middle of the bathroom, his hands covered his face and he began to weep, his shoulders shaking.

"Come here," John consoled him. "I'm doing this as a favour to my family. Strictly business."

"It's just the way she took you by the arm. I've seen it before."

"Look, why don't you have a bath, get dressed and I'll be back for when you come down and join us for drinks? They're all wondering about you…"

"No. No. I'll think about it. I'll take a bath, see how I feel. Yes, fine, I'll be down, yes, I will. Sorry."

"Don't apologise. Just…get dressed. See you later?"

"Yes…yes…see you later. I'll be alright."

"Sure?"

"Yes, I'm fine."

He watched as John just as quickly pulled his clothes on.

"John?"

"Mmm?"

"No, you're right, you're right. I'm a mess. I haven't even unpacked yet."

"See you later?"

Richard nodded helplessly, silent tears wetting his face. John kissed him and gave him a hopeful look before disappearing through the door.

John walked Isadora towards the stables where his father

kept four horses.

"The smell." Isadora laughed. "I have to confess, I'm not a country girl, I'm a modern woman. When I wanted to go riding, I didn't mean on horseback."

"No? What did you mean?" John halted, his pulse beginning to race.

"Your motorcycle, of course."

"Oh, but, well, I…"

"'Oh, but, well, I'…" she mocked. "I like machinery. I like speed. I'm a futurist, not a farmer. I like surrealism not saddle sores."

"What? Well, of course! A surrealist."

"Sorry. I'm being precious. I'm going to study art. That is, my father wants me to study art. I'm more interested in photography. You must let me take your picture some time. You'd make a good portrait. Have you ever heard of Man Ray?"

"Can't say I have."

"You must come to Germany and visit us. I'm trying to talk Papa into buying me a studio in Berlin. He's reluctant. He's says Berlin is full of pimps. He's so funny."

John guided her over to where he'd left his motorbike, propped up near the orchard gate.

"It's a beautiful machine," she said.

John climbed on board and pushed the bike forward off its stand. He turned the key that he'd left in its ignition, kick-started and it roared into life. She yelped with joy and climbed on the back, her body hugging close-up to his, her arms around his waist. He felt that excitement again, gave it a couple of revs and called to her: "Hold on tight!." They tore off along the dirt track that followed the perimeter of the orchard, along into Bluebell Wood that hid his father's land from the main road and divided it off from neighbouring property. He soon got up the speed and weaved the machine along the track and over a small wooden footbridge, into the wood proper. Both wheels left the ground as they dipped into a small meadow and followed the bank of a stream. They powered up the opposite slope and she screamed as they skidded around a cluster of beech trees. She was screaming something but he couldn't tell what it was, he picked up the revs and topped a small hill and down the other side. At the bottom, he made a sharp right turn and slid along some overgrown grass as the machine went away from him, he tried to correct it but too late. He went over the handlebars and she went in some other direction. The engine cut out. John managed to roll to his feet.

"Isadora! Isadora!"

He found her lying on her back among a patch of ferns, mud and twigs in her curly hair.

"God, I'm sorry!" he panted, as he stood over her. When he saw her wide grin, he fell onto his knees, then next to her. She came up to meet him, her mouth meeting his and her arm pulling him down on her. His hand found her buttons.

"Wait!" she said. She frantically undid his belt and trousers and pulled them down around his thighs. He laid back and stared at the trees above, the sun tried to peek through at them. He gently placed a hand on the back of her head.

'This is what she wanted,' he thought.

She stopped as suddenly as she started and pulled him by both hands to his feet. She eased her jodhpurs down around her knees and stood against a tree and held onto it with her back to him. He came to her and felt her buttocks against his belly. After a long moment, he pulled away from her, gasped, and fell onto the ground. She remained standing, getting her breath back, and pulled her pants back up. She pulled him to his feet and helped him with his clothes, brushing them off. He pulled a twig from her hair.

"We must get back," she said.

"Wait, we're a mess."

"Don't worry, we'll tell them the truth."

"What?"

"We came off." They laughed in each other's arms.

They mounted the bike again. John started it up and this time rode all the way back across the open field towards the fountain where he'd found her. The party was already waving to them as they pulled into view. His father was opening a bottle of champagne. Isadora jumped down as John parked the motorbike. He joined them at the top of the steps. His father, beaming at him, handed him a glass of bubbly.

"To business and pleasure," he said.

"Business and pleasure," they all chorused.

"And to family," Meyer added.

"Family."

"Business and pleasure and family," said John.

The clink of crystal filled the air frozen by the sound of a single shot from a revolver from the upstairs open window.

SEVEN

Hard work started the next day. Solov and Decker joined their ranks while Miller took the lead. They headed for the obstacle course outside the camp, in the nearby woods.

The course was tried and tested, constructed in 1942, shortly after the training centre had been opened. It incorporated rope bridges, rope swings, ditches, all the toughened routes the terrain could offer. Mother Nature did the rest. Some of the men suspected Redfearn had been responsible for its demanding lay-out. This was untrue, but he didn't discourage this belief. The Sergeant-Major did, however, operate the old Vickers machinegun, from time to time, from the top of a small hill, overlooking a maze of barbed wire they were meant to crawl through, and he delighted in using live ammunition.

Although crude, the course was effective in reproducing certain battle conditions. It was based on the prototype for commando courses at Achnacarry Castle in Scotland. It was distinguished in claiming three fatalities. Miller's men did three circuits on the first day, with little time for rest. They went on to practise throwing hand grenades at the opposite end of the woods from sand-bagged slit trenches, hurling them into disused oil drums. Then there was target practice with Sten guns, Brens and rifles. Following that, a night-time circuit of the obstacle course and the pattern was followed again into the following week. They slept out in their two-man pup tents, tired, dirty, hungry for hot food and drink. They were often split into two teams when one team would track the other. Later, while one team slept in their tents, the other would stand a perimeter guard, each team taking four hours to guard, then sleep.

Frank Mason was cold and miserable, curled up against a fallen tree. He had nobody to talk to. He scanned the shadows before him.

"What the fuck am I doing here?" he muttered to himself, over and over. He wanted to piss. He knew, somewhere out there,

Barrow, Anderson, Wheeler, Malone and that ponce Decker were huddled away in their own misery on the perimeter. Nobody would notice. He stood up, unbuttoned himself and splashed away, farted, and crouched down again, wondering whether Decker had heard him. Decker was about twenty or so yards to the left and Wheeler to the right. He pulled the top of his tunic over his mouth and felt his warm breath down his chest. He took off his woollen hat and lit a cigarette inside it, cupping his hands around the warm glow, and exhaled pleasurably.

An arm grabbed him around his neck from behind and he felt a knee in the middle of his back as he was pinned face down. His mouth was gagged by a big hand. He could hardly breathe. There were two of them. They rolled him onto his back and grabbed his Sten gun from him.

To the right, he could make out two or three running figures, then voices called out. Above them, there was a familiar boom…Redfearn's.

"Everybody out! Your sentries are dead! You're all captured!" he yelled. Several torches were switched on. Mason was dragged down by the two men towards the tents where the rest of the men were roused from their sleep. Nobody was happy about this.

"What the fuck's going on?" said Armstrong, crawling out of a tent, followed by Scalleni.

"It's an invasion," someone said.

"No, my son," said Redfearn, triumph in his voice. "But one of your sentries might as well have waved us a welcome flag."

Redfearn's patrol had everyone covered with rifles. Decker walked over to Redfearn: "I suppose we should be congratulating you, Sar-Major," he said.

"Thank you, sir."

Solov joined them, followed by Miller.

"Thank you, Sergeant-Major. You did a good job," said Solov. He turned to the others. "Captain Decker and I thought you were getting a little complacent, so we asked the Sergeant-Major to arrange a night patrol to keep us on alert. If they had been Nazis, we would have been captured or killed."

"I thought there'd be a weak link, sir," said Redfearn, enjoying himself, "and we found one."

"Who was it?"

"We saw someone lighting a cigarette. He tried to hide it but not good enough. Right, lads, let's have a look."

Redfearn's men released their hold on Mason and he staggered forward.

"I might have known," said Redfearn. "It's a little squirrel gathering his nuts in May."

"Mason," said Decker, "you're a damn fool."

In the second week, emphasis was laid on close quarter armed and unarmed combat. This took place in the grounds of the training centre where Miller saw to it that rubber mats were placed together on the parade ground. He ran his men through a series of warm-up exercises. They were allowed to strip down to shorts and vests if they so needed. Decker and Solov stood before them.

Decker said: "No need to lecture you here, men. You all know the form. Pick yourselves a partner and fight like hell. Don't hurt each other, we need you all in one piece. It's just practice. It's about getting the enemy in a position where you can easily kill him. Miller, carry on."

Solov observed them grappling together, grunting as they heaved at each other's body weight, feigning punches and kicks to the throat, nose, groin and kidneys. He heard a voice call to him. It was Mason, the funny one, the joker in the pack.

"Major, I see you've got nobody to play with. Why don't you show me how they do it in Russia?"

Some of the others stopped to watch, some of them lay on the ground where they'd been thrown. Solov felt under pressure. This was an open challenge to his authority and he also guessed that Mason was trying to redeem himself for the other night in the woods.

"Very well, Mr. Mason," he found himself saying, with an obliging smile. He removed his tunic and dropped it to the ground. Mason was on him, aiming the firm edge of his hand towards the Russian's neck. Solov stepped back out of reach and grabbed Mason's wrist, his forearm struck the Englishman's belly and pulled him over, letting Mason's momentum and gravity do the rest.

"Feel better?" Solov held a hand out to help Mason to his feet.

"Just lost my balance, that's all," he said, as Solov received applause from the others.

Armstrong stepped forward away from where he'd left Scalleni on the mat.

"Need a new playmate, Major Russkie?" he said. He squared up to Solov.

"That'll do, Armstrong," said Miller

"Training, innit?" said Armstrong, not taking his eyes off Solov. "He can take a little feller like Mason on, but when it's someone his own size…"

Solov raised a hand to Miller to signal it was alright.

"When you're ready, Armstrong," he said. "But I don't think you are ready yet." He turned and walked away dismissively. He heard him coming and ducked down on one knee, swivelled round and caught Armstrong with his fist full in the solar plexus, then side-stepped away, leaving him gasping for air on his knees.

"Now, to finish him I would…" Solov stepped one pace back to the side of Armstrong and pretended to kick him in the ribs but pushed him onto his back with his boot. "…then I would…" He stood over him and demonstrated how he would stamp hard on his throat and grind his heel.

"Go on, Sterl!" shouted Mason. "Go on, big man!"

Sterling Malone towered over everyone. He wasn't particularly bothered. He liked Solov, felt some kind of affinity with him, but this was training, this was work. He strode towards Solov, warily, cat-like. Solov didn't want to get caught by those big arms, those big hands.

"Feel free, big man," Solov taunted. He knew Malone was no hothead like Armstrong, or foolhardy like Mason. He was cool, professional. Solov watched him as they circled each other, looking for openings. Solov lunged forward with a blow to Malone's throat, the Irishman stepped back and then made a grab for him. But it was a feint from Solov who went in low onto the ground and wrapped his legs around Malone's ankles pulling his feet together and forcing him over. Solov was up and swiftly behind him, one arm applying pressure to his windpipe, the other pushing his head forward in a lock. Everyone knew, in a real situation, Malone would have been seconds from asphyxiation. Solov released him and helped him up.

"Nice move, Major." Malone cheerily shook his hand.

The others, apart from Decker and Armstrong, applauded. Nobody else challenged Solov.

The second week showed the men to be pulling closer now as a working unit. They were more alert, more focused and functional as a team. Four more nights in the woods acclimatised them and two more middle of the night raids by Redfearn's Redcaps, as they became known, were repulsed, much to the annoyance of the Sergeant-Major. Individually, they were fitter, leaner and took a more professional interest in their work. The next period, the beginning of May, saw Solov coming more to the fore in their training. To prepare for this, Solov gave them a day of rest. It also gave him a chance to review his training schedule and study maps. Solov was restless. The weather was warmer. He'd been given a message to phone Sevoska in London for an update on his progress. He felt strange speaking on the admin office phone in his own tongue. Sevoska had mildly scolded him, good-humouredly, for not keeping in touch about his work and his movements - "Communication is vital in our work." Solov had apologised and told him that things were going well. Sevoska sounded suitably impressed, though Solov wondered why he should be interested in the minor details of commando training. Through the window, he could see some of the men kicking a football around with troops from another squad.

"It's not the big operation I thought it was going to be, Stefan, but these men are of good calibre, which makes it pleasant enough," he said. He saw Malone reading a book. "Some of them are exceptional. I think as far as public relations go, I seem to have impressed one or two of them..."

"Well done for that anyway, Nikolai," said Sevoska. "I'm glad you're finding your feet..." Solov was interrupted by the adjutant, Lieutenant Carter.

"Sorry to disturb, Major. Just to say that the Home Guards have confirmed they will give any assistance you need in any upcoming exercises. Their commander is a retired Colonel. He said he's only too glad to help out the 'old firm', as he puts it."

"Thanks, Carter," said Solov.

"Back to work tomorrow, sir?"

"Yes." He looked at Carter and indicated the phone, but smiled. He liked Carter. He had made him feel welcome and carried out his requests on equipment, and anything he needed, with a cheery disposition.

"Is there anything else, Lieutenant?"

"Sorry, sir, I know you're on the phone…"

"Yes?"

"With it being a day off, Sergeant Miller and his men wanted to know whether you would like to go to the local pub with them for a drink…"

"This evening?"

"Yes, sir."

"I thought officers and other ranks don't fraternise in your army, Lieutenant?" Solov heard Sevoska snort with laughter on the other end of the phone.

"Well, sir. It's a little more relaxed in this outfit."

"Give yourself a night off, Nikolai," Sevoska urged. "You need a break."

"In that case," Solov said. "Tell them I'll be pleased to have a drink with them. Where are we going?"

"Just down the road, the Horse and Hen."

"Fine."

After the Lieutenant had left Solov alone again, he said to Sevoska: "English beer, is it nice?"

"Better start getting used to it. What was the name of the pub again?"

"The Horse and Hen."

Sevoska burst out laughing again: "So quaint, so English. I love it. Enjoy it. We'll be talking again soon. Keep playing soldiers."

Sevoska's manner had irritated him. He didn't appear to take this part of the work seriously, had almost ridiculed it. He felt mildly offended as this was him practising his profession and he felt the old tension a soldier felt towards a bureaucrat. In the end, that is what Sevoska essentially was. It made him think of what was in store for him after this task. A life living under cover, a double life and it seemed far away from the life he was used to leading. He didn't want to 'melt away'. He wanted to be there, in amongst the action, concrete reality, not lurking in the shadow of lies and deceit. He tried to put it to the back of his mind for the moment. He needed a drink.

The Horse and Hen was an old public inn standing at the crossroads of gritty lanes and dirt roads proudly isolated between two small hamlets. The nearest sizeable towns were Brighton to the south-east and Chichester to the west. It was just five miles due east of the Special Training Centre and within equal easy reach of an American Army Air Force base to the north.

It had been a resting place for peacetime travelling salesmen, and the regular watering hole for local farm workers. In better times, the landlord had provided a well-used bed and breakfast service. Its bedrooms still lay in wait but were infrequently used. The dining area was long since given up to the influx of off-duty servicemen and women, especially the Americans who injected much-needed cash into the place or, more particularly, into the landlord's retirement fund. For the moment, he offered a near-resplendent lounge, thickly carpeted, its bay windows looking out across a canal that cut into some rolling landscape, for officers and their lady friends perhaps. There was a larger, stone-floored bar room equipped with dart board and billiard table for other ranks. The dimly-lit bar room was a cold, uninviting place with the tired faces of hard-bitten farmers nursing a dark pint in their laps, reading newspapers. A mahogany wireless high up on a shelf behind the bar brought its fodder of news bulletins, or BBC comedy shows built around a recipe of catchphrases that gave out the comfort of familiarity. But, come the evening, with the fireplace blazing, allied service men and women, civilian workers, all brought light and life with them as the radio dial found swing music, Hollywood hits and crooners. Bewildered locals either slipped away home or moved closer together in a corner and looked on enviously. Or else they tried to join in and take advantage of any largesse, especially from the Americans - 'overpaid, oversexed and over here'. A few local girls looked for excitement like moths around a light bulb (or, as some of the jealous local men would have it - 'like flies on shit').

Young women working in the Land Army that helped keep Britain fed, or ATS girls in khaki, or women from the munition factory a short bus ride away, all worked hard, and played hard. Some had American boyfriends who spoiled them with gifts and called up dreams of a new life or just a good time. For some of them, it was colour in a monochrome world, their own Clark Gable or Humphrey Bogart.

The older locals would look on, knowingly, play dominoes, allowing one or two Yanks to challenge them to a game if they bought a round. By early evening, it was a lively joint, romance, fun, Glenn Miller, beer and laughter.

Lieutenant Carter slowed the jeep and parked up next to several other vehicles and assorted bicycles. Decker and Solov dismounted. Already, Decker looked bored but dutiful. Solov rubbed his hands together.

"Lead on, Lieutenant," he said.

They walked through a heavy oak door into the lounge. It was half full with assorted tables around the room filled with junior officers talking quietly. There were some young couples talking with their heads together, looking up briefly as they entered. Decker pulled his gloves off, his cap, and placed them on the bar.

"Major, Lieutenant, what will you have?"

Solov settled for a pint and a brandy chaser. Carter had a pint, the same as Decker, who made the order.

"Not drinking vodka then, sir?" said Carter, trying on some bonhomie. "Make you feel at home?"

"Vodka? In England? It's nice, but...well." He smiled. He took his drink from the barmaid who blinked at his shaven head. Silence bore down on them as they sipped at their glasses. Decker looked at something across the room.

Carter whispered: "This bitter tastes watered down. It's foul."

Solov looked around the room too. He took in the reproduced oil painting, a stuffed fish with a gaping mouth, encased in glass.

"There is a war on, y'know," he said.

More silence, underpinned by the sounds of music and life coming from the bar room.

"I take it the men are through there?" Solov pointed at the connecting door that was signed 'bar room' and 'toilets'.

"I should think so. It gets a little rough at times, noisy and smoky. I suppose the men enjoy that kind of thing," said Carter. He led them over to a table for four by a window, a solitary figure sat there reading a newspaper, the Times. He was an older officer, a Colonel. He used the stem of his pipe to guide his reading.

"Sir, is this table free?" asked Carter.

"Yes, by all means," the Colonel said. The bar room noises filtered through each time the connecting door opened and closed.

Carter did his best: "Gentlemen," he said. "I think we can drink to the health of every one of our troops. It seems we're getting somewhere in this bloody mess. We've kicked Rommel out of El Alamein and he's losing North Africa. Your crowd," he said to Solov, "have kicked the Jerries' backsides at Stalingrad, pushed them back from Moscow and are holding out at Leningrad. Hats off, I say."

"I wouldn't say it was as easy as that at Stalingrad,

Lieutenant." Solov raised his glass, nevertheless. "We battered each other senseless for months. We outmanned them and outgunned them. And there's a long way to go yet. Berlin's a long way off."

Decker remained silent.

"Well, at least we're teaching Hitler he can't have it all his own way," said Carter, keeping up the conversation.

"Yes, Hitler tried to take Leningrad, big mistake, then he headed south and came unstuck. Two wrongs do not make a Reich."

Solov's lame joke struggled to stay afloat but the Colonel, at the end of the table, looked up from his paper and said: "Oh, very droll, sir. Very droll," raised his drink and went back to his paper.

Solov smiled as if he needed rescuing. He looked at his watch and downed his drink: "I'll get the next ones." He walked to the bar and ordered the same again. It was going to be a long night, he thought. Best take the edge off: "Make it a double," he signalled to his brandy glass. He could see through into the bar next door. The packed ranks of uniformed hands thrust out pound notes for service as the busy staff manned the pumps, coping as best they could with some humour. "Hold your horses, sheriff," one of them said to a US airman. Someone leaning over the bar caught Solov's eye.

"Major! Major, you comin' round, sir?" It was Mason. He smiled back at him.

"Just give me a moment," he said, indicating the round of drinks he'd ordered lining up in front of him on the bar. He took them back to the table.

"I'll just go through and have a quick drink with the men. I've been invited," he said. "Excuse me."

They nodded and Solov took his drinks through the connecting door. He shouldered his way through the crowded room and made his way until he heard whistling above the din.

"Major! Over here, mate!" Mason again, this time standing on a chair, waving him over to three tables, pushed together. Solov brushed against a pretty woman in uniform. She looked at him. "Hello, lovely man," she flirted. She was guided away by a morose-looking US Sergeant.

"Over here, Major," called Mason, stepping down from the chair. He was handing out glasses of beer from a wooden tray. Armstrong and Anderson played darts with two American airmen.

"Come and sit down here, sir," said Mason. Some of the men cheered him. Sterling Malone held out one of his big hands and gripped Solov's.

"Hello, comrade," he said. "Sure, and it's nice to see you."

"Thought you'd never make it, Major," Mason said

"Thought you'd stood us up," Miller said.

"Stood you up?" said Solov, not getting the vernacular.

"Turned our invitation down."

"No, no."

"Lieutenant Carter said he thought you might 'pop in' and say 'hello'," said Tobey, mimicking officers' tones, "Don't you know, old boy?"

Solov smiled and remembered how Sevoska had mimicked the same upper class twang at the reception in London.

"What you drinkin', Major?" asked Mason

"Brandy."

"Good. I'll get you a pint of bitter."

"Noisy, Major, isn't it?" called Malone, across the table. "It's the Yanks. They insist on letting everyone know they're here."

Solov sat between Malone and Miller. The table was full of empty and half-empty, half-full glasses.

"There you go, Bullet, get that down your neck," said Mason, returning from the bar.

"Bullet?" said Solov.

"Yes, sir," said Miller. "It's our nickname for you. Bullethead. Shortened to Bullet."

"Did the Lieutenant bring you?" Malone asked.

"Yes, and Decker."

"They next door?" Mason asked.

"Yes."

"Let's hope they stay there."

"Don't you like them?"

"Thing is, Major," said Miller. "The Lieutenant's fine. It's Captain Decker we don't much like."

"Got a fucking chip on his shoulder," said Tobey

"A chip? Sorry, some of your phrases..."

"He's got an attitude," Malone helped. "I think he resents you being in charge or something. He's sulking." Malone stuck his bottom lip out. Solov smiled.

"I'm only here a short while. After that, he can have his toys back."

"He was strange even before Bullet got here," said Mason, setting out for the bar again with the tray.

"He's a quiet guy," said Miller "A proper officer. Bit of a stickler for the rules. Seen a lot of action though. He's got a Military Medal. But he's strange, funny. Especially since you've been here."

Solov shrugged: "It's his problem. I'll do my job and leave."

"Y'know, Major," Malone again. "Your English is really excellent."

"Thanks. I did languages at university. The only time I have problems is when you fellows talk about chips on shoulders."

"In fact, Major," said Malone, "for a Russian, you make an Irishman feel a foreigner."

"Irishmen *are* foreigners, you big mick," said Tobey.

"Why have you shaved your head, sir?" asked Barrow, out of the blue, drunkenly leaning over Malone's shoulder.

"I was losing my hair. Think it looks better. Women like it. What do you think?"

"All them Russian peasant women, eh?" said Tobey.

"Well, they're closer to nature, shall we say? And your English women?"

"Now you're touching on a big subject. Passionate, fun-loving…"

"How do you know, Barrow? You're married," said Tobey.

"Fuck off, Corporal."

And so it went. Solov felt himself relaxing, enjoying himself for the first time in a long time. He knew he had more in common with them than the stilted atmosphere in the lounge. It confirmed everything he'd learned about class relations, the gulf between 'them and us', it was international. He knew the workers of Russia, England, France, Germany had more in common with each other than with their own ruling classes. Old Trotsky had been right, an international call to arms on class lines would have been enough to finish off the capitalists who held their workers in national boundaries…oops, this English beer was getting a hold on him, or was he just tired?

"So, Malone," said Solov. "Tell me, did you ever meet James Collony?"

"It's James Connolly, sir, begging your pardon."

"Sorry. Connolly. I'm tired…and this brandy…"

"I saw him speak a couple of times. I sat on my dad's shoulders in the middle of a crowd…"

"We've all done that…"

"Strike meetings and such. But I was too little. I was just turned six when the Easter Uprising took place. My dad saw how an English officer and gentleman kicked Connolly when he lay wounded on the ground, he did. You know what them murdering bastards did, sir? Took 'em all off to Kilmainham Jail in Dublin and shot all the leaders that wouldn't sell out. Then they brought Connolly in, tied him to a chair, a wounded man! Had to pinch his cheeks to wake him up before they shot him, they did. Scum! Fucking British bastards!"

"So, if we're bastards, Sterl," said Miller. "Why are you in the British Army, fighting on our side?"

"Fascism is the common enemy of the international working class. Am I right, Major?" Solov nodded. Malone continued. "That's why I went to Spain, to fight the fascists there. But we were up against Franco, backed by Hitler and Mussolini. No fucking help from Britain and France, mind, just ordinary workers making their own way there, under our own steam, we were. Some of us went on foot, proper foot soldiers. And the Stalinists stabbed the socialists in the back…"

"Oh, here we go," groaned Armstrong, darts in hand. "The Red fucking Flag."

"Fuck you, Armstrong," Malone said, smiling. "Why the backstabbing, Major?" he asked. "I couldn't figure it out. Now I've got a Russian here, I can ask you face to face…"

"It's complicated, Malone. But it's something that has

bothered me when I heard about it. Like I say, I was at the front. I was as horrified as you. I couldn't believe it. I thought it was fascist propaganda put out to divide us."

"Then you Russkies stabbed the fucking Poles in the back in '39, after siding with the krauts," said Armstrong. "What the fuck was all that about, Major?"

"Can we keep it down?" said Miller. "And keep it bordering on respectful. The Major's trying to answer."

"It's something I'm still struggling with myself. But I will explain it. Trotsky explained it. Maybe I will use it as a seminar sometime…"

Armstrong threw his darts derisively at the board.

"Yeah, right, a seminar, I can't fuckin' wait."

"Armstrong, I'm warning you," said Miller.

"No, he's right. Malone's right too. People need an explanation." Solov hadn't quite cottoned onto Armstrong's derision. "I want people to understand. There's no excuse for betrayal, because that's what it was. I'll do something in a seminar."

"All I know, sir," said Malone, "in Spain, and I bet in Poland, a lot of brave socialists, men and women, were taken away and shot, in the name of Stalin, and he's given a bad name to the revolution. He's drowned it in blood."

Solov looked at Malone. "You're right, Malone. In Spain, in Poland, in the Soviet Union too."

The door opened and four American airmen walked in with three civilian women. Heads turned their way. Mason gave a wolf-whistle. One of the Americans looked annoyed but saw the large group of men in uniform and chose to ignore it. The women looked and smiled, appreciatively. One of them, slim with long brown hair fashionably swept off her face, noticed Solov's shaven head and gave him a bigger slice of attention before following her friends.

"She likes you, that one, see that smile? Nice too," said Tobey

"Fuck, if that's what it does for women," said Mason, "mine's coming off tomorrow."

"Go get her, Major," Tobey urged.

"Get in there," said Malone.

"She's waiting for you," said Barrow.

Solov was only too happy to change from matters of politics to the lowest common denominator. The girl seemed to be distracted from her friends and kept glancing over her shoulder in his direction. Her American companion saw her and tried to stare down Solov.

"I had a letter a couple of months back," said Thornton, "off my older brother. He's in Burma, artillery. He said the Japs keep dropping leaflets saying 'Go Home, Tommy, your American allies are in bed with your women'. He said they had a laugh about it. But if he could see what we see, he wouldn't be laughing."

"Been going short, lately, Major?" said Tobey.

"What?"

Miller nudged Tobey and frowned at him for overstepping military etiquette. But Solov paid no heed, if he even understood. Two of the Americans were walking over towards them, one of them a Corporal, stubbled chin and dark face. Behind him was the soldier who had been glaring at him. The Corporal leaned over Solov.

"'Scuse me, bud, my pal here says he seed you making eyes at his girl over there." It was not a question, but a statement. The other American nodded.

Solov stood up. Miller stood too.

"Just a minute, Corporal," Miller said. "Don't you think you should show some military courtesy to the Major?"

The American looked at Miller: "I doan see no military insignia or nothing," he challenged.

"Take it from me," said Miller.

The American looked at Solov, then, Miller, then the others. Sterling Malone stood up.

"Yes, pal, take it from all of us," Malone said.

The Americans looked at the big Irishman.

"'Kay, sir," the Corporal said to Solov, "but it doan mean you can pull rank on a soldier's good time."

Solov acknowledged the American's need to save face.

"I'm sure you're right."

The Corporal nodded and steered his friend away.

"No sense of discipline, them Yanks," said Mason.

Solov watched as the Americans and their friends got up to leave. The brown-haired girl stayed where she was. The young airman cajoled her to follow. He tried to tug her by the elbow. She pulled away. He saw where she was looking. He snapped at her: "Fuck you, you bitch!" and scowled at Solov, then followed his friends outside. The woman looked over to Solov, lit a cigarette, and lifted her glass to him. One of her girlfriends returned briefly, in an apparent attempt to persuade her to leave. No doubt this was a final attempt by the American to get her to follow on. She smiled and shook her head without taking her eyes off Solov. Her friend glanced over, smiled, then hugged her and left.

"I think she needs another drink," said Solov to Miller.

"Go to it, Major," said Miller. Solov approached her.

"Can I buy you another?" he said, indicating her glass.

"Thank you," she said, "Brandy, and soda, if they have some. Brandy and water if they don't."

Solov went to the bar and got himself a refill too. As an afterthought, he gave the barman extra money: "Whatever they want over there, the British Army," he said, indicating Miller and the others.

He re-joined the woman, who self-consciously pulled her hair from her collar.

"What happened to your American friends?" he said.

"They have big wallets, but even bigger mouths," she said. "They buy you a drink, they think you belong to them."

"How will you get back home?"

"I can get a room here for the night. Get the early bus." She met his eye. Solov took a gamble, he had nothing to lose.

"Can you order a room then?"

"Isn't it customary for a man to order the room?"

"I'm a great believer in equality for women," said Solov. She looked at him, got up, then walked to the end of the bar to make the arrangements. Solov looked over to the men. Most of them were talking among themselves. Mason gave him the thumbs up. Solov ignored him. Mason might be a good soldier. He had yet to see the evidence, but he was childish, he decided.

"Shall we drink these and go?" said Solov, when she returned.

"You're eager. I like the direct approach. I mean…have we been introduced?"

"My name's Nikolai."

"Marianne. Are you foreign?"

"Can we talk about it upstairs?"

"I just want to know."

"I'm…Czech."

"Czech…mate?"

"Yes."

"You don't get it, do you?"

"Get it?"

"Come on, let's go."

He followed her after their drinks were finished. She held the door open for him as they entered the lounge.

"Hello, gentlemen," slurred Solov, when he saw Carter and Decker. "I didn't realise you were still here." He kept walking in tow to Marianne. The two officers watched him move towards the stairway tucked around a corner where the bedrooms were. Along a narrow corridor upstairs, Marianne produced a key with a number two tag on it. She fumbled in the dim light and opened the door. Checking that the curtains were drawn, she switched on the light. Solov closed the door behind him and moved towards her. From her handbag, she produced a bottle of something. Solov took it, unscrewed it and drank a burning mouthful. Marianne sat on the edge of the bed and bounced lightly up and down a few times, testing the mattress.

Shit, thought Solov, watching her take her top off, it had been a long time. He needed to slow down. He took a pull on the bottle she'd given him.

"Save some of that for me," she said, unbuckling his belt.

"All yours," he said.

EIGHT

W ithout opening his eyes, he knew she'd gone in the early morning when it was barely light. He'd heard the door close gently, then minutes later, a bus stopped outside the inn.

He looked up and saw his watch still there on the bedside, alongside it a scribbled note with her name and a phone number. His clothes were on the floor. He leaned over and pulled his wallet out of his tunic pocket. His money was still there. He slipped the note in the wallet and swung his feet to the floor. Shivering in his nakedness, he smiled at his mistrust. So, she wasn't a thief, or a prostitute, just someone like himself who wanted some relief from the war.

He lit his last cigarette and savoured the night. Her name was Marianne James. She wasn't married, had no sweetheart in the forces. Maybe some rich American GI would take her away, she'd joked. She'd worked in the local munition factory the last three months. It got her away from her home in Bristol. Said she'd go back soon. Her family was there. She'd made friends easily at the factory and was into the dating game with Yanks at the airbase. When she asked him about himself, he elaborated on his Czech refugee story. He said he'd made it here after the Nazis had marched into his country in March 1939 following the Munich fiasco of '38. Had joined the British Army, been sent back to France and was evacuated at Dunkirk. Solov had improvised and felt quite pleased with himself. Sevoska would have been impressed with his 'undercover work'.

He heard footsteps outside the door, and voices. A loud knocking jolted Solov back into reality. He started to dress, quickly.

"Who's there?"

"Open it!" he heard a familiar voice say to someone. Keys were fumbled into the lock and the door opened on Solov as he pulled on his trousers. There stood Sergeant-Major Redfearn, an embarrassed landlord, and two MPs each barely containing a smile.

"What the hell is going on, Redfearn?" Solov demanded.

"I have orders to collect you, sir." His voice filled the room.

"I'm sorry about this," the landlord apologised. "They just barged in."

"It's alright."

"You running a knocking shop, sir?" Redfearn asked the landlord.

"What do you mean? How dare you?" he said.

"I could have you closed down," Redfearn said.

"You just try it, mate," said the landlord, fuming. "Now get off my property before I call the police. Have me closed down, indeed..."

"I could put this place off limits to our men and that'll cut your trade..." said Redfearn.

The landlord retreated and snarled back at him: "Just get him and then fuck off."

"I'm getting dressed if you don't mind." Solov angrily slammed the door on the MPs. He could hear the landlord's voice receding downstairs with Redfearn following him. Solov was outraged. He realised he was late but he was not in the British Army. He'd be making a complaint about this, being hauled out of bed like a criminal. How far would they go? Could he get recalled? A reprimand? Would he be charged with disgracing himself and the Soviet Union and exploiting the womanhood of an ally? It was stupid. Would he be in trouble?

He gathered his thoughts and decided he would lay off the alcohol. He knew it was a reaction coming out of the extreme battle conditions he'd lived under in the last two years, especially at Stalingrad. It was like battle fatigue. He had hit the bottle with a vengeance in Moscow, waiting to come to Britain. Now he had to restore his self-discipline.

He straightened his tunic and, with a last look at the unmade bed, his own personal Stalingrad, he went down and joined Redfearn and the MPs.

"Let's go," he said.

Sergeant-Major Redfearn escorted Solov across the parade ground, bypassing Miller and the others who were cleaning their weapons on the grass. They looked on as Solov followed Redfearn into Colonel Lawler's office.

"Colonel's waiting for you," said Sergeant Walker to Redfearn.

Redfearn stamped across to Lawler's office, Solov and the MPs behind him. Lawler was behind his desk, at his side was Carter, leaning against the window behind them was Decker. To the side of them, Captain Ferry leaned on a filing cabinet.

"Send your men out, Sar-Major." Redfearn dismissed the MPs.

"Beg to report, sir, found the Major at the Horse and Hen. One of the bedrooms."

"Colonel," said Solov, "is this really necessary?

"I'll have my say, if you don't mind," said Lawler, taking his pipe out of his mouth. "We are all soldiers here, Major," he said. "I know you've worked hard, we've all worked hard, but what does it look like to the men and my officers if some of us can take off willy-nilly and please themselves...?"

"Willy?"

"Willy-nilly, whenever they please," said Lawler. Carter looked down at his hands while Decker, he noticed probably for the first time in a long while, looked Solov right in the eyes.

"...we simply have to behave like officers...set a good example..." Lawler went on, "...but getting drunk and fraternising with a woman like that who is a complete stranger..."

"Well, I'm sorry, Colonel, but I'm a stranger around here myself," said Solov.

"This is no time for sarcasm, Major," Lawler said. "You admit you booked a room with this woman and stayed all night?"

"It certainly looks that way, doesn't it?"

"What was her name?"

"Oh, please, what is this? Are you my father now?"

"Name?"

"I didn't ask."

Captain Ferry smiled. Lawler gave him a sharp look.

"Did you speak about our operations here?"

"Certainly not."

"Do you realise when drunk, it's easy to let things slip out...especially with a girl?"

Solov said: "Something slipped out alright, but it wasn't a military secret."

"I'm warning you, Major Solov, please take this seriously." Lawler banged his desk with his fist.

"I passed myself off as a Czech soldier. There's no risk whatsoever. I give you my word," said Solov, seriously now.

"I cannot rely on words, Major," Lawler said, in a quieter tone. He lit his pipe. "You should have come back with your fellow officers. We've already lost this day now. You were to have started the next phase of the training..."

"Colonel, we've lost..." he looked at the clock on the wall..."a couple of hours..."

"I'm afraid I had to inform your Mr Sevoska of your conduct this morning. He's very angry. He's sent for you and you are to leave immediately. My driver will take you, and the Sar-Major will accompany you. That will be all. On your way now."

Solov was stunned. He saluted then left to change his uniform.

It was a silent, restless journey in the car to London. Solov sat alone in the back with his thoughts, smoking, and looked out the window. What lay in store for him? He could hardly believe what had happened. It was petty. Had he disgraced himself? What would the consequences be? How would Sevoska react when he turned off that friendly, avuncular style? Was he, after all, the hard-nosed Party man when things went wrong? Was he the kind of bureaucrat he knew so well back home? He tried to squeeze Lawler, Sevoska, Decker, Carter and that bastard Redfearn out of his mind with thoughts of the night.

They reached London shortly after noon. They drove through streets being cleared of bomb wreckage and a few houses being demolished. Then, deeper into the city, into Mayfair, Regent's Park, even some of the homes of the rich hadn't escaped the Luftwaffe. Solov felt hungry. He hadn't eaten or even shaved. He felt he was going to panic.

"How much further?" asked Redfearn.

"Ten minutes maybe, Sar-Major," said the driver.

"Time for another cigarette," said Solov. He wondered about Carter and Decker. They must have gone straight to Lawler this morning. He bet Decker did all the talking. Decker wanted him out. Miller and the others had said as much. That Captain Ferry had told him Decker didn't like him. He didn't particularly want to be there. How were ten men meant to open a second front - even a small scale one? Ridiculous.

The car turned off the street through some wrought iron

gates, bringing Solov back from his thoughts. He recognised the Russian embassy car park at the rear of the main building. They stopped alongside two black limousines, each flying the red hammer and sickle pennants on their bonnets. After a brief stretch of the legs, Solov followed Redfearn across the car park to the black door framed by a pair of white pillars. He noticed a curtain move on the second floor. As they approached the door, it was opened by a friendly man in a suit.

"Enter, please."

Redfearn stepped inside behind Solov. He was more deferential as, technically, he was on Soviet territory now. They followed the receptionist down the corridor and signed in a book on a desk. They turned into a larger reception area where Redfearn was ushered to a leather Chesterfield.

"If you would remain here, sir, my colleague will bring you refreshments."

"Thank you." Redfearn removed his cap and smoothed his hair down, seating himself. Solov was taken upstairs, along another corridor. His guide left him in an ante-room while he entered an office without knocking. When he returned, after a few moments, he held the door open for Solov. Inside, Solov was met by a wall of books surrounding a fire. Standing with his back to him, looking out of a window, eating sandwiches from a plate, was Mr. Sevoska. He turned, placed the plate on his desk, wiped his beard with a napkin, and greeted him with open arms and his familiar cheery laugh. Stefan Sevoska embraced him like an old friend.

"How are you, old chap?" he said, in what Solov took to be his mock-upper class English accent. Then, in Russian, he said: "You look remarkably fit, I'll tell you that. Drink?"

"Tea or coffee," said Solov.

"Whisky?"

"I'm trying to cut down."

"Just the one. I'll order coffee and more sandwiches. Just one shot should put the colour back into your cheeks."

Sevoska poured them both a whisky. He pressed the intercom and ordered coffee and sandwiches.

"I gather you weren't expecting this reception?" Sevoska took them over to two armchairs by the fire. He gave him a long Kazbek cigarette he kept for special occasions. "You're probably wondering what old man Sevoska finds so amusing?"

"I'm a little surprised to find you in such good humour. Colonel Lawler told me you were furious when he spoke to you on the phone."

"I had to give the fool that impression."

"You mean, there's no problem?"

"I thought it was time we had another chat. I didn't want you to think I'd forgotten all about you. His phone call gave me the pretext to send for you. By the way." He winked. "Marianne gave you a high rating on last night's performance."

Solov looked back at him.

"Don't worry, old man, you weren't the first. You won't be the last. All in the line of duty for her. Loves her work, that one, cut out for it."

"She's one of ours?" Solov said.

"Absolutely. You have to understand, we have to do more than one security check. You passed with honours. You can think on your feet...er...and your back. That Czech refugee story was good. But don't worry about it, Nikolai, we all have to be checked once in a while. Loyalties can shift like sand. We don't take risks with anybody."

"Amazing. She was good. I was sold. She really had me fooled that I had her fooled. I thought she was just a lonely British factory girl. No trace of accent. Is she Russian?"

"To the core, Nikolai. She's been here for six years now. She's one of my many girls and boys. She's done some good work for me. After your work finishes with the commandos, you'll be joining my embassy staff, legitimately. You'll have to start growing your hair out because, in a few months' time, we'll have a new identity for you, our latest entry into the British population. That's when your real work begins. You've been briefed on this by Colonel Bosck, of course."

"Yes. I'm to 'melt away'. That was the expression he used."

"That's exactly what you'll do. Initially, there'll be courier work, information gathering, as a member of a team. Your code name will be 'Renegade' in regard to any radio or Morse communications. You'll be a link in a whole number of chains up and down the country. We've got Marianne, that's not her real name as you've probably guessed, she's normally based in Bristol. She's a useful link over to Ireland and the secret military installations in the Welsh mountains. She also does special jobs for us like last night. You can imagine I keep her busy."

Solov watched Sevoska coolly as he accepted another shot of whisky as the coffee and sandwiches arrived. He felt a lot of admiration for him. He realised that, beneath that carefree smile, the laughter, the down to earth humour, the talkative man of the world, there was a competent, professional, ruthless spymaster. He felt the ruthlessness, if necessary, could be turned on him without much pause for thought.

He was relieved Sevoska was being honest with him. Solov reminded himself he was a soldier, not really the same as a spy. He would learn to fight in this different kind of silent, dirty, undercover war.

"How's life in the commandos' playpen?"

"Just fine. Quite straightforward stuff, really. The troops, the men themselves, are good. I like them on a personal basis."

"The British are so slippery. How long have we been

demanding a second front? They make promises when we all know they will fight the Nazis to the last drop of Russian blood, if we let them.''

"So now they've trimmed this operation from a battalion to just ten men to create havoc," said Solov. "It's ridiculous. They'll just send them to their deaths and the results will be negligible. Their only chance, and I will inform them of this, is to select a target or two for maximum impact, instead of an overambitious campaign of hit and run."

"Nikolai, we are bending over backwards for them. You know Comrade Stalin has agreed to close down the Comintern? And what do they do in return? Put off a second front till next summer, a whole year. They want the Nazis to bleed us to death…"

"He's closing down the Comintern?"

Solov kept his counsel. Stalin seemed to be turning Lenin and Trotsky's revolution increasingly on its head. The Comintern, or communist international, was the original organisation that had been a rallying point, almost a beacon, for uniting and co-ordinating international co-operation between revolutionary workers worldwide. Stalin, in effect, was renouncing world socialist revolution, exactly what the capitalist powers wanted to hear.

"Yes," said Sevoska, "it's a nod and a wink to the West. The organisation was moribund anyway, especially since that bastard Trotsky formed the Fourth International in '38. He tried to divide communism against itself. He was always a splitter…until he finally got his own head split in Mexico, eh?" Sevoska laughed, and pushed the last of a sandwich into his mouth.

Solov remained silent and chose a thin slice of ham.

"But, Nikolai, the commandos are not your main concern. They were a useful way of getting you into this green and pleasant land. Like I say, your real work begins in a few months. Your first task will be the elimination of a couple of our enemies before you 'melt away'."

"Elimination?"

"Yes. I've selected a couple of targets we would like to disappear. Two counter-revolutionary scum who need to be rubbed out, because if we don't, they're going to develop into a couple of running sores. Eat your sandwiches first, then get a bath, smarten yourself up, then we'll talk in more detail. Shall we re-convene in, say, two hours?"

"Yes. Yes, of course."

"Meanwhile, I'll bring my department head up to date."

Events were moving way too fast for Solov. He soaked in the oasis of Sevoska's bath and tried to digest everything he'd been told and everything that had happened since leaving the rubble of Stalingrad. Everything seemed so straightforward in Stalingrad - kill or be killed, stay alive.

But then he'd always learned to stay alive, he didn't need a war to teach him that. It felt like he'd been at war for most of his life, certainly since the age of sixteen when he broke his promise to his father and donned the Tsar's uniform.

His father Giorgio had told him he understood why. Nikolai had been conscripted. The Imperial Army had lost hundreds of thousands of men, since 1914, especially in the opening battles of Tannenberg and the Masurian Lakes. Russia had lost tens of thousands more; wounded, in desertions or incapacitated by vodka. By 1916, the Russian Empire was militarily on its last legs. His father was a Bolshevik and, as such, he had to leave his job as a train driver and go into hiding. But he was still active in his political work.

"Papa," Nikolai had explained, "even though the Tsar is conscripting me, I will go as a Bolshevik. I'll agitate with my fellow soldiers. We need to get the troops on our side for your revolution."

"Our revolution, boy." Giorgio had accepted this. But Nikolai knew he only joined the army because he did not want to go to prison or to a penal colony. Political agitation was secondary to him. But when he joined the frontline, there were no attacks on the German positions. He only took part in defensive actions in the trenches. Squalor, disease and drunkenness were all around him. When officers beat a soldier for refusing to advance, some of those same officers were shot, or beaten to death, to save ammunition.

The front was close to crumbling by January, 1917. When the revolution broke out, Nikolai and his fellow soldiers were already back in Petrograd joining the strikes, the demonstrations, the workers' committees, the soviets - then Nikolai became a true Bolshevik like his father, alongside his father, his mother, his uncles and aunts, his family.

When Nikolai volunteered for the army a year later in 1918, it was Trotsky's Red Army, and he joined with his father's blessing to fight the counter-revolutionary forces in the civil war, and against the foreign armies of intervention that tried to strangle the revolution in its cradle. His father took to driving one of the many trains that shunted Soviet forces from one front to another. Nikolai remembered jumping down from every carriage or wagon at most stops and running to see if this train or that was driven by Giorgio. It took six or seven months before he found him at a stop somewhere in Georgia, and they embraced, their tears wetting their faces.

Stefan Sevoska threw two manila envelopes onto his desk and indicated to Solov to open them. Solov leaned forward in his chair and took the one on the top and ripped it open. He took out a folder. On the front was a small black and white photograph attached by a paper clip. A man stared out from behind a typewriter. He had a severe short back and sides haircut, a moustache and bright, piercing eyes. On the front of the file was typed 'George Orwell' and beneath - in smaller type, in parentheses - was the name 'Eric Blair'.

"Heard of him?" asked Sevoska. Solov pursed his lips and shook his head.

"A little known writer in England, known mostly to the intelligentsia," said Sevoska, as Solov began leafing through the file. There were newspaper clippings, pictures of book covers under the name of Orwell, pictures of him in cricket teams, rowing teams, as a policeman in a pith helmet, more recent ones as a soldier, an irregular soldier in what looked like Spain where he towered above others, or amid a group of men gathered around a BBC microphone that stood in the middle of a table.

"Comes off a family of the impoverished middle class. His father worked in India. He went to Eton, you know, where they educate their next generation of empire-builders," Sevoska continued. "Then he joined the imperialist police in Burma. Stayed out there for a few years. Up to then he saw himself as a 'Tory anarchist', then he saw the light about how the British exploit the Asian peasant masses and threw it all in to become a writer."

"Very noble," said Solov.

"He starved for his art, well, he sponged off his wealthy relatives while he tried to sell articles to newspapers about tramps. Ever read 'Down and Out in Paris and London'?"

Again Solov shook his head.

"Claimed he was 'going native in his own country'. Anyway, he wrote a few shitty novels, one based on his experiences in Burma, one about his tramping days, another about a fucking priest's daughter who went off the rails, and one about a failed, miserable writer, pretty much autobiographical. Then he got noticed by a few left-wing intellectuals. He got commissioned to write about the English working class conditions…heard of 'The Road to Wigan Pier'?"

Solov shook his head.

"Shit, Nikolai, I thought you studied English at university?"

"Before this guy was published. It was all Dickens, Shakespeare and H.G. Wells."

"Oh, well. Then he went to Spain, on the Republican side, of course. He was a member of the Independent Labour Party. They put him to work based on the training he'd had with the Burmese Police. Got shot in the throat and was invalided back to Barcelona. He was a supporter of POUM."

"I remember them. The Spanish Trotskyists."

"That's right. Trotskyists, anarchists. They wanted to take it all too far, dividing up the land for the peasants, workers' control of the factories. They pissed a lot of our people off. They were undermining our Popular Front policy so we had to intervene and try to keep things together…"

"Then we lost," said Solov.

"You were at the frontline, weren't you?"

"Yes. We didn't know that while we were fighting the fascists, behind our lines we were fighting among ourselves. It was time to go," said Solov.

"Yes. Well, Orwell was with POUM and when we clamped down on them, he scuttled over the border to France."

Solov remembered that time with bitterness. But he wasn't about to tell Sevoska. In the first place, he'd volunteered to go to Spain to get away from the military purges Stalin was beginning to instigate in 1936 in the wake of the Moscow Trials. It was safer. He knew, somewhere out in the Siberian wastes, his father Giorgio toiled in a labour camp, never to return along with many other old Bolsheviks. He'd kept his head down, lived to fight another day and carried his shame with him. "I'm just a soldier", was the mantra he'd kept on repeating to himself. He couldn't be a good Bolshevik like his father, so he'd be a good soldier. He was a military advisor and had fought alongside a ragtag of International Brigade troops from all over the world, yes, and among the bravest and selfless were members of POUM. And he remembered a whole company of them being disarmed and loaded into trucks and taken away singing the Red Flag. He'd protested to his Spanish commander, a man called Suarez. But he would do nothing. Suarez had explained they were Trotskyists, fifth columnists, working for Franco. In reality, he learned, the Stalinists in Spain were keen to keep their Popular Front together, a common front between the Communist Party and the liberal capitalists and the bourgeoisie. His own side preferred to back these people than the real revolutionaries.

"Hadn't we seized the land and the factories in 1917?" he'd said to Suarez, who only shrugged his shoulders.

"I can't help them. They are dead men," Suarez had said, as the last of the trucks pulled away. They had to fill the gaps in the frontline the best they could. Within a week, they were falling back. Stalin and his bureaucrats had believed in 'socialism in one country' and had no intention of spreading the revolution across the world not when he had the lid on the revolution at home. He didn't want to provoke the Western powers. Whereas Trotsky had held that only the spread of the revolution could save our own. But if Stalin couldn't rule, he would ruin. It was this non-Marxist theory that led to the contradiction of the Nazi-Soviet Non-Aggression Pact in '39 that gave Hitler the chance to deal with the West which, disastrously for the Soviet Union, gave him the chance to turn his forces against the USSR in '41.

But now, as then, Solov kept his head down. He wasn't about to bring all this up with Sevoska.

"When he got back to England, Orwell wrote a book in support of the Trotskyists in Spain, 'Homage to Catalonia'."

"Never read that one either," said Solov. But, he thought, one day he'd like to have a look at it.

"He upset a lot of our people, our supporters on the left in Britain. It wasn't a best-seller but the intelligentsia didn't like it and it didn't make us look good. Ever since Spain, he's always attacked us, and our people here. He's practically a pseudo-Trotskyist. Shortly after the war broke out, he was back to scraping a living in the press and he joined the Home Guard. He was calling for it to be made a 'People's Army'. Then he got a job with the BBC, broadcasting to India and Asia. Only a few weeks ago, he lambasted us in a broadcast to Malaysia about our having wound up the Comintern. Portrayed us as traitors to democratic socialism in so many words."

"Malaysia? How damaging is that? The Japanese are in Malaysia."

"Very damaging. The Malaysian resistance is led by their fast-growing communist party. We have a lot of supporters in the resistance throughout Burma, Malaysia, French Indo-China, Indonesia and the rest of South-East Asia. Believe me, when the British, French and Dutch had their arses kicked by the Japs in '42 they had their images as imperialist masters severely shaken and the local nationalist and communist forces have taken note. Do you really think they'll welcome the imperialists back after the war, especially as the Western economies are going to be severely weakened? These regions are going to look to us, of course. And we don't need the likes of Orwell blackening our good name."

Solov nodded. He could see the opportunities opening up for spreading the revolution. He wondered how Stalin's policy of 'socialism in one country' fit into this. Would a thousand Spains be repeated if liberated people took their revolutions too far?

"But, more worryingly, at least for my department here," said Sevoska, "on our own doorstep, we've had a number of our people exposed as 'communist infiltrators' in the BBC by none other than Orwell. He's compiling a list of 'undesirables'. We think this is his prime purpose for being at the BBC, to root out any of our so-called 'fellow travellers'. We've had a few of our people side-lined, tactfully moved aside, others dismissed under any trumped up charge. We have this on good authority. The British may refer to Comrade Stalin as 'Uncle Joe' but we know they are looking ahead to when the war is over. The last thing they want is a communist-friendly media. And this is where you come in, Nikolai."

"Kill Orwell?"

"You've got it. It will be your job to eliminate him, then there's this other bastard we've got in mind."

Solov tore open the other envelope and took out a similar file. The photo clipped to the front was a man with thick hair, parted to the right, a pleasant face, but firm-jawed as he looked past the camera. This photo was taken at some meeting; other people were around him, but out of focus or cropped out of the shot.

"Edward Grant," read Solov. He raised his eyebrows. "So, how has he upset us?"

"You won't have heard of him, or his organisation. He's the National Secretary of the Workers International League. They're affiliated to the Trotskyist Fourth International. Needless to say, at the present time, they are the strongest Trotskyist faction in Europe. They're only small in numbers, probably 150 – 200 active members with branches in London, Liverpool, Glasgow, Yorkshire, South Wales and Durham. They are very active in amongst the coal-miners' unions and the dockworkers. Over the last twelve months, there have been more unofficial strikes since the General Strike of 1926, numbering hundreds of thousands of workers downing tools. Our comrades in the British Communist Party are losing control to these bastards who are gaining a foothold. These workers are essential to the war effort if we want the British to open a second front and keep supplying the Soviet

Union. In a way, I would say these people are more dangerous than the likes of Orwell. They are working on the ground, where it matters. Even Herbert Morrison, the Minister of Labour, has been forced to investigate them but his new regulation banning strikes has been ignored. This, more than pithy articles and broadcasts, is probably more dangerous to us and I think is deserving of our attention. The Workers International League, like POUM in Spain, is a mad dog that needs to be put down, starting with Grant."

"Is he easy to get to?"

"They run their operation from an office in a builders' yard in King's Cross, would you believe? But don't underestimate them. That's how our Bolshevik Party started. They have a newspaper called 'Socialist Appeal' and a magazine,'Workers International News'. It's already putting out stuff about Stalin finishing up the Comintern and they're organising rallies and public meetings. This is the last thing we need, more anti-war strikes with an anti-Soviet flavour. You know the English saying - 'great oaks from little acorns grow'. We can't ignore the impact this small, but effective organisation could have."

"You want Grant dead first?"

"I think he's a priority. As soon as your work with the commandos is finished. Myself, I think the British will be secretly pleased."

"And Orwell?"

"Might prove trickier. But he's got enemies. Could be made to look like a German job, or a Mosleyite. He bashes them as much as us."

"I'll get to work on it as soon as I return."

"Good. It'll be time to stop playing soldiers and get down to some real work for Mother Russia."

NINE

The journey back from London was easier.

Solov prepared to act out the role of a subordinate stung from a superior's reprimand. In fact, he felt relieved and relaxed that there had been no rebuke. He also felt a hurt pride in that he'd been so easily taken in by the woman, Marianne, though he now knew that was not her real name. He also felt disturbed about what he was being asked to do by Sevoska. Not asked, but ordered.

Is this what he'd become? An assassin?

He'd always hidden away from the dirty side of politics by engaging in the dirty side of war. He could justify his actions as a soldier, kill or be killed, using your strength, wits and skills, sometimes your innate brutality, especially working behind the lines with the partisans. War was war. But assassination?

He could justify some of the things he'd done, killing non-combatants in a war zone, but these were civilians in a relatively safe urban area. These were Trotskyists too, like his father, like the men driven away in trucks in Spain. He was being ordered to kill people who stood for the original aims of the revolution like his father and his family, what he himself had fought for in the Red Army in the Civil War. He knew this was the predicament of his political 'quietism'. This was the price he was always going to pay some day. His father had paid with his life for refusing to compromise. Now he was paying for his own betrayal of his father's principles. That's what sickened him, what he knew had been tearing at him all these years. He couldn't follow his father. He'd been lost somewhere along the way.

He tried to push the thoughts out of his head and he thought about Marianne and what her real name was, and where she came from in Russia. Mother Russia! When Sevoska used that phrase it made him want to spit. Sevoska was a chauvinist. The revolution had given birth to the Union of Socialist Soviet Republics of which 'dear Mother Russia' was supposed to be an equal component. But he knew that most of the elite who dominated it were Russian, apart from people like Stalin himself, who wanted to be Russian. Stalin was a Georgian but had traded on patriotism, yes, on 'Mother Russia'. Yet he'd suppressed any independent thought throughout the smaller republics. Stalin the Georgian, Hitler the Austrian, and they both called on bigger states to do their dirty work. Mother Russia and der Vaterland!

He wondered if she came from the Ukraine like the love of his life, Anya. She'd been so loving and warm, this stranger, Marianne, loving like Anya, though he'd never suspected the calculating mind ticking inside her. He wondered how many men had passed through her this way. How many times had Sevoska used her like this? Did she always seduce men she worked with, or had it just been orders? Or had she made him the exception? Gazing out of the window, he promised he'd try to see her again, soon. He had her number.

He felt he hadn't known that feeling of abandon since he'd been together with Anya way back in 1927, at university, when things didn't matter, didn't weigh so heavily, or at least he pretended they didn't.

The Soviet economy had started to pull itself up by the bootstraps by the mid-1920s. At age 27, the same time his father had been sent to a labour camp for 're-education', Nikolai had taken the chance to go to university. He'd long been relieved from active service in the army. He was still officially in the reserve, but wanted to return to the education he'd missed because of the war and the revolution. He was not the only older student. The USSR needed to train and educate its workforce for the mammoth task of dragging what had been, pre-1914, a semi-feudal society into the 20th century as Stalin was hijacking Trotsky's original idea of mass industrialisation. It was time for stabilisation and the Kremlin wanted to demonstrate that socialism could be built in one country and rid itself of its pariah status. Already, the new democratic German state had been among the first to officially recognise the USSR. The Soviet Union not only needed scientists, engineers, architects, but doctors, diplomats and linguists if it was to make its way to the centre of the world stage.

Trotsky's idea for industrialisation had been ridiculed by Stalin and his cronies, but then taken, distorted and presented as their idea. The Stalinists had enforced it, rather than developed it via democratically planned and organised workers' committees. Tens of thousands of peasants were enlisted into the factories, grain confiscated from the Kulaks, or rich farmers, who were to be destroyed as a class. Solov had entered university to study modern languages. He felt he could play a small part in spreading the revolution in his own way if he was allowed to travel as an interpreter one day. He'd studied hard and played hard. At 27, long deprived by upheavals of war as a youth, he now played out his teen years like he'd suffered arrested development. That's how he met Anya. She'd studied engineering, never before dreamed of for a woman in Tsarist times. She didn't believe in marriage. She believed in exploring life and breaking through those social barriers that had been closed off to women down the ages. They attended debating societies and he'd initially taken part in them as much as she did. Then, he knew it was only to impress her with his knowledge and experience.

"Saying you believe in world revolution won't get me into bed, Nikolai," she often said.

"No, but it will do until I can think of something better," he'd joke. They attended a few Left Opposition rallies, before the Stalinists started breaking them up when Trotsky was coming under increasing pressure. Solov had pulled back from attending them when he heard his father had been arrested. She scolded him for his reluctance to support the Left in the wholesale faction fight. He tried to turn her away from her political activities. She was neglecting her studies. Then Trotsky himself was arrested in 1929.

"It's time to step back and lie low, keep our heads down,"

he said.

He could see her anger. They saw less of each other. She became involved with someone more committed to the cause. He returned more to his studies. She was expelled from the university. Later, he heard she was arrested, along with her new lover. He never saw her again, so he kept quiet. By 1930, a post-graduate, he re-joined the army, the only safety he'd known, where he could hide.

Solov watched the English countryside flow by the car window. He forced himself to think of the job at hand. Espionage, he thought? I'd better start thinking like a spy.

Time to play a little game to amuse himself and keep his memories at bay. He made a mental note of small landmarks along the way, keeping something of a map in his head from London to the training centre. They were roughly eighty to a hundred miles south-west. There was an old war memorial before a picturesque hamlet, a river that ran through it on the left. Further, along the way, a watermill, a derelict church fifteen or so miles beyond that. A railway station came next with a billboard by it with its poster flapping in the breeze.

Solov lit a cigarette, enjoying his game. They ran along a country lane. On the right was a row of trees packed tightly together barely concealing a barbed wire fence. At the end, the loud rumbling they heard became louder. Solov thought it was a train, but then they saw a huge four engine American transport plane climb towards the sky.

"Wonder where that's off to?" mused the driver.

"Transporter," Redfearn said. "Who knows?"

They now came to the familiar woods that led to the training centre, the journey nearly over. Once in the camp, Solov reported to Colonel Lawler's office.

"How was the trip?" Lawler asked, from behind his desk, like a headmaster.

"Very good, thank you, Colonel. Made quite a good progress report," he said.

"And your interview with Mr Sevoska? Did he talk to you?"

"He was displeased with my conduct. Gave me a lecture. Told me not to be a naughty boy."

"All water under the bridge, Major Solov. No hard feelings. I do hope there won't be any rancour about this affair."

"Colonel, consider the matter closed."

"So, what's on the agenda? Decker's been putting them through their paces."

"For the following week, I'd like the men to take part in survival training, especially eluding the enemy, on their own, as individuals. If we call them together this evening, I can put them in the picture. If you could make arrangements with the local Home Guard units, they can pretend to be our Germans. I did outline it in my schedule."

"Yes, Decker and Carter have made contact with the Guard."

"I would also suggest, Colonel, we make enquiries about a specific mission, not just a raid, but something that will have an impact on a whole region of France, that may reverberate throughout the country, something to…I don't know…how do you say it?…stir up a hornet's nest? Rather than a series of individual raids which I think will deplete the men's strength…a quick, high impact hit and run."

"I'll make enquiries at Combined Ops. They have lots of contacts in France, of course. I'll do that right away. What do you have in mind?"

"If you can come up with something headline grabbing, I'll devise something. That's why I'm here, sir."

"Very well, leave it with me."

"For the next seven days," said Solov. "You will take part, as individuals, that is on your own, in a big game of hide and seek."

The men were assembled in their billet, sitting on their cots, pulled together, facing Solov at the front. Captain Decker was at one side, listening to Solov's outline.

"Starting tomorrow, you will be hunted men. Colonel Lawler has kindly arranged for you to be hunted down like dogs."

There was some laughter.

"You'll be hunted by the local Home Guard."

"You must be joking," Mason said. "Us being chased by a bunch of pensioners and war-dodgers?"

"You're to keep within a radius of twenty miles. You'll be wearing uniforms to make it more difficult for you. You're to live on your wits, live off the land and live with the elements anyway you can. You'll each wear a yellow armband so you can be identified. Try and stay free for as long as possible, by any means possible, within reason, of course. Please don't kill any of your Home Guard. If you're still free after seven days, come in and surrender, there'll be a hot meal waiting for you."

Decker produced a small box of armbands and handed it to Miller who began doling them out. Decker took one himself. He intended to take part.

"I'll be scanning the countryside for you with the Home Guard," said Solov, "so your hiding places had better be good. I know all the tricks. We start tomorrow. Any questions?"

There were none.

By early afternoon of the next day, Ed Barrow had reached Oxford train station. He propped the bicycle he'd stolen against some iron railings and caught the 2.30 train to Coventry. He paid for the ticket out of a roll of cash he'd stashed in his boot. He had to hurry, his train was about to leave. Settling in a seat by the window, he smiled contentedly at the passengers opposite him. He wasn't as dumb as some people thought he was. He'd be back before the seven days were up and he'd have had some nice unofficial leave with his missus.

Corporal Harry Tobey reached the safety of a hay barn at a farm by mid-afternoon some twelve miles away. He made himself a comfortable nest in its loft and decided to stay there until nightfall, despite his grumbling stomach. He planned on stealing one of the chickens he'd seen out in the farmyard.

Phil Armstrong waited in the woods soon after Solov had signalled for him to leave, as he had with the others at five minute intervals. He'd run into the bushes and waited. He knew Joe Anderson wouldn't be far behind. Half an hour later, Joe found him. Armstrong heard him coming and sent a low whistle for him. They ran together deeper into the woods, selected a tall oak, hauled themselves up and secured themselves among the thick, broad boughs.

"We're okay here till nightfall," Armstrong whispered. He pulled out a coil of copper wire. "Get a couple of rabbits with this and we're fixed up."

Solov told Lieutenant Carter he could give the go ahead to the Home Guard, that the hunt was on. He then joined Redfearn and two MPs in the jeep.

"Where do you think they might head for, Sergeant-Major?"

"Haven't a clue, sir," Redfearn muttered.

They pulled up at nearby Caseby village hall and met an elderly Colonel Howard, commander of the Home Guards. The retired Colonel had been only too happy to get his men involved in this exercise.

"It'll help keep 'em occupied," he said. "Busy soldiers are happy soldiers."

He had about 150 men under his command. Solov asked him to deploy them wherever he felt best, crossroads, bridges, hilltops and to send a number of patrols through fields and woods for the more fitter Guards. As the days passed, Solov kept in radio contact with the Home Guard units. He and Redfearn and the two MPs criss-crossed the area in the jeep. They drove up and down lanes, searching any wooded areas, across moorland and poked around old farmhouses, cottages, ditches, caves, potholes, even weed patches.

On the third day, it rained heavily but none of the men were flushed from cover. On the fourth day, however, Solov caught sight of a figure moving stealthily across a meadow. The man dived into some long grass. Solov sent Redfearn after him. He came back triumphantly with young Tony Scalleni, dirty, damp and hungry.

"Never mind, lad, you gave us a run for our money," Redfearn said.

"Shit. I couldn't lie low anymore."

"That's fatal," said Solov. "The solitude gets to you, doesn't it? It makes you nervous, impatient, careless. It can kill you. Next time you'll know. If this was real, you'd be dead now." He gave Scalleni a cigarette. "Let's get our little fish home."

When they got back, the Home Guard radioed they were bringing Tobey in. A farmer had found him in his barn, along with the remains of two chickens. The farmer had been angry, thought he was a deserter and wanted to phone the police. He was given compensation and sent on his way.

"You stayed too long in one place," said Solov. "You got too comfortable, too complacent. The farmer might have shot you."

On the fifth day, Frank Mason came out of his hole again. He'd dug out a small foxhole in a dried out ditch at the side of a lane not far from a derelict house, which he thought would be too obvious a place to hide. He'd taken a sheet of corrugated iron from there and used it as a cover for his den, weaving pieces of bracken through some of its holes. He only came out at night to relieve himself and had lived on young potatoes from a neighbouring field. On the fourth day, he supplemented his diet with unripe blackberries which made him want to relieve himself even more, which was risky. A number of times, he'd seen Home Guard patrols stroll by.

He thought he'd done well. But he was only a hundred yards away from the Horse and Hen pub. He'd taken a couple of pounds with him as insurance. They were burning a hole in his pocket. He swore he could smell the beer drifting over to him. He decided that, after dark, he'd chance a pint and a pork pie, despite his unshaven face and dirty appearance that might bring suspicion on him. That night, he made his way along the lane, keeping a lookout for Home Guards. He reached the bar room entrance. He caught the stares of the landlord and some of the regulars, not a uniform in sight.

"Bloody hell! Has the invasion started?" someone said.

"Pint of bitter and two of them pies, please, mate." Mason threw a pound note on the bar. Mason took his drink and pies to a seat in the corner.

"Jesus, I needed that," he said to himself as he put away the pint and started on the first pie. He ordered a second glass of beer and made a start on the other pie. The barman brought him his second drink.

"You're hungry, mate. Not eaten for a while?"

"I'm training, aren't I?" he said.

"Pie eating contest, is it?"

The door opened and four Home Guards walked in with their rifles and took off their forage caps. They were old, grey-haired men. One of them noticed him and smiled. Mason froze, one hand self-consciously moving up to hide his yellow armband. One of the guardsmen pointed to Mason: "Fancy another pint, mate?"

"Go on then. Cheers," said Mason, sheepishly. "I'll have a bitter."

"And another bitter," the guardsman ordered and looked back to Mason, "We'll have these, then we'll take you in."

John Decker was curled up in the entrance to a pothole up on Caseby Hill. He'd pulled up a large shrub to hide the entrance after sweeping away any footprints outside. It was dark, smelled of earth, almost womb-like, he felt so warm he had to undress to his shorts. He'd covered his face and body in dirt and felt secure enough to stay there most of the time. If he needed the toilet he crawled deeper into the recesses of the pothole to relieve himself. He decided he would see how long he could fast. He took his drinking water from the limestone ceiling that dripped moisture. At night, it was pitch black. He could see nothing. He was practically entombed. He only saw the pictures in his mind. They pulled him back. He couldn't differentiate between day and night and his hunger made him feel feverish but kept his mind active. Sometimes, he didn't know if he was awake or asleep. When shafts of light penetrated between the leaves of the shrub, he scratched another line on the wall with a sharp pebble. When total darkness returned, his mind took him for another ramble.

He drifted back to the face of Isadora. He thought about the sex and death of their first meeting and found it hard to separate the two. Richard's suicide had been like a bomb going off, not only at the family gathering but in his life. Decker remembered the single shot of Richard's pistol and pushing past his father's guests, all their heads turned to the open bedroom window. He was the first to reach the room, followed by his brother, Tom.

Richard was on the bed, the top of his head blown off. He'd fired under his lower jaw. The wall behind him was sprayed with blood, brains and fragments of bone.

"God!" Tom was frozen by the door, his hand to his mouth. There were footsteps behind him, more laboured. His father came in.

"Good God!"

Decker could hear his mother's voice.

"Keep the women out," said Decker. His father's face was ashen.

"We need an ambulance," he said, finally.

"Too late for that," said Tom.

His father went out to meet some of the guests climbing the stairs: "Keep back everyone, there's been a dreadful mishap. I think there's been an accident with a gun."

The police had to be involved, of course. Luckily, Bernard Wise, the family solicitor, was there to handle that side of things. There was an inquiry. Decker told them he and Richard had roomed together at Sandhurst, that he'd known him for over a year. He'd had no signs of depression that were obvious. His record as an officer cadet was impeccable, the commanding officer at Sandhurst confirmed this as the investigation wormed its way on. There was no history of suicide in his family. The Decker family attended the funeral, condolences were given. The obituary notice gave causes of death as a 'tragic shooting accident' that 'ended so prematurely a life so full of promise'. The Meyer family gracefully stayed on an extra two weeks to attend the sad ceremony and old man Meyer and his wife were so supportive. The incident seemed to cement the new business relations with them. As far as business was concerned, it couldn't have worked better if the shooting had been staged.

Decker remembered how beautiful the Meyer girls looked

in black veils and dresses, especially Isadora. After the wake, they returned to the Decker home. In the dark of night, Isadora came to his room, to the bed where Richard had killed himself. She still wore her veil but nothing else when she removed her dressing gown. She said she felt so good to be alive. She left him as dawn was nearly breaking. He was in a kind of shock. She told him her invitation for him to visit her in Germany was still open. Two days after the funeral, the Meyers left for home. The deals were done.

Decker wrote regularly to Isadora. True to her word, she'd persuaded her father to put aside his objections to her studying art and photography in Berlin. They hardly mentioned the shooting in the letters, only once or twice Decker referred to 'that unpleasant business'. As part of his cadet training in Sandhurst, Decker was fortunate enough to be seconded to Potsdam, outside Berlin, to study military strategy as part of an exchange programme. He'd been given the choice of Berlin or Heidelberg. For Decker, there was no choice - to be at the centre of Prussian military tradition and to be near Isadora was exactly where he wanted to be. He was there for a year, thrilled to be able to be so close to Isadora. By September, 1934, he and six other officer cadets were based at Potsdam with the crack 23rd Infantry Division whose commander, General Count Erich von Brockendorf-Ahlefeld, was of the traditional aristocratic Prussian mould. Decker was almost disappointed when the General had no monocle or visible duelling scars, but old school he certainly was. He regularly heralded his British visitors with evening meals of venison and the best Rhenish wines at his private home and told them stories of his military career, his time as a cadet.

"Blood and iron, old Bismarck told us and, by God, that's what we got. I was at the Lichterfelde Cadet School. One foot out of place there, one lapse in discipline. See these?" He lifted up the bottom of his shirt to reveal two sets of symmetrical scars below either side of his navel. "I was made to sew my trouser buttons on my own skin! That's the kind of discipline we had."

During the week, Decker pored over theories of strategy, observed training exercises, studied logistics and military history, attended lectures. In the evenings, he was swept away by staff officers, invited into their homes or went to hunting lodges near the Wannsee. At the weekends, he visited Isadora in the Neukölln district of Berlin. The contrast was a chasm. The district she lived in was rundown, not especially working class, but more than a hint of the bohemian, artists and students. She lived in an old tenement block. Her apartment was scattered with books of photographs and some of her own work, portraits of people, street scenes, architectural photography, snatched scenes of photojournalism.

She'd been pleased to see him. Their first meeting had concerned him. Before setting out for Germany, he'd set the record straight with her. He'd written to her about his previous political affiliations, his involvement with Mosley's Blackshirts, his dabbling with fascism, his anti-Semitism, but how personal experience and maturity had changed all that, especially after meeting her and her family. They'd spoken about it during their first night together in bed.

"People are allowed to change," she said, "for better or for worse. Everyone has the capacity to change. I'm glad I've been a part of that change."

"But, surely, it must rankle with you? I mean, the way things are here with the Hitler government?"

"People wonder about that. Yes, they speak ill of the Jews, but many think he used that as an electoral ploy. It's a dubious one, yes, but Hitler isn't the only politician and his is not the only party to spout about the Jews. It's happened down the ages."

"Yes, and not only in this country."

"Exactly, but they're only words. They haven't actually done much to us. He's railed against Jewish Bolshevism, he's railed against Jewish financiers. He needs to make his mind up. What are we, capitalists or communists? Surely, we can't be both? As you've seen in the newspapers in June, he silenced the more radical Nazis when he put a stop to Ernst Röhm and his SA cronies. It's mostly they who spouted the anti-Jewish stuff on the streets. No, Hitler knew they could only talk racism for so long, the majority of the German people don't care and don't believe it anyway. Yes, I'm a Jew, But I'm like any German woman..."

"You're not one of the more visible, orthodox Jews."

"No. Never been a synagogue-goer. I'm a modern woman. The orthodox Jews are a minority. Most of us prefer to assimilate. We're Germans first. A lot of Jews fought bravely in the war."

"It was mainly the humiliation at the end of the war..."

"Versailles."

"...that Hitler wants to wipe out. As long as his eyes are to the East, against the Soviets, I think Britain, France and the rest will be happy. As long as that communist baboonery is kept in check nobody really cares," said Decker.

"So, John, what made you into a Jew-baiter?" She smiled at him. He looked briefly away, embarrassed, but he knew she was doing the baiting now.

"Ignorance, narrow-mindedness, you name it. Social background, maybe? Then it was compounded by Eton, mixing with the ruling class-in-waiting. I suppose I wanted to be accepted by the people my father hates, the 'old money'. My father's a self-made man so I became one of the opposition, I suppose. He didn't mind it when I helped break the picket lines on his factories with my fascist friends. Richard and I helped organise that."

"Why did Richard kill himself?" Again, Decker looked away.

"I really don't know. He was moody. Maybe he suffered from depression? I suppose we'll never know. Strange how my best friend died on the same day I met you."

Decker had wanted to ask Isadora to marry him that night,

but it wasn't the right moment. He visited her in Berlin as often as his schedule allowed. He went away for three weeks' winter manoeuvres, to the region of Grafenwőhr in south-east Germany, from November into December.

As he travelled with the 23rd Infantry, their trucks and armoured cars streamed along the pride of the new Germany, the Autobahn. He marvelled at the network of direct motorways and was told by one officer that they were built with the military in mind primarily, easy access to the borders.

All staff officers and their guests were invited a week before that Christmas to a ball at the private home of General Brockendorf-Ahlefeld. Mischievously, Decker invited Isadora and borrowed a Mercedes to pick her up. She was thrilled to be taken, not only because of the resplendence of the occasion but because of who she was and where she would be, in among the 'master race'.

Decker introduced her proudly to his fellow British officers, then to those German staff officers with whom he was acquainted. She was beautiful in a black and white dress. She barely concealed a smile as each officer clicked their heels and gave a stiff bow before kissing her offered hand. If only they'd known! Then they danced mostly to Strauss, and sometimes to dreadful Bavarian folk music, but the wine and champagne flowed and they didn't care. She even met the General himself.

"Delighted, young lady. I like to see the Germans and British together. And your face." He flirted well for an old Prussian General, "Your face is worth a declaration of war on its own."

Decker remembered how proud he was of her, and they laughed so often afterwards about their deception. She told him she loved him that night, but he wasn't sure if it was only wine or passion or both.

They celebrated seeing in 1935 at the Meyer household where her parents greeted him warmly. The Meyers' business partnership with the Deckers had been profitable for both sides, especially since Hitler's government came into power. The new rearmament policy meant machine tools and engineering were going to thrive and, as promised, Hitler put paid to any union militancy by banning them, creating a Labour Front, and imprisoned all the socialists and communists. For old man Meyer, whose family had suffered at the hands of the Russian Revolution, this was most pleasing. All the Nazi talk of ridding Germany of the Jews had come to nothing, mere electioneering talk. Yes, Herr Meyer acknowledged, there were stories of assault, arson and abuse on the streets, but these seemed to be confined to the ruffian element, Rőhm's SA organisation. Hadn't Hitler himself done away with Rőhm and his street-fighters the previous June in the so-called 'Night of the Long Knives'? Rőhm and his stormtrooper leadership had been executed or thrown into prison and cut down to size.

"Rőhm had been useful in street fights and breaking up communist political meetings, but the Fűhrer had no further use of them, and the more conservative element, especially the army, would no longer tolerate such behaviour. Nasty business, of course, but getting Germany back on its feet again, well, there were bound to be a few bloody noses," he said at the family table.

"Heidi, here," said Frau Meyer, smiling, turning to Decker. "She's not against the Jews, are you, Heidi?"

The young housekeeper stepped forward and began to collect the dinner plates. Her blonde hair tied back in a bun, she self-consciously swept a strand of hair behind her ear.

"That's hardly a scientific experiment, is it, Heidi? She works for you, Mama. That's unfair, isn't it, Heidi?" said Isadora.

Heidi smiled as she balanced the plates.

"Not all Germans are anti-Jewish, of course not. Not all Germans support Hitler." She smiled at Isadora.

"And that business with you, Ruth, on the way home from college?" said Isadora to her younger sister.

"There's always been bullies," she said.

"But they were spitting on you, calling you 'Yid'?"

"That'll do, Isadora," said her father.

"And the shop signs - 'Jews not welcome'. They don't mind taking our money though."

Her father was beginning to lose his patience.

"Isadora, there has been anti-Semitism since the time of Moses. There was always that element, well before we even heard of Herr Hitler. Almost two years he's been in power, and nothing has materialized. He's done away with the socialists and the unions, which can't be a bad thing…"

"We're next," said Isadora.

"Isadora! Show some respect!" said her mother, sharply. Her father calmly raised his hand.

"That's enough. For your information, dear daughter, there was talk of driving the Jews out of the professions, so a few university lecturers and lawyers have lost their jobs. Here am I, a successful businessman, working in the vital arms industry. They haven't touched a hair on my head. Only in November, I had a visit off three businessmen offering to buy me out. The nerve of them. Of course, I refused. They were offering rock bottom prices. They said I'd better settle for that because it was the best I'd get. Nonsense, I said. My firm is worth twice, three times the price they were offering. What nonsense. The name above the factory gates is still Meyer."

That night, Decker slipped out of his bedroom in his dressing gown. In his pocket, he had a small box, in the box was a diamond ring. He could wait no longer. Down the landing, creeping carefully not to make a noise, he arrived at Isadora's room. He was going to ask her to marry him. His trembling hand grasped the door handle and gently turned it. There was a low light on as he pushed the door slowly open. He looked around the door. Fast asleep in the bed, nakedly entwined, he saw Isadora and Heidi. He swiftly withdrew and made his way back, gasping for air, his hand almost crushing the box in his pocket. He returned to his bed and buried his head under the pillow.

With the darkness warm around him, Decker opened his eyes. Shafts of daylight made him blink. He was in the pothole. He picked up his sharp stone and scraped a line through four others. Five days he'd been hidden from the Home Guard patrols. He felt he was hallucinating from lack of food. Hunger was heightening his memories. He stretched his body and rolled over onto his back. His feet disturbed some loose rocks that tumbled down further into the dark tunnel. The sound of falling rocks reminded him of that summer's military manoeuvres in Germany, in the back of an open truck. Two rows of German infantry smoked and talked. Ahead and behind, more motorised infantry. They were driving to meet with a panzer regiment to practise combat techniques and co-ordination. They followed a road through open fields. They neared a crossroads where the traffic almost came to a stop but crept along.

"Look, boys," a soldier pointed.

Across one of the fields a group of convicts were hoeing. They were shaven-headed and wore thick-striped uniforms. Most of them looked haggard, thin and hungry. Their uniformed guards looked bored. One of them waved. Two convicts pulled a cart heavily-laden with rocks. One of them, his age indiscriminate, slipped in the mud. The other couldn't stop the cart from tipping up and most of the rocks tumbled out onto the ground. The nearest guard strode purposefully over to the man on the floor. He knew he had the soldiers' attention.

"Get up, you lazy swine!" A vicious kick in the ribs rolled the prisoner over.

"Give it to the Jewish bastard!" shouted one of the soldiers from the truck. Some of his comrades cheered. The guard took the stick from under his arm and began to rain blows on the helpless man who rolled on the ground, his arms trying to protect his face.

"Give it to him," yelled the infantryman, now on his feet.

"Sit down, Kramer, you fucking idiot! Or I'll do the same to you," snarled the Corporal called Schwarz.

"It's probably just a Jew, Corporal," Kramer protested. His friends laughed with him.

"I'd like to see that bastard with the stick come at me like that," said Schwarz, "by God, I would. Now sit down and start behaving like a soldier."

Decker had hardly seen Isadora since he left her father's home that January. He'd told her nothing of what he'd seen that night. He tried to put it out of his mind and get on with his job. He'd visited her twice in her Berlin apartment and she'd welcomed him as always. They'd slept together, as always. She made him promise he'd come and stay with her once the manoeuvres were over in mid-August. She was as warm, wicked and as full of mischief as ever. How could he resist? She infuriated him, but he was drawn to her. He knew he could forgive her in time. She was totally oblivious to his broken heart. Slowly, he was mending it himself, restoring it carefully, restoring his faith in her.

By August, he joined her and they went everywhere together, the theatre, the cinema. Isadora was not happy with what was happening on the cultural scene. Anything remotely modern was so hard to find.

"Modern means radical, means Bolshevik, means Jewish, means decadent," she complained, as they sat outside a café in the warm, bustling night along Kurfürstendamm.

Decker looked on as he noticed people at some of the other tables stare at her. He felt exposed.

"Shall we finish our drinks and meet the others?" he said. They emptied their glasses. Isadora had, over the months, introduced him to her circle of friends. They were like her, students. There was only one other Jewish person among her friends, a likeable man called Johann. He'd felt threatened when he first met him, some of his old prejudices being raised, thinking that, perhaps, he and Isadora were lovers while he was away.

"Don't be ridiculous," she'd scolded him. "Why do you think that? Just because we're Jewish? For your information, and just to put your mind at ease, John, I've fucked more Gentiles than I have Jews."

Decker had winced at the time. He didn't much care for the way she swore, especially in public. He knew there was little he could do to stop her. If he protested, he knew, she'd do it all the more.

They left the café and took a cab over to Neukölln. They stopped off at her apartment so she could change into something more comfortable. The restaurant where they were meeting the others was just three blocks away. They'd walk. It was a hot night. As they turned a corner, they saw a small crowd.

"What's going on there?" said Decker.

"Who knows?"

There was some shouting. Decker looked and saw someone on the ground and a pair of hands roughly pulled the man to his feet. The crowd were pushed back by men in uniforms. The man's hat was rolling across the pavement.

"In the gutter!" he heard someone shout. Three young men from the Hitler Youth looked on as their leader was occupied with the man. Under the light of a streetlamp, Decker could see it was an old man. Worse still, the Hitler Youth were young boys. The oldest, who was doing the beating, couldn't have been older than sixteen. His hair flopped over his cruel eyes. One hand brushed it back while his other hand gripped the old man by his throat.

"Dirty, old Jew bastard!" he snarled. His three companions looked on eagerly, and helped keep the small crowd back. Their leader tripped up the old man again and he fell heavily, a cut on his forehead dripped blood down his face.

"John, leave it. Don't get involved," said Isadora, as Decker turned to watch. Before he realised what he was doing, he was crossing the street.

"What the hell d'you think you're doing?" he shouted

The Youth leader stopped as he was about to pull the old man to his feet again. His three friends stopped laughing and the crowd quietened down to watch this new addition to the show.

"We're showing this filth where Jews belong," said the leader, looking over his shoulder for back up.

"I'm a British officer," said Decker. He felt instantly foolish. He was not in uniform, neither did he carry any ID on him. He looked back across the street. Isadora watched.

"Ein britischer Offizier?" one of the younger boys said.

Their leader shrugged. This was about losing face, losing authority. His lips curled and he said: "And?"

"This is no way for men in uniform to behave. Leave this man alone."

"This has got nothing to do with the British Army. On your way, Tommy." One of the younger boys stepped forward, the others moved up with him. Suddenly, they seemed to be more menacing. They appeared to forget the man on the ground who was slowly beginning to crawl away. One of the young boys stepped over to the man and delivered a vicious jackboot to his head.

"You vile shit!" Decker yelled, and he stepped forward. The Youth leader blocked his way and held his eyes with a cold stare as he ordered: "Carry on, boys!" The three of them stood around the old man and began to rain blows on him with their boots.

Decker pushed the leader aside and walked towards them. He punched one of them on the side of his face, but was grabbed from behind, around the neck, as the others turned and jumped on him. The first blows hit their target. He heard his own cries, then those of Isadora. The crowd moved in around them looking down at him. The leader stood over him and raised a long truncheon. He felt the first three strikes, then nothing. Just blank.

On the last day, only three men had been caught - Tobey, Scalleni and Mason. Solov thought they'd done well, for what it was worth. He acknowledged that, in a real situation, Mason would not have ventured out to a pub, and Tobey wasn't going to argue with a farmer's shotgun. He believed if they'd taken it more seriously, nobody would have been caught. In the end, he wasn't really concerned. He knew he was just passing the time, going through the motions.

Ed Barrow stood on the doorstep of his terraced house in Coventry. His wife had cooked him a good dinner and was now kissing him goodbye, bravely.

"You'll have to hurry or you'll miss your train, love. I don't want you getting into no trouble."

"Alright, I'll be off then."

She stepped out onto the street to wave him off: "Bye, Eddie, take care. Write me another letter."

"Bye."

"Look after yourself."

Barrow made it back to the training centre shortly after six on the Friday evening, the last day of the exercise. He hadn't shaved since going away. On his way back, he roughed up his uniform in the woods and joined his fellow commandos in washing and shaving.

After they finished cleaning up, the squad gathered again in the briefing room to hear Major Solov congratulate them on their satisfactory performance.

"But before the success goes to your heads," he said, his eyes darting over to Captain Decker, who had also managed to stay undetected. "Beginning tomorrow is our second week. The next exercise will be a group effort. Same thing, stay free, but working as a team. Again, you'll be hunted within the twenty mile radius and you will have set tasks. We've set up a dummy ammunition store, you'll also undertake a raid on the Home Guard HQ and we'll let you hold a couple of ambushes on a convoy. I'll give any help that's needed. I may even come with you on some of the tasks, perhaps as a neutral observer. And remember, don't kill any of the Home Guards. Britain still needs them."

The next morning they drew their equipment, dummy grenades, Sten guns without ammunition. Robert Thornton took a Bren gun and strapped it across his back.

"You look like a real soldier now," Malone told him. Thornton was almost his equal in height.

"Give me a Bren, Sterl, and I'll take on the whole German army. Well, some of 'em," said Thornton.

"Just remember, it's only the Home Guards, and a lot of 'em wanna keep drawing their pensions," said Malone.

"Fat chance. I'm only firing fresh air."

"What a waste. All this fucking training," said Mason. "We should be out there, in the thick of it." He jerked a thumb in the approximate direction of the Channel.

"Practice makes perfect," said Miller.

"And you need it, pal," said Armstrong. "Especially against

those big, mean pensioners who brought you in from the pub."

"Fuck you, Armstrong," Mason spat.

"The big, tough guy brought in by tin soldiers on walking sticks," Armstrong mocked.

"Cut it out, you two, right now," said Miller. "Armstrong, since you think you're so tough you can go and do the obstacle course twice before we set out."

"Fuck that!"

"Right now, unless you want trouble?"

"Sticking up for Mason, as usual, your little white hen?" Armstrong stood his ground and shrugged off Joe Anderson's hand on his shoulder.

"You heard me." Miller squared up.

"Fucking make me. Just try and fucking make me."

"Armstrong!" It was Decker. "You'll do exactly as Sergeant Miller orders or you'll be returned to your unit. Do you understand?"

Armstrong continued to glare at Miller.

"I said, do you understand?"

Armstrong snapped out of it, shouldered his Sten and said: "Yes, sir," without taking his eyes off Miller. They moved out to the obstacle course.

"Bastard," Armstrong muttered beneath his breath.

After they went through the course, they rested while Armstrong went around a second time. Decker then led them out into the woods. He felt elated, lifted out of his low mood. He was actually back in command of his squad again. He'd been pushed into the background and had lost his voice among the men.

Putting Armstrong in his place had helped reassert his authority.

Out there in the wilds, he was pleased to be on his own. He could live off the land. From his pothole where he'd lay hidden the last week, he'd looked out on a criss-cross of small country lanes and fields like a gigantic relief map spread before him. He'd seen a couple of platoons of Home Guards briefly as they disappeared into woods as if they were out for a picnic. Fun and games, this was not the real thing. He thought he'd spotted Solov's jeep speeding along and had smiled to himself. Satisfied that Solov would pass him by, he wasn't as good as he made himself out to be, Decker thought. Solov was specifically hunting him down to further humiliate him in front of his men. Officers don't treat fellow officers like that. He hated the way Solov played up to the men, drank with them like some kind of class warrior, the communist bastard. In another week or so, Solov would be gone, back to wherever he came from and he could get on with what he had to do.

"...a brilliant starting point for your men to begin their campaign, Colonel," Solov was nodding enthusiastically. "It would make a huge impact, possibly set the ball rolling to cause maximum havoc."

Colonel Lawler had not been idle. He'd listened to Solov's comments over the previous weeks. He agreed with the Russian. He'd got together with Lieutenant Carter and made enquiries through the Combined Operations Executive in London. He'd appreciated Solov's political grasp of the situation. He knew Solov was earnest in saying that the project had to be salvaged from a throwaway gesture to appease both the British and Russian sides, a gesture that would probably throw away the lives of his men in an aimless operation in France. With a goal, an aim, there might be something worthwhile in the undertaking.

Solov had suggested a military target that would strike

terror in a whole region and signal some kind of reaction from the Nazis that would probably cost many French civilian lives in reprisals but, nevertheless, would help stir up something of an uprising. It was a gamble, a bloody gamble. The alternative was to drop the men in and hit any targets they came across, so random as not to have any effect. They'd be operating like any other resistance outfit. Operations would be too scattered and sporadic, with little impact.

Using French contacts, Combined Ops had found out that in the regional town of Villette, south-west of Paris, a regiment of Waffen SS were to move their barracks from the east of Paris and its arrogant commander wanted a show of strength with a parade through the streets to the town square to be greeted by the mayor and all the local dignitaries. Simply, Solov's idea was to have the men lying in wait for them and stage a wholesale massacre from the rooftops and other strategic positions. Staged as a French underground operation, the fall out would be dire in terms of civilian reprisals, such as took place in Czechoslovakia at Lidice following the assassination, last year, of Heinrich Himmler's right hand man, Reinhard Heydrich. It could be the call to arms that many French patriots needed. The squad would then link up with the resistance and support them. Perhaps then something of a mini-second front, or at least a diversion of more German troops, would have some impact on the war and demonstrate to the Soviet Union that it was not entirely being left with the main burden of the struggle. It was a gamble for the men but, if they didn't try, nothing would happen.

"This region," Solov had noted, "is particularly quiet. The strongest resistance centres are in the urban areas led by Communist Party members. If we can stir up the rural resistance and revive the Maquis resistance in this area, it can only be a plus. Before we know it, we could have a new partisan war here similar to the one in Yugoslavia under Tito."

"It's got to be worth a try," said Lawler. "It's got to be."

"I still think it's a bit risky, sir, attacking in broad daylight," said Miller.

Decker, Miller and Tobey were tucked away amongst the bushes on the edge of a small thicket overlooking the dummy ammunition store guarded by the Home Guards. Small groups of Guards patrolled the area around the target perimeter. Decker looked through his binoculars. The stores were kept in an old country home with a large backyard surrounded by high walls. In the yard was an arrangement of cardboard boxes posing as ammunition crates. The only entrance was by two wrought iron gates at the front. A hundred yards or so down the road was an old village hall used by the Guards as an assembly point and barracks. At the rear of the property was a thickly wooded area.

"That's the whole point, Sergeant. The element of surprise. They don't expect the unexpected."

But these are old men, not Krauts, thought Miller and caught Tobey's eye.

"Well, let's not worry about that now," said Decker. "As far as we can tell, they rotate the guards every ninety minutes at the ammo dump."

"So we catch 'em when they're changing guard?"

"That's the idea," said Decker.

Decker led his group to within twenty yards of the ammunition stores, crawling through long grass and ditches parallel to the main road. Behind him were Tobey, Mason, Malone, Wheeler and Scalleni. He checked his watch and guessed that Miller and the others would be in position to ambush any reinforcements from the village hall when the action began.

Decker was sweating profusely. He changed hands with his revolver. His mind was racing. Not long now. He watched two officers strolling past the iron gates, one with a cane under his arm. They stopped to speak to one of the two sentries. The sentries looked old, probably from the last war, he thought. He looked at his watch again and licked his lips. He checked the men behind him, they were fanning out just inside the tree line. Decker checked the Sten gun on his back, took a grenade, pulled the pin and threw it across the road at the gates. He yelled and he and his men launched themselves onto the road as the grenade bounced against the gates. They had them covered.

"You're either dead, wounded or prisoners, gentlemen!" Decker yelled as the Home Guards looked on red-faced and shocked.

The shock over, the two sentries grinned and started to help open the gates.

"Steady on, chaps," said one of the strolling officers to the sentries. "Don't help them, you're dead."

"Oh, yes, sir, sorry, sir."

Decker signalled to Malone and Scalleni to follow him and they got to work fixing handfuls of putty to the cardboard boxes as if they were laying charges.

The rest of the men stormed through the house shouting: "Bang! Bang!"

Down the road, reinforcements were hobbling on their way, around twenty men, many of them overweight.

Miller and his men stepped up from behind low hedges on either side of them and pointed their weapons.

Miller shouted: "You're all dead meat!" The men, startled, threw up their hands. One muttered: "Oh, fuck's sake!" and carefully lay down in the road. The 'barracks' and the 'ammunition stores' were officially destroyed.

In the next few days, Decker and his men struck hard and fast. They captured and 'destroyed' the Home Guards' HQ along with two jeeps. On the fourth day, they were joined by Solov who had been searching for them for a while. Although pleased with their work, he said he'd been concerned that he'd been able to find them too easily.

"But, apart from that, Captain Decker, you've done very well. Now you have to destroy bridges, railway lines, block main roads, anyone who tries to clear the lines of communications, blast them. Constant harassment, the more enemy deaths, the lower the morale, the higher the fear." Decker managed something of a smile, but wasn't really listening. He didn't need Solov to tell him he'd done well.

Over the next few days, the squad ran rings around the Home Guards and accomplished all their tasks. None of these results surprised anyone, but it was a good exercise for the men to think on more of a combat footing having been out of action for more than nine months, since Dieppe in August, 1942.

They were called in out of the field two days earlier than expected. They were to be rested for a few days, they were informed. Solov was given the privilege of announcing to them that, in three days' time, they would receive a briefing, owing to deadlines, then they were going into France. His work with them was finished.

"As you're sticking around for the briefing, sir," Miller said, about to go for a shower, "could we get permission to go for a drink together, a sort of farewell?" Lawler and Solov looked at each other. Lawler seemed put upon, it was a sore point after last time, but he was decisive.

"Yes. Yes, I don't see why the hell not. You've served us well here, Major. Why not?"

Solov turned to where Decker had been. He wasn't there.

TEN

This time Solov went with the men, together, to the Horse and Hen. His work with them was practically at an end and he envied them. They were going up for battle. They knew where they were going and what was expected of them. Solov felt apart from them, yet close and thought of his own work ahead of him - the assassinations Sevoska was lining up for him. In comparison, it was underhand, dirty work. It had been troubling him. One consolation was that he'd arranged to meet Marianne. He'd phoned her, amazed it was her real telephone number, and she'd agreed to meet with him.

He shouldered his way through the crowded bar with the others and they commandeered three tables again, pulling them together. There wasn't room for all of them to sit but they started their binge.

"Get spent up, lads," Miller said. "We won't be needing money where we're going."

"A pity Captain Decker couldn't join us," Solov said.

"No chance, sir," Tobey said. "He's a boy scout. He'll be having an early night with his map and compass."

"You're entitled to a chaser, Major, seeing as you've put your money in the kitty," said Mason.

"But, I haven't..." Solov got the hint, smiled and took out his wallet and dropped five pounds into the large pint glass. "Drinks all round."

"Jesus, he's still loaded," said Mason.

"So what do you think of British soldiers, Major?" Malone asked.

"I've only seen this small group," said Solov. "Right now, I'd give anything to be going into France with you, after working with you. I think you're a fine bunch of men."

"Sterling's winding you up, Major," said Tobey. "He's Irish. Anything to have a swipe at the Brits."

"But it's true."

"What about the Yanks?" asked Mason.

"Americans? I don't know. I've seen some Western films, y'know, cowboys, but…"

The men laughed at that.

"There's a few over there," said Mason. Solov looked over and remembered the night he met Marianne. She'd been with some Americans. These were not the same men.

"Alright, Yanks?" Mason called over to them, raising his glass.

"Hiya, Limey!" one of them returned.

"Not tonight, Mace," said Miller. "A bit of peace before the war starts again."

"They're on our side, y'know?" said Tobey.

"Have a go at the real enemy - the Irish," said Miller.

Mason tweaked Malone's biceps: "You're fuckin' jokin', aren't you?"

"You mentioned Spain to me once, Major," said Malone, "You promised we'd have a talk about it. What was your Spain like?"

"Hot, sunny. Sweaty, dangerous sometimes, boring. Met a lot of good people. Saw some of them killed. I was in Catalonia, and near Toledo."

"I was in Catalonia too!" said Malone.

"Did you read a book by…George Orwell?"

"'Homage to Catalonia'. Yeah, I read that book. Opened my eyes up to Stalin even more. They stabbed the revolution there in the back. They had a straight choice, back the workers and peasants or back the capitalists of the Republican government. They shot the wrong side. I didn't stay long after that. The writing was on the wall," said Malone. "I was in a hospital in Barcelona with a leg wound when all that stuff was going on. It was a civil war within a civil war. Shit, I might've bumped into Orwell myself. He was recovering from a throat wound there too."

"So you became disillusioned with communism?"

"No, Major, not with communism or socialism or whatever you want to call it. What happened in Spain or in Russia, since Stalin took over, has got nothing to do with Marx, Lenin or Trotsky. What kind of true Bolshevik signs a non-aggression pact with fascism? He's blinded with power, that man."

"I agree," said Solov, startling himself by being able to utter those words at last, openly, fearlessly, for the first time in years.

"This is getting too political for me," Mason said, opting out to rouse some of the others to play darts.

"Scared he might learn something," said Miller. "But, y'know, it's hard to understand and sympathise with communists who treat their own people like Hitler treats his."

"Make no mistake," Solov said. "The Russian Revolution was probably the greatest event of this century in terms of human and social development. The workers took power, ran the economy. But, don't forget, we had to fight a major war, a revolution, a civil war, surrounded by hostile states. We were exhausted. The other revolutions in Europe were betrayed by workers' leaders who were not socialists, who channelled their movements into collaboration with the capitalists. Then the USSR was isolated. When Lenin died, bureaucrats stepped forward and took over the party. Stalin was their leader. Then Trotsky was isolated. Stalin traded on the gains Lenin made and expelled Trotsky and hijacked his ideas in a distorted way. He stifled democracy."

"That's about it in a nutshell," said Malone, swigging his

drink. "Stalin wasn't interested in world revolution, was he? It might've inspired his own workers to complete the revolution and undermine his power base. That's why he purged all the Bolsheviks, the Left Opposition in Russia, in Spain, in France, Germany and that's why old Trotsky was murdered."

"Stalin knew," Solov picked up Malone's thread now, "that the capitalist West feared communism more than anything. The last thing the capitalists wanted was Russia calling for revolution so they backed Hitler in the '30s, as a buffer zone against communism. Stalin tried to...placate?...yes, placate them by killing off any kind of revolutionary movement. He even got the British communists to hold down the workers in your General Strike in 1926. He refused to unite the German communists with the German socialists. He split the left and paved the way for the Nazis. When the West refused to unite against Germany, Stalin recognised this as the West appeasing Hitler. Remember how your king supported Hitler? The one who abdi, abdi - how do you say it?"

"Abdicated. Anyway, he was not my fucking king," said Malone.

"Edward VIII," said Tobey.

"Yes, him, he was a close admirer of Hitler," Solov went on. "Some circles in the West backed Hitler's crusade of anti-Bolshevism. In the end, that's why Stalin thought he was safe when he split the Nazis from the West with the Non-Aggression Pact in '39. But it was Hitler who was too clever for Stalin. As soon as he defeated France and Britain, he attacked Russia, and here we are."

"On the same side, fighting Nazis, the way it should be," said Malone.

"What d'you reckon will happen after we've beaten Hitler?" asked Miller.

"Mark my words," said Solov, "the Soviet forces will be in

the centre of Europe. It'll be a race between us and the Americans as to who dominates the continent…to the victors, the spoils. Then the wolves will begin to devour each other."

"What about us?" said Tobey. "The British Empire, the Commonwealth?"

"The Brits?" Malone laughed. "Fuck 'em. They'll be holding onto Uncle Sam's shirt-tails pretending they've still got a fucking empire left, with Mr. Roosevelt's permission, of course. Don't be fucking stupid."

"I'm not stupid, my friend. The British Empire has still got a lot of fight in it, y'know," said Tobey, loyally.

"Kiss my arse!" laughed the Irishman. "You were fucked in the first big one and before that you struggled to fight a bunch of Boer farmers in South Africa. You're only any good when the odds are in your favour, like tribals with spears, and even then you're struggling. Even the fucking Zulus gave you a run for your money. Oh, and you're good at sending in the Black and Tans, y'are, against women and children, oh yeah, that's an easy one."

"If we were so shit," Armstrong barged in on the conversation, "you big, thick Mick, how come we've got a world empire?"

"I just got through telling you, and what's all this 'we' shite? You're fucking ignorant! So, two hundred years ago, you chased the tribals away with your muskets and cannon, you couldn't even hang on to America."

"Hey, buddy, tell it like it is!" one of the American GIs called over. "No taxation without representation!"

"And a lot of them colonials was Irish sent into exile," Malone added.

"And Scotch, my family were Scotch," said another GI.

"Don't fucking encourage 'em," Mason piped up. "C'mon, Yanks, let's have a game of darts. Best out of three wins the world."

Solov was enjoying himself with the camaraderie of these men again. Why, he hadn't spoken like this since those heady days in university when he used to attend the Left Opposition debating societies with his beloved Anya, all the radical political talk! Now there was no Left Opposition…and no Anya. He looked at his watch as the others were sorting out who was playing with the 'colonial contingent'. He said to Malone and Miller: "Listen, I've arranged to meet that woman, in the lounge. Do you mind..?"

"Major, how could we?" said Miller, shaking his hand.

"I'll hold the revolution up for you until you're finished, Major," Malone said, "Enjoy yourself. It's been marvellous working with you, an honour." He gripped Solov's hand with the two of his. "It's been a real honour, believe me."

She smiled at him as he entered the quieter lounge. He returned the smile, leaned over, kissed her on the lips and sat down.

"I didn't think you'd want to meet me like this again," she said.

"I might be working with you soon. Did you think I'd be angry because you deceived me so well?"

"I wondered."

He smiled. There was an awkward silence.

"I've…got a room for the night…Renegade," she said, with an impish smile.

"Ha. Do you want another drink?"

"No."

"Shall we go upstairs?"

"I'd like that. I've managed to get the same room."

"Our room."

In his room, on his bed, Decker rolled over onto his back and looked at the ceiling. In the dark, the room resembled the one in the hospital where he spent nearly eight weeks recovering from the vicious attack from the Hitler Youth gang. The first ten days, he'd been in a coma. His skull had been fractured, an arm and leg broken along with a few ribs. He could remember drifting in and out of consciousness for days after he came out of the coma.

Decker looked at the photograph of Isadora in his hand. He'd received visitors, he'd been told by the nurses - his British colleagues, and some of the German officers he worked with, the uniformed police, but he mostly remembered Isadora. He was told he was out of danger, but he'd need time to recover. He was also told that the police investigations could not trace the youths who did this to him. Mysteriously, no one could give a good description, and it had been dark. The military liaison officer from the embassy had visited him and he'd registered a complaint with the Hitler Youth organisation. He'd received a warm telegram from his parents and a card was brought by Isadora from her family telling him how horrified and ashamed they felt that some of their countrymen could do this. He was more worried and concerned about Isadora than he was about himself.

She'd been visibly upset the first visit and he drew strength from this, guilt perhaps? Or more than that? Did he really have to go through such an experience to elicit her feelings? Each time she came to visit, he was getting better, but she looked worse than ever. By the ninth week in hospital, nearly the end of October, he was able to walk slowly on crutches, his leg and arm in casts. She'd walk alongside him in the hospital gardens.

"Got a letter of profuse apologies from the Ministry of the Interior, no less," he said. "They sincerely regret the incident and are still making enquiries into who the perpetrators are…but no luck so far," he said.

"Predictable," said Isadora, sullenly. "Those killers will get away with it. They always do."

"Oh, I don't know. The police are trying their best. I got a personal note off the General the other day."

"Well, hooray for the General," she said. They walked in silence for a few moments.

"What's the matter, Isadora?"

"Nothing."

"No, something is eating you. You don't look well. You haven't looked well for weeks. I look better than you."

"Thanks."

"You know what I mean."

She knew she looked terrible. She looked pale and drawn. There were dark shadows under her eyes. She wasn't eating regularly.

"Oh, it's everything." She sighed, and helped him by holding one of his crutches while he eased himself onto one of the garden benches. Other patients and their visitors strolled by, some on crutches like himself, or being pushed in wheelchairs. Some of them nodded in recognition. Decker wrapped his dressing gown around him. It was a fresh October breeze, but it was better than being cooped up in bed.

"What? What's everything?" He reached over with his good hand and took one of hers. He looked at her face: "What's everything?"

"I'm living with Mama and Papa now."

"At home?"

"At home, for now."

"And university?"

"It's over, finished."

"But you've only just started."

"And now it's finished."

"Why? I mean, how come? I thought you liked it?"

"I did. I do. But," she shrugged, "I'm Jewish, aren't I?"

"What do you mean, you're Jewish?"

"That's what I am. Oh, John, haven't you read any of the newspapers recently?"

"You may have noticed I've been in a coma?"

"The new laws?"

"What new laws?"

"Hitler's introduced new laws, the Nuremberg laws, against Jewish people. They've kicked us out of universities, out of businesses, out of professions. It's hard enough trying to find food, a place to live, medical aid even. We're personae non gratae in our own fucking country."

"The law? That's the law?"

"I feel most sorry for Papa. Do you know what they did to him? Those business people told him if he didn't accept their price for his factory they'd report him to the police."

"They can't report him to the police for refusing to sell his business."

"You remember Heidi?"

"Yes." He remembered Heidi alright.

"Well, we're forbidden, that is, Jews are forbidden to have German females under the age of thirty-five working for them. They've got Heidi to make a statement. She's made Papa out to be some kind of pervert…they've obviously offered her a large amount of money. Papa's sold out so he can stay out of prison. It'd kill him."

"My God. And the house?"

"We've still got the house, but he has no income, only his savings that are dwindling fast just to support us all."

"Does my father know of this?"

"Well, what can he do?"

"They're business partners."

Isadora shrugged.

"I must write to him. I'll send him a telegram. He can write letters of protest to the government. He can refuse to do business with them. They usually listen when it's a question of losing money."

"John, there's nothing you or your father can do. My father has lost everything. It won't be long before they come for our house. He may have to sell that anyway just to stay afloat."

"I'll get better. When I get back to England, I'll start the ball rolling with my father. Why don't you come with me?"

"I can't. I have to stay here with my family. We've all had to register. We have to carry ID papers stamped with the Star of David on them."

"What? Look, we can work something out. God, I feel so helpless here."

"I'm sorry, John. Sorry I have to put all my troubles onto you like this."

"Isadora, I'll do everything I can to help you…and your family. My time's been up in Germany a while back but for this." He slapped the leg in plaster in frustration. "The doctor says as soon as I'm able to walk with a cane, I'll be able to be shipped back to England. Surely, they can't stop you from leaving with me?"

"Even if I could leave, I have to stay with my family. Many are leaving, but they're saying we can only leave with the clothes we stand up in. We'd have to give everything up."

"Outrageous." She leaned in towards him with her head on his shoulder. He could feel her body shaking. Soon, she composed herself. He'd never seen her like this.

"Marry me," he said, out of the blue.

"Oh, John."

"Marry me. I know I haven't chosen the most romantic circumstances…"

She began to laugh, then cry, then both at the same time.

"What?" he said, seeing something of the absurdity of it, he felt himself smiling. "What?" he said.

"You," she said.

"Yes, pretty bloody stupid, I know."

She put a hand on his face and said: "Pretty, yes. Bloody," she looked at the healing scar on his head, "yes. But not stupid."

"Are you sure about that?"

"Yes. Very sure. You're not stupid. You are a lovely, lovely man, and a good friend…"

"But you don't want to marry me."

"I would marry you."

"But you don't love me enough."

"I do love you."

"But…"

"No buts."

"Then what?"

She put a finger on his lips to stop him. "I want to live," she said.

Decker looked at her photograph as he lay on his bed in the darkness.

"I want to live."

After they finished, Solov and Marianne lay under the covers in each other's arms. He'd stopped her from explaining when she tried to say sorry for deceiving him. He smoked a cigarette salvaged from his jacket that lay on the floor. She turned onto her side and watched her hand slowly rising where she placed it on his chest.

For the first time, she spoke in Russian: "This fucking war."

"You were doing your job," he said.

"I'm ashamed. I deceived you."

"You were acting under orders. You must have had to do it before..." He stopped himself too late.

"Yes. I'm a state-controlled whore, and you're a name on a file. I know we are both more than that, much more."

"While I'm fighting for my country, you're fucking for it. We both have to do things we don't like, that seem alien. It's for a good cause."

It was a different, new kind of war he was getting into, Solov thought, a different kind of soldier was required. Where the battlefield sapped your strength, constant undercover work must sap your will. There was something sad, melancholic about her that concerned him. She had to pretend to be someone else. Could he do that? Why not? He felt like he'd lived undercover in his own skin for years. It had saved him from the purges, from the labour camps that had killed his father. Could he go on like this with no respite?

"Sevoska told me you've been here for years. How much longer do you expect to stay? I mean, is the rest of your life going to be lived as a lie?"

She lifted her head. "When you've served your purpose, well, that is for them to decide. If you are successful and you're recalled, you're guaranteed the good life. But, well, when can that happen? The more years you invest in establishing an identity, a life, then why spoil that investment? You can't request a transfer, like in the army. No. They let you go home when they alone are ready to let you go. When you take a job like this one, you must assume it's long term. They really haven't prepared you, have they?"

"You make it sound like a prison."

"It is. Do you think I've much chance of seeing home again? Home..." She began to cry. Solov put an arm around her. What was he supposed to do?

"So there's no way out?" said Solov.

"Only two alternatives," she said, dabbing at her eyes with her fingers, once again in control. "Go double for the British or make a run for it and hide somewhere they can't find you."

Solov was shocked to hear her talking this way. This was the woman who had taken him in so perfectly the first time around. He wondered why she was so openly putting herself in danger of being exposed by him on their second meeting. But she was reflecting some of the feelings that had burned in his mind long ago...to escape, to get away and to live an open, honest life, without fear. A life that wouldn't be closed off. He dreaded this new work with Sevoska. He would far rather have the open, honest work of a soldier.

"Why do you trust me?" he asked.

She propped her head up on one hand and thought about

this, taking a cigarette off him.

"I think, after six years in this work, you know when you can trust people. You learn to read people more precisely, quickly. Apart from the stuff I've read about you. You learn to pick up on characteristics, make judgements…"

"How do you know I won't tell Sevoska about you?"

"You are honourable, Nikolai." She used his name for the first time. "So am I, deep down, beneath all these layers. You have your own idea about how a soldier should be, and serving your country, and it has nothing to do with this devious, shadowy stuff."

Solov smiled again. He felt like he was having his palm read by a gypsy at a travelling circus. He wondered what else she'd read about him.

"I've got a plan," she said, suddenly. "I've thought it out over and over in the last eighteen months or so. It started as a dream, and the desire grew bigger and bigger". She heaved a deep sigh: "When I tell you, just tell me whether you think it's good or bad and whether you want to join me. It's made for two."

He looked hard at her. His next reply could seal his fate one way or the other.

"Go on," he said.

"Over the years, I've stashed money away. I've got nearly eight thousand pounds. I can hire a boat to Ireland. From Dublin, we can go by liner to South America or perhaps Mexico. We could settle there. Easy, simple, straightforward…"

"…and we'd be running for the rest of our lives, at least, looking over our shoulders. Remember, they even caught up with Trotsky in Mexico."

"Don't let's flatter ourselves. We're small fish compared to Trotsky. And he was not publicity shy. We'll live the quiet life. You could grow your hair, grow a moustache like Emiliano

Zapata." She giggled.

"Zapata?" said Solov, fingering an invisible moustache.

"What do you think?"

She made it sound so simple. He knew from experience that, usually, the simplest ideas were the most effective. Take a boat to Ireland, yes, then a neutral Irish liner to neutral South America, a whole continent to get lost in. He spoke excellent Spanish. There were big European communities out there. What then? Well, maybe the possibilities were endless, or they could just disappear?

"I'm not saying anything," he said, cautiously. "You're right though. This isn't my idea of soldiering. I'll think about it. It'll be the most important decision of your life. There'll be no turning back."

"Anything is better than this shadow world I live in."

"You might think differently when you come face to face with a man with an ice-pick in his hand," said Solov.

"I'm not afraid to die. I don't want a living death. So, you'll join me? Think about it?"

"I'll keep in touch. This could be another cheap loyalty test." She shook her head. "Now you've got it all off your chest, you might feel better to have got your fantasy out of your system and turn me in. Shit, why did I let myself get mixed up in all this? I'm just a soldier."

"I'm just a girl from a fishing village on Lake Ladoga." She shrugged.

"Lake Ladoga? Some nice places there. Some nice skiing places." He also remembered the winter of '41-'42 when the lake froze over and supplies could be trucked over to besieged Leningrad.

"We lived in Propinsk," she said, dreams in her voice.

"There's eight in our family and we lived on a commune. We were lucky, we had a little boat too, for the lake. I got to university, did languages…"

"Me too, in 1927-30."

"Joined the army in '33, volunteered for secret service work a year later, was transferred to London by early 1936, then they asked me to…"

"…melt away?"

"I'd already practised living as an English girl before I came out here, voice coaching, you name it, dialects, the lot…"

"How to hold a cup of tea? What's your real name?"

"Petra Petrova."

"I like it. Sounds like an actress. Which is what, I suppose, you are."

"Playing one role for life."

"Or death."

"I'm getting stage fright so it's time to drop the final curtain…"

"Oh, very good. I did all that English training. The correct pronunciation and stuff: 'Wolverhampton Wanderers win on Wednesday'…

"'Which way was the wind wafting'?

"'Wade waist deep in the whirlpool'?"

"Anyway, after all that," she continued, "we came out here, three girls together. Ostensibly employed as secretaries at the embassy. Nothing to do with the ambassador, we were under Mr. Sevoska…"

"Lucky, Mr. Sevoska. I get the feeling you don't like him?"

"He's dangerous. He took advantage of our lack of

experience, each of us in turn…"

"I see, you really *were* working under him?"

"Ha. I suppose you could put it like that. He's in charge of several networks in London, southern England, the Midlands. He's got a lot of people on his team, including twenty-odd girls. I'll bet he's tried most of them out. Most of them have gone willingly. He is a charmer. But, underneath, he's dangerous, ruthless. He's ordered a lot of deaths, our own people as well as the opposition. At first, I thought he was fun. The two girls I came over with, he paired one off with one of his bodyguards, while he took me and the other girl into his bed. But, later, I heard a few stories…likes to use whips and things. He liked me to mess with my friend while he watched. When I got assigned my present post, I guess others have taken my place in his bed. But, any instructions off him…I never refuse them. He's a dangerous man."

"He sounds corrupt, like the whole system," said Solov, shaking his head. This was the other side to the man he'd met so many weeks ago in London. Somehow, it didn't really surprise him in this murky world of espionage he was about to enter full time.

"Look." Solov sat up. "I've got to go now. I've got an early call tomorrow, planning operations with the commandos. I'll be going back to London in a matter of two days or so." He began to get dressed. "Sevoska told me I could be working with you in my new post…what's the matter?" She wasn't listening.

"I'm afraid," she said, "you might betray me."

"I thought you said you knew you could trust me?"

She nodded, but wept nonetheless: "I know."

"Can I phone you again?"

"Give it a couple of weeks. Wait until maybe we work together, I don't know."

"Look, I'll have to go now," he said, pecking her cheek. "Please trust me."

He walked to the door and whispered: "Goodbye for now," and closed it softly behind him. He tried to clear his fears from his mind and bring some order and logic to his thoughts, but his plans were crowding in, getting in the way.

ELEVEN

"Gentlemen, you are going to do what you have always trained to do," said Colonel Lawler, "Kill Germans."

"Now you're talking, Colonel," Mason called out. Everyone seemed in agreement with him. They were gathered in the briefing room.

"If our Russian allies want a second front," Lawler continued, "They may have to wait a while longer, maybe next year. In the meantime, the commandos are going in to stir things up and let the Jerries know we're still here. You may have noticed this training centre becoming increasingly emptied out of troops? We know we lost a lot of our boys last year at Dieppe." He looked over at Decker who nodded and looked down at the floor. "Captain Decker remembers that well, and some of you will. This time, we'll show them what kind of hornets' nest we can stir up with just one squad of commandos. Most of our men are being deployed to the Mediterranean theatre. They're getting ready for the next big push down there. They'll be jumping into Sicily most likely, that's pretty much an open secret but that information, of course, doesn't leave this room. But for us, we're going in to hit the Nazis hard, anything to oblige our Russian allies. The commandos have never flinched from that. If we can divert more Nazi troops away from the Eastern Front, we will have achieved our objective. Our operations in Norway alone have caused 300,000 more German troops to be stationed there, troops Hitler can barely spare. Our campaign in North Africa prompted the Führer to occupy Vichy France. Now we intend to keep him on the run, hither and thither. He'll be like the little boy in the dyke with more leaks springing than he can cope with…we'll be a part of that. Captain Decker?"

Decker stood up and walked over to the large table behind them that was covered with a sheet. He removed it to reveal a scale model of a town crudely but effectively put together over the last few days by Lieutenant Carter and a couple of men from the RAF's photo-reconnaissance people. The men were told to gather around. The table was covered in mostly green paint with darker green patches representing thicker wooded areas, contour lines denoting hills and a winding blue path showing a river running through it. Decker took a long stick to point with as he began his briefing.

"This is Villette, a sizeable regional town, some manufacturing. At the centre, the old town, lots of narrow, winding streets, two main streets cutting across the centre that feed onto the main town square where you'll find the town hall - Hotel de Ville - municipal buildings, a church, commercial buildings, here, here and here, very picturesque. The mayor is a man called Simon Cardogne. Our sources say he is not active in the resistance, and is probably hiding behind his badge of office just this side of open collaboration with the Nazis. No protests came from his office, apparently, when members of the local Jewish community were rounded up and their synagogue dynamited. It's known that in other areas where similar things have happened, some French civilian authorities have, at least, registered some form of official complaint, ignored by the Germans, of course. The 301st Waffen SS Panzerbrigade has been relocated from its former base to the east of Paris to six miles outside Villette which lies to the south-west of the capital. We believe they are to be a part of the German defence build-up against any likely landing in Northern France, which the Colonel has already referred to, that may take place next year. Its commander is a Heinz Schrenk, a full Colonel. Our friends in France inform us that now his brigade is settled in its new home, he's been touring the area with his troops and is planning a military parade through Villette to the town square, at the invitation of Cardogne."

"Pretty much rubbishing his non-collaboration credentials," said Malone.

"Correct," said Decker. "We expect the parade to take place on Sunday afternoon at 2pm on June 21st, three days' time. Speeches will be made to the troops by Schrenk, and they'll be welcomed by Cardogne. That, gentlemen, is when we simply hit them. We aim to be in place here..." Decker pointed at the roofs around the square, "here and here". He indicated a department store and what appeared to be a guest house. "This will give us maximum field of fire, and over here..." He indicated one of the backstreets away from the square and across the river on a walkway alongside a park... "we'll have two mortars letting them have it. We'll also have men posted for back up and to defend our main shooters' line of escape. We will be working closely with some French resistance people who will guide us in and out and provide us with a base of operations."

"Sir," said Miller "Roughly, how many Krauts are going to be lined up in that square?"

"At an estimate, we're talking a couple of hundred, as many as can realistically fit the space. It will be a token force, not the complete brigade, of course. The square just wouldn't hold that many. Remember, it's just for public show, to let the local population know they are there. They'll be in a confined space. They won't be expecting us and we'll be hitting them from all directions."

"Won't there be a lot of security?" asked Tobey.

"We anticipate that French police will line the main route, few and far between, they'll be a negligible presence. We'll be in civilian clothes, carrying French ID. They'll be led to believe this is a French initiative."

"Obviously," Lawler cut in, "since Hitler's directive last year that commandos either in or out of uniform are to be shot, this is neither here nor there. However, it's important they believe this to be a French operation for it to be successful. We expect high German casualties and high reprisals against the local population. That's part of the point of the operation, to stir up reprisals that will act as a recruiting sergeant for the resistance."

"We want the German reaction to provoke an uprising, to set the whole region, maybe the whole country, ablaze," Solov said. "A partisan war."

"A lot of innocent people will suffer," said Malone.

"A lot of innocent people are already suffering," said Tobey.

"It's war, isn't it?" said Armstrong, lighting a cigarette. "What difference does it make if it's the French or the Krauts?"

"Don't beat about the bush, Armstrong, tell us straight," said Mason. Armstrong shot him a sharp look.

"Although I wouldn't put it that way myself," said Solov. "Armstrong has a point."

"Men," Lawler took over. "You'll be dropped in the day after tomorrow at 0100 hours, twenty miles south of Villette and you'll meet your contacts who will take you to your base of operations, where you'll stay overnight. The next day, after nightfall, you'll trek over to Villette and will be in position before dawn. It'll be a long wait through Sunday morning and it will be hot on those roofs. By 1400 hours, the show starts. Any more questions?"

Silence.

"Study the model. Work out the details about who's doing what. We have maps for you. This is just the beginning of your campaign. You'll then withdraw into the hills of the Central Massif and await further instructions. If your position is tenable then continue to lend the resistance support in destroying other targets. If things get too hot, you call in our flyboys and we'll whisk you out to fight another day. Good evening, and good luck to you all."

Solov also wished them luck. His mind was not on the briefing. He knew his work here was finished. He was due to leave first thing in the morning. His thoughts were on Petra and the ideas she'd put into his head. He wondered how long it would be, if he fell in with her plans, before the Kremlin sent some of Stalin's strong arm boys after them.

He imagined some place like Mexico where they could be staying, one of those traditional adobe-walled affairs, the air thick and heavy, windows open. The killers would be armed, of course, and they'd come in the middle of the night, or just before dawn. They'd be roused from their bed, read their death sentence, made to kneel and shot in the back of the head. Perhaps they'd just shoot them as they lay sleeping, or make it look like a domestic murder and suicide? That would be more fitting. No investigations, nothing. Just two dead bodies and a shocked neighbourhood, shocked at the death of a happy couple, such a tragic end.

"Anything to add, Major Solov?" said Colonel Lawler, killing his thoughts.

"Colonel, Captain," he nodded. "I think you've pretty much covered most things you need to. I wish…a part of me wishes I was coming with you to see this through. I wish I could change my nationality as easily as I've changed my uniform. But, I've got my own work to do. I will say this, it was a pleasure and an honour to work with you all. You are among the best soldiers I have worked with and I wish you luck again."

The men applauded.

"And thank you, Major," Malone called.

"Send us a postcard when you get back to Russia," said Mason. "We'll leave a forwarding address, care of Adolf Hitler, Berlin. Sure he'll see that we get it."

"I'll put my name to that, Major," Lawler said. "Men, by the time you land in France, the Major will be back in London, getting ready to go home…"

That night, Decker remembered when he went home. His recovery in Germany had been remarkably good. He was given sick leave until the new year of 1936. It wasn't long before he no longer needed his walking cane and he feverishly waited for his medical officer to confirm him fit for duty. He was due his new posting. In the meantime, he convalesced at his base in Dorset. He wrote letters to Isadora and her family. He sent parcels with food and medical supplies. He contacted the Red Cross on their behalf. He then went to see his parents. They were relieved to find him safe and well. His scars were healed, the scars on his body.

"There must be something you can do, Dad," he pleaded with his father. His parents were shocked at what he'd told them about the Meyers' circumstances.

"They always gave us assurances that Hitler's government only railed against Jewish people, that it was harmless electioneering talk," said his mother.

"It's not just talk, Mother, believe me. I've got the marks to prove it."

"It must be awful," she said. "And they don't intend moving away, to another country, to England maybe? We could help them much more effectively if they came here. We could sponsor them."

"Yes," said Thomas, his father.

"They're afraid they'll lose everything then. The authorities won't allow them to bring anything with them. No money, no belongings, just the clothes they stand up in," said Decker.

"You know, John, I'd like to do everything in my power to help those people..."

"Can't you use some of your influence through the business?"

"What do you have in mind?"

"Well, start with a letter of protest, through the embassy, or directly to those people who have practically stolen their business from Herr Meyer? He's like you, Dad. He built up his business from scratch, even more so because he got chased out of Russia when the Reds took over. Put yourself in his position. How would you feel?"

"Terrible, of course, just terrible," said Thomas, holding a match to one of his cigars.

"Maybe some form of...I don't know how these things work...a trade embargo, a boycott of our exports until they're either given their business back or given the right amount of compensation. They got a pittance. They're on the verge of losing their home, they're in that much debt. I can't afford to keep sending them money, not on a junior officer's pay."

"I'll see what I can do. I can make a start by writing a few letters maybe..."

"That's just a start, anyway. Then, maybe, if you threaten to hit them where it hurts, in the pocket..."

"How do you mean?"

"Well, like I say, a trade embargo. Refuse to do business with them until something is done."

"Are you mad?" said the younger Thomas, his brother. "What good will that do? We'll be cutting our nose off to spite our face. We can't just stop trading with them."

"You're making enough in the home market, aren't you?" said Decker.

"Yes," said his brother. "Enough. Nothing like the money we're making in Germany. They're massively expanding their arms industry, they're building ships for their navy. It'll be the making of us."

"To the cost of our partners, the Meyers, our friends?"

"You're just being sentimental, we're talking business here. Mother, talk some sense into him, will you, please?"

"John," she said. "Your father has already said he'll do what he can to help them."

"Letters are a good start, but they won't be enough, Mother," said Decker. "Do you seriously think one letter from Dad will make them change their minds? These are vicious people behind the friendly façade. I've seen it in action. I saw its vile underbelly on the street in Berlin."

"Just a bunch of high-spirited thugs," said his father. "You'll find that in any city, especially in the poor districts. You were in the wrong place at the wrong time. The people we're doing business with are like us…"

"When did we blackmail anyone?" Thomas the younger said. "When did Dad use the law to rob somebody of their livelihood? When did he use force to get what he wants?"

"Oh, now, boys, no arguments, please," said their mother.

"How about 1926?" said Decker. "Remember how the picket lines were cleared off?"

"Oh, yes," smirked Tom, "when you used to be a Nazi, I remember. Now you've become what you always used to hate - a Jew-lover!"

"So I can change. Remember those Jews? They helped make this family a lot of money."

"And we'll continue to make a lot of money," said Tom, helping himself to one of his father's cigars. "You need to be realistic. Stick to what you're good at, John. Just go away and get back to marching up and down."

"Boys, please!" said their mother, again. "We've had enough. Thomas, please talk to them."

"I will do what I can to help the Meyers, John," his father said. "But, as for some sort of embargo, it's really out of the question…"

"Mustn't lose any profits, eh?"

"It's not only about profits. It's about responsibility. I'm responsible not only for our livelihood, but for the livelihoods of twelve hundred employees, and their families, the people who supply us, and their families. We're slowly coming out of this Depression. How many people have been out of work? It doesn't bear thinking about. I can't endanger all that on a whim because one family is losing their home."

"What about the responsibility of friendship? What about personal loyalty?"

"Oh, don't be pathetic, John," said his brother. "Of course, we've been loyal. Anyway, what's that got to do with anything? Dad's already said where his loyalties lie."

"Don't put words into my mouth, Thomas," said their father.

"You know, Dad, what this is all about, don't you?" said Tom. "It's about Isadora. John is still carrying a torch for Isadora. He'll do anything to win her hand, even risk the family going to ruin."

"Now you're being pathetic," said Decker.

"Tell me I'm wrong."

"The business is thriving like it's never done before," their father interrupted them, "both for us and our German partners. I have absolutely no intention of risking that relationship, rest assured. But I promise I'll send a letter asking them to reconsider the welfare of the Meyers..."

"It'll go straight in the waste paper basket," said Decker.

"...then I'll write to the Meyers and ask them if there's anything I can do to help alleviate their conditions..."

"Too little, too late," said Decker. "It's a poor show when we can't support our friends." Decker turned away.

"Oh, la-di-da, poor show, is it? Not cricket, eh, Lieutenant?" Tom sneered.

"Go to hell!"

"John!" his father snapped. "I will not have language like that in my house, and in front of your mother!"

"What language would you like? Sieg Heil?"

With that, Decker left the family home and returned to Dorset. He'd carried his anger and disgust for the next few months. He wrote letters to Isadora. She replied infrequently, but gave assurances that, though they were struggling at times, they were getting by. They had help off friends and relatives, even neighbours in the apartment block where they now lived. She helped her mother and sister earn money or bartered for food for repairing or laundering clothes. Her father did what he could, took out loans if they really needed anything, but he was finding it increasingly difficult to get credit. Often he was depressed, but gained strength through the way the family was sticking together.

Decker received his first posting in March that year, a few days after German troops moved into the Rhineland boldly breaking the Treaty of Versailles that was meant to keep it a demilitarised zone. Nevertheless, Decker was sent to Egypt and threw himself into his work. He was in the spiritual home of one of his boyhood heroes, T.E. Lawrence, 'Lawrence of Arabia', stationed with the 7th Hussars in the Light Armoured Brigade under General Hobart. This was part of the Mobile Force that patrolled the deserts and coastal roads as far as the Libyan border, which was under Italian control. His unit was very much looked down upon by the corps commanders in Cairo, who were old school cavalry men and still believed in real horsepower, as opposed to the mechanical kind. They scoffed at the Mobile Force - or 'Immobile Farce' as they referred to it. General Hobart was keen to master armoured warfare, was something of a pioneer in his field, and recognised that tanks and motorised infantry were where the future lay in warfare, especially in the wide open spaces of the desert.

Decker was busy learning his trade in desert warfare, learning how to command and lead troops. He had fewer letters from home, which dwindled down to Christmas and birthday celebrations, initiated, of course, by his mother. Worryingly, even fewer letters came from Isadora. He was eighteen months in Egypt before he heard from her, early 1938. The letter had been waiting for him back at his HQ, in Cairo, to where he returned after months at the Libyan borderlands. She seemed in good spirits, despite her father having suffered a mild heart attack. She said that, when he returned to England, she'd like to try to come and see him. If that was not possible, maybe he could visit her and they could catch up with each other? She told him her father was beginning to think more of applying to take the family to England - his father, Thomas, had apparently suggested that possibility in several letters - as now things looked like they were not going to change in Germany as the anti-Jewish atmosphere was more and more oppressive. More shops were being ransacked, more beatings were taking place and only the other day she saw some old men being forced to cut their beards and then scrub the streets.

Decker sent replies to her, encouraging her to keep strong and to try and persuade her father to make the move to England, anywhere where it will be better for them.

That summer, he received a telegram from Isadora. The family were on the move toward Trieste, at the head of the Adriatic, on the border between Italy and Yugoslavia. They were planning to move to Palestine. In subsequent letters from Trieste, Isadora explained how her father felt he could no longer tolerate his family living under those oppressive conditions, that he felt they were only going to get worse, not better. He could smell war coming around the corner, he told his wife and daughters, and with war came persecution of perceived 'internal enemies'.

'My father said our family have been in that predicament before and he didn't want us to suffer any more. Hitler has already moved into Austria and was making noises about the Sudetenland in Czechoslovakia. He said things are beginning to accelerate and we saw how the Jewish community in Vienna were treated and the West does nothing. Thousands of Jewish refugees are being refused entry in countries you would expect to be more welcoming, even Britain and America. So now, we are in a house with five other families near the docks in Trieste. We are trying to raise money between all the thousands of refugees here to charter passenger ships to Palestine. My father is throwing himself into this work with others. He's tired, we're all so tired. My mother looks old before her time and Ruth is now a grown woman, she's been through so much. So, dear, dear, John, we may be seeing each other a lot sooner than we thought. How far is Cairo from Palestine? I know it's not a great journey. I will let you know when we are coming. Perhaps you can meet us? It would do us no end of good to be greeted by a friendly, familiar face.'

It must have been so difficult for them, Decker thought. To lose their business, their home, the second time they'd been chased from their country of choice. He smiled grimly to himself. He remembered the first time he met Herr Meyer in his pinstripe suit. The old man had scoffed at the idea of a homeland for the Jews in Palestine and could he picture him wearing sandals in the sand? He decided he would do his utmost to meet them. He had plenty of leave saved up, having not taken any the whole time he'd been in Egypt. He began to save his money and stopped socialising so often with his fellow officers in the clubs in Cairo. After promotion to First Lieutenant that November, there was news of the 'Kristallnacht' in Germany, a near pogrom of the Jewish community they blamed for the assassination of a secretary to the German ambassador in Paris, and they were blamed for the 'international conspiracy' against Germany following the Munich crisis, when Neville Chamberlain and Daladier met with Hitler and Mussolini to decide the fate of the Czechs.

Decker, like everyone else, sensed there was a war coming. The Munich conference was a stalling tactic that bought time. It only bought time for the Nazis. By March, 1939, they marched into the whole of Czechoslovakia. Before, Hitler had only claimed the lands where German-speaking people lived. Now, he'd invaded foreign soil. It was time for the West to wake up. This, of course, did not interrupt his father's business arrangements, he was told, in a long letter from his mother that finally reached him. He knew his mother was doing her best to heal the rift between him, his brother and father. But Decker had more pressing matters.

By the end of March, he received another telegram from Trieste. It had taken them months to raise the cash, what with having to pay their way just to keep afloat, but hundreds of families had managed to charter three small ships that would ferry more than fifteen hundred people across the Mediterranean. Isadora expected to land at Haifa harbour in Palestine, on April 8 or 9. Decker requested, and received, three weeks leave from the 4th of April, packed his clothes and boarded a train to Alexandria, then took a coastal steamer to Haifa.

His colleagues in the mess had ribbed him: "You're going on leave to Palestine?" There was ongoing trouble there with an Arab uprising against the British Mandate and increasing Jewish immigration.

"A few Arab terrorists do not concern me. I'm meeting old friends there," Decker had told them. He was genuinely moved when his fellow officers made a collection for the Meyers after he explained exactly why he was going to Haifa. He managed to shop for a few small welcoming presents for the Meyers around the bazaars - a selection of silk scarves for Ruth, a necklace made from onyx for her mother, a pair of sandals for Herr Meyer as a kind of running joke, and he still had the diamond ring for Isadora. He imagined a dockside proposal, but thought better of it. He'd give it some time for them to get settled.

He found a good hotel in Haifa and sent a telegram to Trieste to say he was waiting. He waited for two days before a reply came. It read: "We're setting off this evening, darling. Can't wait to see you, love Isadora."

The voyage took six days, a lot longer than anticipated. The ships were in poor condition. There were crowds at the dockside as they came into view. They looked like rust buckets, Decker thought. The second ship was listing heavily to the left. As they drew nearer, he could see people crammed onto the decks. He tried to spot the one the Meyers had boarded but the names had rusted away. He moved closer to the quayside as the ships slowly came to rest. He saw the crammed passengers begin to disembark. He couldn't believe the humanity that was packed into what looked like floating hell holes. Relatives surged forward to greet the faces they recognised. Decker found himself being swept along and had to quickly step aside. He saw a wheelchair being eased ashore, helped by a sailor and three women. He could just make out the face of Herr Meyer, his face thinner, his hair thinner too, and nearly totally grey.

"Frau Meyer!" he called. "Ruth! Isadora! Over here!"

He pushed through. Frau Meyer saw him and let out a cry as she held him tightly, crying into his shoulder.

"It's okay. As long as you're safe. As long as you're safe, thank God." Her daughters were helping to push their father's wheelchair, to turn it around.

"Let me help you," said Decker.

"Thanks, John," said Ruth.

"Isadora...?"

She turned to face him. It was a nurse smiling back at him.

"I need to try and get Herr Meyer out of this heat," she said. Her patient was staring into space. Decker turned to Ruth.

"Where's Isadora?"

"She's not on board, John. Had to be quarantined," said Ruth. Decker looked at her.

"Quarantined?"

"Cholera."

Decker looked back at the ship still spewing people out of its belly.

"John," said Ruth, a cracked, sympathetic smile on her lips, "she died."

"Died?"

"Isadora died two days ago."

"Dead? Isadora dead?"

"They had to bury her, like all the others. They had to bury her at sea."

The touring car that belonged to Colonel Lawler swept through the country roads leaving the Special Training Centre and its surrounding woodlands behind. Soon, they passed the US airbase where, Solov knew, the commandos would be gathering that night to leave for France in the early hours of the morning. He remembered other landmarks as they came up and bid them a silent farewell - the church tower, the billboard on the side of the rail station, the ox-bow lake and the Roman milestone then on to London. The driver stared straight ahead as the roads were eaten up and, in the rear seat, Sergeant-Major Redfearn relaxed at attention. This was the best part of Redfearn's assignment, Solov suspected, delivering him back to where he came from, playing postman for the British to the Russians. Solov would be glad to see the back of him, too. He knew the British Army had never experienced democracy like his Red Army once did in the revolution. There had never been any soldiers' committees where there would have been no room for the likes of this bully. However, he'd experienced a genuine feeling of regret saying his goodbyes to the men that morning.

"Come back and see us after the war, Major," Sterling Malone had smiled.

"You're alright, Bullet," Miller had said.

"Look after yourself, mate," Mason had said, seriously for once. He'd pressed hands with Thornton and Wheeler. Young

Tony Scalleni's eyes had tears in them as he shook hands. "Arrivederci," Solov had grinned.

Armstrong had remained cool and aloof and barely touched hands.

"Hope you get your stripes back one day," he'd told him.

"Yeah," he said.

Decker had stood off in the background. To hell with him, Solov had thought.

Colonel Lawler had made a big show of shaking hands, his teeth clamped around his pipe, like the headmaster he probably used to be, for all he knew. He had given another speech of thanks about what Solov had achieved for promoting 'goodwill' between allies. Lawler had then waved Lieutenant Carter forward who was carrying a paper parcel.

"…on behalf of His Majesty's government…" Oh, no, Solov had thought, the pomp… "the men and myself are pleased to present you with a little gift of thanks…"

Solov had torn open the parcel. It was the uniform he'd worn in the training.

"If ever you fancy a change of army, put this on and think of us," Miller said.

The car cruised through the streets of London. It was almost noon. Solov saw some of the cabled barrage balloons looking lonely and obsolete. He rubbed his crown and scratched at the stubble there. He was going to have to grow his hair out so he could 'melt away'; one of the first changes required. Solov had been awake for most of the night, turning his thoughts over in his head. He'd thought of Petra's plan to run and the life of a hunted dog, forever looking over his shoulder. Then, the thought always came back to him, whether or not to tell Sevoska about her. Maybe he already knew and it was another trick? He decided to trust his instincts and see how things played out. He'd survived this far. He touched the stubble on his head again and sighed as the car turned into the rear car park of the Russian embassy building.

Solov climbed out and took his bag and the parcel he tucked under his arm. He shook hands with the driver, then leaned in the passenger window.

"Farewell, Mr. Redfearn, it's been a pleasure."

"Yes," said Redfearn. "Driver!" he snapped and the car pulled away. Solov watched them go, smiled then shook his head. He wondered whether he'd been a little childish with Redfearn, insulting him by not using his rank to address him.

"Fuck him," he breathed to himself. The door behind him was opened by a young, black-suited man. He greeted Solov with a smile.

"This way, sir," he said, leading the way down the corridor. The dim passageway yawned like a mouth devouring him.

TWELVE

S tefan Sevoska looked up from the papers he was reading on his desk and was grateful to be disturbed. He stood up and walked around to greet Solov, embracing him almost like a brother.

"Hello, my boy, how are you?"

Solov was put at his ease, as usual, despite Sevoska's seniority. Sevoska offered him a whisky.

"At last, I'll have someone working for me who likes to drink," he said, over his shoulder as he returned to his desk. Solov took the glass and looked at the whisky inside it. He tried to sound pleased. He remembered what Petra had said about this man. Was he really so dangerous, so corrupt? He didn't find it so hard to believe. But, maybe, the more she assassinated his character the more he would believe her story, or the more easily he would be persuaded to join her? Sevoska sat behind his desk, shoved aside the sheaf of papers and raised his glass: "Welcome to the team."

"…and farewell to the British Army." Solov raised his glass.

"What's that?" Sevoska eyed the parcel.

"Parting present. The British uniform I wore."

"Ah, that's nice. The British can be so sentimental behind the stiff upper lip, you know. I see you've already started to grow your hair out?"

"A shaven head is not very fashionable in British society."

"Now that your stint with the British commandos is over and your…er…shall we say, your loyalty is proven by that dirty little trick I played on you, I'm sure you'll want to know more about some of our future plans for you?"

Sevoska opened a silver-plated box of cigarettes, gave one to Solov and lit one himself from the cone-shaped, ivory lighter on the desk.

"If you write up a report of any significant events or information about the commandos or the Combined Operations organisation that you may have picked up, that will be fine."

"Nothing significant to report. But, of course, I'll write something."

"As I was saying, your future with us…"

Solov leaned forward in his seat and sipped his drink. He pushed everything else out of his mind, the commandos, the girl, Redfearn, and focused on Sevoska.

"For the next month or so you'll be undertaking a training schedule here at the embassy. I'm afraid you won't be leaving this building very often. We have all the facilities you need in our basement, there's even a gym and a swimming pool. You may begin to feel like a caged tiger but that's part of the course. You'll build up the role you'll be filling as a member of the Great British Public, his identity, work, personal history, all of which you will have to learn by heart. You'll read his dossier inside out and backwards. You'll be located in the area of Bristol. You'll work with our friend, Petra, from time to time, another reason I got her to meet you. Your job, initially, will be to support any of our agents, any sabotage jobs, perhaps some courier work, one or two assassinations…"

"Speaking of which," said Solov. "You mentioned a couple of assassinations at our last meeting, the writer fellow, Orwell…and that Trotskyist guy, what was his name?…Yes, Grant?"

"Edward Grant, yes. They will be your first assignments before you leave London."

"Which one is first?"

"Probably Grant. He's already organising Trotskyist rallies against us after Comrade Stalin announced the end of the Comintern, like I told you. He can go first."

"Fine. Everything seems to be worked out."

"That's the way we work. I've been in this business longer than I care to remember. I have to smile when I think the natives still think I'm attached to him upstairs," Sevoska cackled, pointing a finger to the ceiling approximately in the direction of the ambassador's suite. He poured Solov another drink, swapping his empty glass for another one. "Before you start work, I think you need to relax a little. We've got some beautiful women right here, you know? Tonight, maybe, we can get you acquainted with one or two of them?"

"One or two? Sounds promising," Solov smiled back. His mind raced back to Petra's words. She'd been telling something of the truth. Sly fox. He grinned at the bearded face across from him, those gleaming eyes. No, he thought again, sly wolf! The way he could win you over, all the personal touches, cool but calculated, then he floored you about fucking his female staff.

"Consider it as part of your fitness training." Sevoska winked. "I feel a bit of a swine, but our girls are good operators, good workers, like Petra, she does an excellent job, can't fault her. What more can you ask of a girl?"

Solov wondered. Yes, what more could Sevoska ask of her? He used and abused her, by pulling rank. Solov swilled the whisky around his mouth. He swore to himself he wouldn't allow Sevoska to abuse him in any way, no matter how many whiskies or women he threw at him.

"Excuse me a moment, will you?" Sevoska pressed his intercom. "Josef, bring it in, please, will you?" He looked at Solov again, silently. He shuffled his papers on his desk and drained his glass in one gulp. The door behind Solov opened. A suited man appeared, presumably Josef. He nodded at Solov.

Sevoska began: "Trust, my friend, is a priceless asset, in anyone's language. It can be bought, but even then it isn't really secure. It can be bartered for but even then it remains suspect. One way or another, it has to be felt deep inside." He tapped his chest. "Here. Trust always goes hand in hand with loyalty. Even our friend Hitler recognises this. His SS organisation has the motto: 'Meine Ehre Heisst Treue' - 'Loyalty is my honour'. Unfortunately, there's little honour in this world, no honour among thieves, as the British say, nor among spies."

Sevoska's eyes glanced past Solov, then towards Josef behind him.

"I hope what I'm talking about strikes a chord with you, Major Solov."

Solov sensed something to be wrong.

"For a soldier, Major, you seem to display a disappointing lack of both loyalty and honour. Loyalty to your leaders, your government, your party. Yes, I'm afraid you've been found out. Our friend Petra is an example of that loyalty and she did her duty again and has made a full report of your collusion with her story to…elope together."

Solov turned his head. Josef had a hand stuck inside his jacket pocket.

"What do you mean, exactly?" He tried to feign puzzlement,

"It was another test of loyalty like before. Tedious, I know, but necessary. I'm disappointed in you, Nikolai."

"Tell me what I've done wrong." Solov sat up in his chair.

"I can refresh your memory."

"Am I under arrest?"

Sevoska ignored the question.

"You'll recall your meeting with Colonel Bosck, in Moscow, when you were summoned from Stalingrad? Why you were sent here was all bona fide. You were part of a goodwill package to encourage the allies to begin a second front, to encourage better East-West relations, to work as an expert in partisan warfare. You would have made an excellent operative for my network. Alas, this is where the plot thickens. You have no respect for the party, like your stupid father. You insulted officials, superiors, commissars, quite the little rebel hero to the men and some of your fellow officers, officers like your friend, Vatutin. It's all here in your file."

"This is ridiculous."

"You are ridiculous, Major. You and your friends have made one remark too many. They will, one day, find themselves shipped off to a labour camp. We didn't want to do that with you, Nikolai, thought you'd be useful. We didn't want you wasting away breaking rocks in Siberia, like any Trotskyist scum. You still did a good job for us with the partisans. Somebody in Moscow, Bosck himself I think, had the idea of giving you a chance with us so I could knock you into shape. I had orders to put you to work with your talents here in Britain, out of the way, put you to the test. So, I put Petra onto you. She's good, she's loyal. Knows how to get men talking, you get the picture. Our girl is clever, it was obvious, but you fell for it. This, to me, shows lack of socialist fibre, low morale. Your head is burned out. You weren't going to give her away, were you? It was your secret from me. Now we return to the theme of loyalty and honour."

"Socialist fibre?" Solov interrupted him. "You call yourself a socialist, you and all those other bureaucrats, all the way up to Stalin himself? You feather your own nests and the rest of us do your dirty work for you. Trotsky was right, a revolution betrayed. You called my father stupid. Sevoska, he was a socialist, a true Bolshevik. I was always afraid of his fearlessness. I kept my head down while he stood up, yes, like Trotsky and the others. You and the other Stalinist gangsters cut them down. You can kill the man, Sevoska, you can't kill an idea. Now, I finally know, in that real sense, my father lives on through me."

"And now he'll die again...through you."

"Then I'm dying in better company than this." Solov sat back in his chair. "So, what happens now?" he said.

"My orders were to employ you if you proved useful, eliminate you if proven otherwise. You've thumbed your nose at us once too often." Sevoska leaned forward. "You asked whether you are under arrest. The answer is no. You are under sentence of death. It's a pity. I would have enjoyed working with a man like you, with your talents. But, as it is, Josef here is armed and you will accompany him down to the basement. He'll execute you and your body will be placed in our incinerator. If the wind is blowing in the right direction, perhaps it will carry your soul back to Russia. Now go."

Josef pulled a revolver from his pocket and tapped Solov on the shoulder: "This way, please, Major."

Solov was shaking with fear. He placed his glass on the arm of his chair, grabbed his parcel, and stood up. He hugged the parcel to his chest. Josef turned to open the door, his eyes and gun aimed at Solov's head.

"Mr. Sevoska, can I please offer an explanation?" His voice trembled. His shaking hands dropped the parcel.

"Pick it up!" Josef ordered.

Sevoska looked down at his desk and ignored him: "Take him down, Josef!" he ordered.

Solov bent down to pick up the parcel, swung it around and slapped the gun aside then rammed his head into Josef's face who crumbled to his knees. Solov scooped up the gun from the carpet, turned to Sevoska and fired twice, hitting him in the arm, then the chest. Sevoska stood up, held his chest then slumped forward over the desk, spilling blood over his unfinished paperwork.

Solov turned to Josef and closed the door. He placed the muzzle of the gun against the back of his neck, thought better of it, then brought it down hard on the top of his head and continued hitting him until he drew blood. Solov grabbed his parcel. He carefully opened the door. Surprisingly, nobody was in the corridor, but it was eerily quiet. He boldly walked down the passage towards the rear door again. He was halfway down the corridor when the young man who had admitted him walked out of the reception room towards him. The young man smiled. Solov held Josef's gun down by his side.

"Sir?" said the young man.

"The door?"

"Straight ahead."

"Thank you."

He walked on. He turned and saw the man reaching inside his pocket. Solov fired and hit him in the face. He picked up the doorman's gun. He was just alive, on his back, spraying blood on the expensive carpet. His legs were kicking, trying to gain purchase.

"I'll let myself out," Solov told him.

He tucked the parcel under his arm and, outside, he passed two more men in plain clothes. They'd been waiting outside to be let in. They watched Solov walk to their car where he ordered out their driver at gunpoint. Then he climbed in behind the wheel, looked back at them. They watched as he drove away.

THIRTEEN

Nobody seemed to be following him. Solov drove at a steady speed through London, looking through the rear mirror, then checked the petrol gauge, just over half full. He didn't want to attract attention to himself, the further south he went the less bomb damage meant he could locate main roads all the better. It would take time to locate the route he was looking for out of the city. Had the authorities been alerted? What would they tell the police? They'd have to cobble together some kind of cover story, maybe tell them he was some Nazi agent or something? Or would they cover it all up? It didn't look good, a shoot-out in the Russian embassy.

If they kept a lid on it, they could alert all their own people who could be anywhere watching for him. He reversed the car up a side street, near a row of dilapidated terraced houses. On one side, a few homes were still occupied. Children played games in the street. He took his hands off the wheel, they were still shaking. It was 3.45. It would be dark by nine or so, that gave him around six hours to find his way out of the city. He grabbed the parcel he'd thrown onto the seat next to him. As he got out, the children were starting to gather around to look at the car. Two little girls smiled at him from where they were sitting at the kerbside, playing with rag dolls. He walked into one of the empty houses.

Broken glass cracked under his boots as he made his way up the hallway. He entered what looked like the kitchen. The rear wall had fallen outwards into the backyard. The kitchen floor was covered in plaster and masonry. Solov took off his Russian uniform and changed into the British one, complete with beret. He checked the pockets. It was a stroke of luck, he found the War Office ID papers. That would help if he ran into any police. He finished dressing, then buried his Russian uniform under some of the rubble.

"Oi, mister! This is our 'ouse. Wot you doin' 'ere then?" It was the two little girls.

"Just changing my clothes." He smiled. Behind them, other children were beginning to gather. He didn't have time for this.

"You a German spy?" one girl said.

"No, I'm not a spy. Don't you recognise my uniform?"

The girl turned to her friend: "I think he's on our side."

The other girl sighed: "Does he know our dad?"

"No, I don't. There's lots of men in the army, you know." Solov stepped by them, and they quickly moved out of his way, then followed him out onto the street. A crowd of children had now gathered around the car. Mothers were peering through net curtains or standing in twos on some of the doorsteps. He waved and smiled, got into the car and drove away. The children followed the car out onto the main street, the bigger ones running after it until they ran out of breath.

A couple of miles later, feeling less vulnerable now, he saw a policeman walking along the street and pulled over.

"Officer," he asked. "Could you tell me how I get to the Brighton Road? I've lost my way." The officer stepped back and looked at the car. He looked at Solov's epaulettes as if he was looking for a rank. There was none.

"Can I see some identification, sir?" he said.

Solov showed him the War Office ID. The constable took a look at it, then at Solov.

"Russian officer, eh? Joined our lot, have you, sir?"

"Special Training."

Solov hadn't been far off course. Once he left London, he headed south, south-west. So much for security. If the Nazis invaded, all they'd have to do to find their way was to ask a policeman. Once in the open country, he put his foot down, still glancing in the mirror, then he kept a lookout for any familiar landmarks. He cursed himself for not having the presence of mind to take his bag from Sevoska's office, or take some cigarettes from his desk. He badly wanted a cigarette. He had no money on him either.

Sevoska. How things had turned around since their first meeting weeks ago. Now he was glad he killed him. In killing Sevoska, he knew he'd finally stepped across the line he'd always feared to cross. The line his father had crossed. He'd channelled his fear into warfare, fighting for a system of government he never believed in. Now he could begin to feel even better about his father's memory. He was glad he'd killed Josef too, a kind of symbolic killing of all the butchers who killed without question, the faceless executioner got his comeuppance. And that doorman lackey, that was good too. He'd probably been a young careerist party man, no doubt, working his way up as a bootlicker, ink-stained fingers turning the pages of personal files, rubber-stamping untold numbers of future deaths. Yes, he was glad he'd stopped that career in its tracks. He thought how he'd like to kill Petra now. He shook his head. Just kill her, a bullet in the head.

At least now he knew where he stood. His life would never be the same again, but he felt free, free to go anywhere. He knew where he was going.

Yes! He stood on the brakes, and reversed a few yards, the old Roman milestone. He was on the right road. Another thirty or so miles, yes, the oxbow lake. Another twenty and there would be the tattered billboard on the side of the rail station. He eased up on the accelerator to conserve his fuel. The daylight was beginning to dim, next came the church tower. He stopped and switched off the engine and got out to listen. He knew the US airbase was around here. He flagged down a farmer on his tractor and got a cigarette off him. That felt good. He drove on. Two cars passed him. They were civilian. His tank was nearly empty. He guessed he had about ten or fifteen miles left. He stopped again and smoked the other half of his cigarette. It was almost dark, then he saw the beginning of the hedgerow that shielded the barbed wire fence. It was the airbase. He knew a mile or so further would bring him to a fork in the road, if he took the right fork it would bring him to the main gates. He looked at his watch, 9.15. He parked the car on a side lane. He had to bluff his way in. He checked his two revolvers. If the War Office ID failed him, he'd have to rely on these. He crossed his arms on top of the steering wheel and rested his weary head.

He woke suddenly, 12.15. Someone had called his name. He'd been dreaming. It was one of those dreams about meeting his father on a train station in the civil war more than twenty years ago. "We have to go, Nikolai." His father's dirty face smiled. Time to go.

He drove the car slowly along the road following the fence by the meagre light the blacked out headlamps allowed. He kept watch on the perimeter fence, occasionally broken by a dark mass of trees. He turned right at the fork. He spotted the main gate entrance. At the side of the black and white barrier there was a small sentry post. He pulled up at the barrier. The sentry approached his window he'd already wound down. It was an American MP with a flashlight.

"Sir, you got a pass?"

Solov shielded his eyes, and offered the War Office ID. The light pointed down at it.

"Major Solov?"

"I'm linking up with a British crew going out tonight. I lost my way from the Training Centre..."

"Those limeys? They came through a while back. You say you're who?"

"I've been working with them..."

"You Russian?"

"Yes." The flashlight looked his uniform over again. "I'm

supposed to be with my men, leaving tonight for France."

"A minute. Hey, Corp, we got a limey crew going into France tonight?"

Solov heard a murmur from the sentry post.

"'Scuse, sir." He took Solov's papers. Solov felt the butt of one of the revolvers. Had word got ahead of him? The MP returned.

"Problem?" said Solov.

"No, sir. Just have to let my Corporal take a look and stamp it. Just ride over to the next checkpoint, sir, night officer's there. He'll give you directions."

The barrier was raised and he drove through to the next checkpoint. A young MP Lieutenant came out of his office. Obviously, the main gate had phoned ahead.

"Evening, the guard said you'd direct me to my men. British commando squad going into France tonight."

"Kinda late, aren't you, buddy?" the American said, looking down at his ID. "Sorry, sir, Major Solov. Russian, huh? Say, folks on my mother's side of the family are from the Ukraine."

"I know Ukraine well."

"No kidding? Kinda late, aren't you, sir?"

"I had to pick up my ID. Changed my uniform and forgot my ID, can you believe it?"

"Happens all the time."

"Had to get a last minute briefing, completely forgot."

The Lieutenant folded the paper and gave it back. He knew about these Combined Ops guys, a weird bunch of operators.

"Hut Thirteen. Picking up their 'chutes. Thirteen, right? Hope you're not superstitious. If they've got their 'chutes, try

Eighteen, that's where they're departing from. Just follow the track between the white stones. Hey, Johnson!" the Lieutenant called over one of his men from the office. "You wanna escort the Major to Hut Thirteen?"

"That's okay, Lieutenant."

"No problem, sir. Just a security measure."

Johnson got into the passenger seat.

"Thirteen, sir, no problem."

They let the barrier up and Solov drove the car through. He heard a huge roar.

"I never get used to the sound those birds make," said the MP.

"They're a little early, aren't they?" said Solov.

"They have to warm those crates up, they'll be high-tailing it soon."

The car stopped outside Hut Thirteen.

"Can I hand this car over to you.? Leave it here until I get back?" Solov said.

"Sure. Wow! It's a pleasure, sir. I'll park her up in the motor pool for you. When you get back, huh? There's confidence for ya. I like that. Good luck, now."

They shook hands. Solov got out and slipped inside the doorway. He was in a storeroom, shelves up to the ceiling with a pair of step ladders behind a counter where a store clerk sat dozing in a chair with his feet up. He stood up when he saw Solov approach. He saw no insignia.

"Another Brit? Shit, thought you were my Sergeant, man. Can't let him catch me sleeping on the job again." He smiled.

"Need another parachute. Came a little late, have to catch up with my squad."

"Those Brits just passed through here, earlier? Sure." He turned and reached up to one of the shelves and pulled down a parachute pack.

"Just sign here, if you don't mind, buddy."

Solov took the pack.

"Hut Eighteen, thataway."

"Can you spare me a cigarette?"

"Sure, pal, getting nervous?" He offered Solov a full pack of 'Luckies'. "Take 'em, you'll need 'em more than me wherever you're going. It's okay, I got another pack at the back."

Solov was back out into the cool night air, the roar from the twenty Dakota bombers was deafening. He lit a cigarette from a passing air ground crew. He hoisted the parachute over his shoulder and watched for a few minutes as some of the planes began to taxi and line up at the beginning of the runway. Other planes were being towed out of several hangars. Solov remembered from Lawler's briefing they were part of a five hundred bomber raid on the Ruhr, the heavy industrial area of north-west Germany. The commandos' Dakota would peel off, once across the Channel, and head south over France. Solov strolled almost leisurely as ground crew moved around him, too busy about their business to pay attention to just another Brit. He walked towards Hut Eighteen, its windows blacked out, he kept his distance. In the dim light, he saw a Dakota warming up its engines nearby and saw crouched figures carrying equipment cases towards the plane. That would be their mortars and ammo. He made out the hunched figure of either Sterling Malone or Thornton, both men of similar height, with a Bren over his shoulder. He took another deep pull on his cigarette, then threw it away. He put on his parachute and hastily adjusted the harness about him. He tugged at his collar and fitted the beret closer to his head. As he walked, head lowered towards the plane, he saw the rest of the squad filing out in ones and twos, to wait at the door of the aircraft. He could make out Decker patting their backs as they scrambled aboard. As he got closer, he could make out their civilian clothes. Some of them wore leather jerkins and round-necked sweaters.

He tagged onto the end of the line, a few paces behind the last of the men, their voices drowned by the sound of the plane's engines. Solov's hand held the butt of one of the revolvers shoved in his waistband. He saw Barrow hand a radio transmitter/receiver into the hatch then a pair of arms helped to pull him inside the aircraft. The men directly in front of Solov turned around to light a final cigarette away from the draft of the propellers. Their eyes met. It was Sergeant Miller. He took the cigarette out of his mouth.

"Fuck! What are you doing here, Major?" He yelled in his face so he could hear.

"Change of plan," Solov forced a smile. "I'm coming with you. Be more exciting than London." Solov looked over Miller's shoulder as the men were climbing aboard. Miller was next. Decker saw him.

"Solov? What are you doing here?" Decker yelled. "You're not down for this show, Major. You've no authorisation to be here. You'll have to turn back. Get on board, Sergeant," he told Miller.

Miller looked at them both, then climbed aboard.

"Not you. Major, you're staying here."

"No, Captain. No, I'm not." Solov pulled a revolver out and pointed it at Decker's face.

"No time to argue, Decker, get on the plane."

Decker looked at the gun. He stood his ground. Everybody was on board. The roar of the engine would drown out the sound of the revolver. Decker knew this.

Solov made a decision, he hit Decker hard on the head with the gun. He fell forward and Solov caught him over his shoulder and pushed him into the plane's hatch. Miller helped him pull

Decker on board. The two of them closed the hatch.

"What's going on with you two, Major?" Miller said. The other men were sitting hunched against their parachutes, only one or two had noticed Decker being pulled on board.

"You don't need the gun, Major," said Miller. "Just tell me what's going on."

"I think the Captain had an attack of last minute nerves. So I'm coming with you."

FOURTEEN

I t took a while for Decker to regain consciousness. His head throbbed and he realised that part of the ache was the loud drone of the Dakota engines. He began to remember what happened, and where he was, and felt nauseous. He raised his head and opened his eyes in the dim light.

There were voices. The men were talking in the background, just nervous talk. A voice nearer to him was talking to Miller, Malone and Corporal Tobey. It was Solov.

"...so I had to kill this Sevoska man. Quite an important figure at the embassy, two of his aides also, though I can only confirm one of them dead. If I go back, I'm under sentence of death. It was him or me. I had no choice. I had nowhere to run. I'd rather take my chances fighting the Nazis than my own people. Where else could I have gone? My father died in one of Stalin's labour camps. I was a dead man."

"Looks like that girl caused you a lot of trouble," said Malone.

"I know that now."

"So just because you spoke out against Stalin, they sentence you to death?" asked Miller.

"That's about it." Solov didn't tell them he was intended to be a spy in Britain. That would have complicated matters.

"Shit. If we got shot for slating fucking Churchill, there'd be nobody left to fight the fucking war," said Tobey.

"Couldn't you have claimed political asylum?" asked Malone.

"I couldn't take that chance. They might have considered it a Russian disciplinary matter, not wanting to sour relations with an ally. I'm up against the whole bureaucracy."

"Yeah," said Malone. "Look what happened to Trotsky.

They'd send someone after you, sooner or later."

Their words were interrupted as the plane began its swing to the right as it reached the French coast and began to leave formation and head south towards their drop zone. Miller looked at his watch: "Another forty minutes or so, fellas." He looked out of a window. "There they go off to Krautland. Give 'em hell, boys," he said.

"What are you planning to do after we land, Major?" asked Tobey.

"Stick with you until I get my bearings? You never know, I might come in useful. After a few days, who knows? I may head for Spain or Portugal, somewhere nice and neutral. I won't get in your way. I don't want to step on Britain's toes. I need all the friends I can get. This is Captain Decker's show."

"You're in a mess, Major," said Miller. "I won't stand in your way." He looked at Decker who was slowly recovering. He held his head, propped himself up on one elbow and looked at Solov.

"I'm sorry I had to do that," Solov said to him.

"Sorry nothing," Decker snapped. "You've committed a serious offence. You assaulted me and obstructed me in the course of my duty. You've jeopardised our mission. You'll be placed under arrest..."

"I won't be present in any of your courts, Captain," said Solov. "I'll never darken your green and pleasant land again. Remember, you've got work to do down there. Concentrate on that. I won't get in your way."

"Hand over that gun."

Solov shook his head.

"Sergeant, I want a permanent guard on this man until I decide what we'll do with him. I could have you shot for this, Major."

"Sir, he's given his word…" Miller said.

"Damn his word. I'm telling you to take his gun. If you've anything of a soldier about you, you'll do as I say."

"Begging your pardon, sir," said Malone. "A good officer will not order a soldier to do anything he's not prepared to do himself."

Decker looked at them, Miller, Tobey, Malone, then at Solov's gun. Solov shoved the revolver into his waistband.

"So now I can add incitement to mutiny to the list of charges," Decker said.

"Your men are not mutinying, Captain. They're questioning your order to help you see reason. I'm just a passenger on this trip. This is your command. I'll keep out of your way."

"In my book, it's mutiny."

"Let's just calm down, sir, and relax. We're nearly at the drop zone in another few minutes," said Miller. He crept down the fuselage to check the others, making sure they were ready, checking their equipment. One of the airmen helped them drag their cases near the door, ready for the drop. Tobey helped Decker check his gear. Decker sat still and allowed him to adjust his straps like a sullen child.

"I don't care who's in charge," Mason said to Barrow. "As long as he doesn't get us all killed." He jerked a thumb in Decker's direction. The Dakota began to descend gradually and the red light came on.

"Not too late to change your minds, lads," said Mason. Nobody laughed.

"Hook up, guys!" yelled the airman.

"Check your gear again, lads!" shouted Miller. Everyone stood up in a line, hooking their lines up, making last minute adjustments.

"Put that cigarette out, Mace!" Miller said.

Thornton and Malone hung their Bren guns across their chests, barrels pointing down.

"Mother, where are you now?" Malone crossed himself.

The red light bathed everyone in a warm glow. The airman swung open the hatch allowing the noise back in as the air filled the plane. "Standby!" he yelled.

The green light came on. Miller and the airman pushed the cases out. Then Miller screamed: "Go! Go! Go!" Thornton, Malone, Tobey, Wheeler, Scalleni. Solov waited for Decker to go ahead of him. He followed Decker. Miller was the last out.

Mason's parachute had carried him some distance away from the drop zone into a small wood. He'd crashed through the tops of the trees, but somehow, he landed straight to the ground without getting caught, dangling in the air. His parachute was torn and he escaped with a few minor scratches to his face.

"Fuck!" he swore, easing some of the tension he'd not let out between the Dakota and the ground. He'd located approximately where the others would be and released himself from the harness, quickly gathered up the silk bundle and began to stash it in among some bushes.

"'allo!" It was a woman's voice. "'allo, m'sieu!" He spun around. It was a young French woman. She stood only a few feet away, out of breath. "Come quickly," she said, and grabbed his hand.

"We've been waiting. I'll take you to the others," she said.

"I'll follow you anywhere, darling," Mason said.

"But you must be silently," she said, a finger to her lips.

A tremble went through Mason's body. "I can be silently, oh yes," he said.

They walked quickly through the wood. She was wearing a man's jacket, too big for her, and it caught on some of the undergrowth. They came to a small path and they followed it. She stopped at the edge of a road and took out a small lamp. She flashed it twice and received the same signal in acknowledgement from among some bushes. They ran across the road and met with a short, squat man. He spoke in French with the woman and shook hands with Mason. He had a deep voice that vibrated as if he had an infection. He took them through to a small clearing where they met with Tobey, Wheeler, Scalleni, Thornton, Barrow, Decker and Solov.

The vibrating voice rasped at them in English, after using his lamp to signal again: "Here are the others."

Another Frenchman, Marcel he was called, led Miller, Anderson, Armstrong and Malone, each carrying their parachutes like bundles of laundry.

"Keep close to the man in front of you. We will walk for two, maybe three hours."

It was a long, tedious trek through the night. They had to avoid the roads in case patrols had spotted the drop. They were later joined by four other men who had picked up the equipment cases. They'd found the mortars but the shells were missing, rendering them useless. One out of the three cases of grenades was also lost. But they couldn't afford the time to stay out looking for them. They moved along a small river, then headed uphill through another wooded area. Through a long, winding ravine, they came onto a meadow where they could make out the outline of a farmhouse. As they approached the main building, the door opened and a young woman with flowing black hair greeted them quietly.

"This is Lucille," said the vibrating voice. "She has made a meal. Food for you."

Inside, Lucille lit several lanterns after the men drew the curtains. There was a log fire almost gone out. A stairway led to a balcony with two rooms leading off it. A huge table commanded the main room.

"We will put your cases in the barn. Our captain will arrive in the morning at ten. Sleep if you can," the man named Marcel said.

"I'm Solov."

The Frenchman took his hand in greeting: "I'm Marcel. That's Francois, Jean, Lucille and Sascha. You'll meet our commander in the morning."

"Their captain? Who the hell's he?" said Tobey.

"It's a good enough name for the man in charge," said Solov. "We'd better get something to eat, then rest."

"Did you see that girl outside? Think I'm in love," said Mason.

"Hands off, Mace," said Barrow.

They spaced themselves out around the room, propping their weapons against a wall, eased off their knapsacks. Lucille brought out a huge pan of soup. Marcel brought the bread.

"Shitty French soup," muttered Armstrong. "How's a bloke to survive on this shit?"

"Better than nothing," said Anderson, too tired to talk.

Few of them slept for long. They were still fuelled by the adrenalin shot of the parachute jump. Most of them just relaxed, smoked and drank coffee. Solov handed a few of his 'Lucky Strikes' around that the American store man had given him. He resolved to stay in the background from now on. He wrapped himself in one of the blankets they'd been given and thought about the last twelve hours. He kept seeing Sevoska's body slumped across his desk. He knew his life had changed now, forever. He felt some kind of release. He was glad he'd killed Sevoska. He felt he had it coming anyway.

Phil Armstrong stubbed his cigarette out against the skirting of the wall where he was bedded down. He was watching the bedroom door upstairs on the balcony where he knew the girl called Lucille must be sleeping. She reminded him of one of his friend's sisters. That long, black hair was exactly how she had it. His friend had been overprotective of her but he'd secretly had the pleasure of her, several times. She'd had the same innocent face. He could read women.

"Funny thing about that tart in there. She reminds me of an old girlfriend, Joe," he said to Anderson.

"Leave it, Phil, we're here to work."

"Personally, Ray, I don't give a fuck what he's done," whispered Malone to Miller. "I happen to like the man and he can come in handy for us out here. A sight more than Decker would be. He's lost his nerve, that fella, mark my words."

"Far as I'm concerned, Bullet is a passenger. Decker's calling the shots and from now on, what he says, goes," said Miller.

"That's not what the lads think…"

"Fuck what they think. Decker's in charge. We take our orders from him. We do the job at hand and get out if we have to, understand?"

"Whatever you say, Sergeant Ray. What do I care? Do or die, brother."

FIFTEEN

Miller reminded everyone to check their weapons by first light.

He'd woken up to the sound of birds singing and heard someone moving around in the kitchen. He woke Solov first then nudged the others with the toe of his boot. Soon, the room was full of the men's moans and the metallic ring of their weapons being checked as ordered. Miller opened the windows to let in some air.

Mason stretched to his full height. "I was having a great dream," he said, to no one in particular. "Trouble was, it was all in French."

He was the first to light a cigarette and he stood by one of the windows looking out. Across the field in front of the house, he saw the girl who had found him in the woods at a distance, Sascha, leading someone towards them. Someone tall, carrying a walking stick like he was out for a pleasant stroll.

"Ed, we've got visitors. Isn't that the little beauty of the forest who found me?"

"Yeah, yeah," said Barrow.

"You married blokes, mate, I dunno."

Francois appeared on the porch outside the window. He waved to them. The man waved his stick. Francois opened the door.

"It's our Capitaine."

"He's all yours, Captain Decker," said Solov.

Decker ignored him.

The newcomers entered. The Capitaine stood and looked around the room. He saw Solov in his British army uniform.

"You are in charge?" he asked.

"No. This is Captain Decker," said Solov.

The Capitaine shook hands with Decker.

"I'm Andre Lacloche. I'm only called the Capitaine because, well, I am a Capitaine, late of the French army. I'm pleased to meet you all. Shall we get to business? Er…why the uniform?"

"It's all I had to wear. I'll get a change of clothes if possible. I'm Major Solov."

"Solov?"

"I'm Russian. It's a long story."

"Russian? I'm honoured to meet a comrade. I'm a member of the Communist Party too. I joined the resistance after June 22, '41."

"I'm sorry to disappoint you. I think my party card got lost in the post."

Lacloche shrugged: "Be it on your own conscience, comrade."

Solov did not want to be drawn into a political debate so remained silent. He felt the sooner he got away from here the better for all.

"I will try to be as brief as I can. We have an important opportunity with this operation," said the Frenchman. "We need to be in our positions before noon tomorrow. Our Nazi friends will be starting their parade into town, we think, about 2.30pm. We expect around two hundred SS troops to be goose-stepping their way into the town square. The Germans like to bluster and intimidate us. Little do they realise, a lot of them will be goose-stepping to their final resting place."

"It'll cause a lot of reprisals to be taken," Miller said.

"Sergeant, that's the whole point of this operation," said Decker.

"Correct," Lacloche said. "It's hard but it's what we need. Sometimes, an uprising needs the whip of repression. You must realise, Sergeant, you have already met the entire active resistance in this area. A mere handful with a few rifles and pistols. This way, we take the battle directly to the enemy. As soon as we hit them, we pull back into the hills. We will have our base there, then watch the volunteers flood into our ranks. Then the fighting really begins."

"How do we get to the town?" asked Decker.

"Francois will bring a friend's truck. We drop you off at different points. We'll take you to your positions, then you wait. Whoever drops you off will guide you back to our rendezvous points. If anyone fails to show up, or you miss us, you make your way back here as best you can. Marcel, the maps."

Marcel opened a briefcase and began to hand out clearly drawn but crude maps of the way to the farmhouse.

"You will have two hours to get back here. If you are late," Lacloche continued, "don't bother. We will be gone. These maps are for you to memorise. Hand them back to Marcel when you think you've learned the way back. He will destroy them. If the Germans get hold of one of them, they will be waiting here for you. We guess the confusion caused by our attack will delay them considerably. All you have to worry about is shooting straight then get out of there, preferably alive," he said.

"For a small operation, Capitaine Lacloche, you seem to be organised. What outfit were you with?" asked Decker.

"Tanks."

"Tanks? They had it rough in '40."

"Yes. My battalion was cut off and badly cut up near Sedan when the panzers broke through. We drove like madmen to get back to our fallback positions, or where we thought they were. Four or five days on the road, pounded by Stukas. We had to abandon our vehicles and walk. France was finished. I threw away my gun and walked. I deserted an army that had been deserted by its government."

"Won't you find yourself in trouble after the war?" asked Decker.

Lacloche scoffed at the idea. "The old government is finished. Questions will be asked but it will be people like myself who will be asking the questions. Communism will go from strength to strength. It will be a different kind of France after the war."

"Sounds like a good idea," said Solov. "Let's hope it doesn't go the same way as my country did."

Lacloche chose to ignore him and went on: "I didn't return home. I lived in the forests. Farmers would give me food and shelter. One farmer's son was a communist. He was in hiding too. Ah, the conversations we had about politics. He filled me with hope. I like the theory and now it's time to put it into practice. Our group was about twenty men. After five or so actions against the Germans we were up and running, but somehow we were betrayed and the Nazis broke us up. This action tomorrow will reset the balance."

"We'd better go over our plans," said Decker.

Monsieur Simon Cardogne, the Mayor of Villette, was going to need a lot of nerve to see himself through this day.

He was a small man but the owner of a strong, commanding voice that he used to some effect on the people who worked for him.

He had risen early that Sunday morning. He still had a lot to prepare for Colonel Schrenk's arrival. The bunting had been put up over the last few days, his welcome speech had been written and re-written, his best suit steamed and pressed, the banquet was almost ready. The local brass band were having a run through that very moment in the square. Outside the window, workmen were raising the Swastika and tricolour banners above the main oak doors of the town hall, on the stone steps technicians were busying rigging up a public address system.

He remembered the apprehension, two weeks ago, when he received the swastika-headed letter from Paris. Any official letter from Paris meant government, government meant the Germans, the Germans, in this particular case, meant the Waffen SS, and the Waffen SS meant bad news.

He'd been told to expect Schrenk and a large armoured brigade which was being re-located from the east of Paris. He didn't know why, but who was he to ask questions? He was required to accommodate three hundred and twenty troops who would pass through his town for a parade, at the Colonel's request. It was only a small part of his 15,000 man command, but it would be a show of strength and solidarity with the French people, so they said.

Cardogne knew that, in some respects, the German presence would be good for local business, the shops, the restaurants, the cafes, the bars. He'd always shown his willingness to co-operate. He'd even endorsed his police chief's men, helping the Gestapo round up the local Jews. Even he had benefited in taking over one of their hotels as his personal business.

His biggest fear was if, when Schrenk arrived, he'd inspect the town, find it to his liking, and may well requisition his hotel for his own use. This would leave a huge gap in his personal income.

So he'd have to keep on his guard. He'd possibly recommend the hotel of one of his rivals, someone he didn't like. Hopefully, Schrenk was like a lot of Germans, they had aristocratic pretensions and might prefer a hunting lodge in the country. There were a few of those he could recommend. Yes, maybe he could do that? He could come out of this quite well. He'd do business with the Germans.

SS Gruppenführer Heinz Schrenk picked his nose with a spent matchstick. The movement of his Mercedes irritated him.

He barked at the neck of his driver to slow down to marching pace. After all, there was no hurry for the sake of the French. They could wait.

He had a deep dislike of the French, in fact, he had a dislike for most non-Aryans. He grinned dreamily as his eyes scanned the shadowy forests on either side of the road. He and the SS were made for each other.

He fit the bill for the Führer's master race - tall, blond-haired, blue-eyed, like a Nordic prince. He knew he looked classy in his smart, decorated black uniform as he now indolently twisted the baton in his hands.

He shot a glance at his second-in-command seated next to him in the open Mercedes. Willi Viertel and he were old friends and they'd accompanied each other through it all. They'd been in the same troop together since Kristallnacht, in 1938, when they first worked together, cracking Jewish heads, making them crawl on all fours in the street through the broken glass. Willi had cracked him up when he'd forced a Jewish grandma to eat dog shit. Then the war had started. Poland had been good. They lost count of how many Polish prisoners they'd shot, as if it had been a competition. Then France, kicking the Britishers' arses all the way home. Then a stint in some of the camps - Belsen and Mauthausen, dreary but profitable. Now France again. The war wasn't going too well, especially in Russia, but theirs was a good war. French women and wine. They were getting it while they could. Now they had their own brigade, it felt like they could do as they pleased. They knew the war was coming to them, sooner or later, so they were grabbing what they could and shipping it back to Bavaria. Antiques, jewellery, gold ornaments, paintings. It was like a working holiday.

When he'd learned he was returning to France, he seriously considered volunteering for the Eastern Front. But not since Stalingrad. Within six months of coming to Paris last year, he'd worked his way up to his present position. He even had his own secretary, Trudi, who would swap her typewriter for his bed at a moment's notice. Then some bastard suggested a tour of this region as if his brigade was moving there and he'd been landed with it. But he and Willi had packed ten years of high living inside as many weeks.

He turned his head and looked behind and smiled proudly at the troops in their trucks and carriers, stretching down the road. He and his men had debauched themselves, drinking cellars dry, like Vikings only a little more civilised, but not much more. They'd been careful not to tangle with the local Wehrmacht units, inter-service jealousy and all that.

Schrenk threw the matchstick into the road. He sniggered to himself, his own private army, a private army of pleasure-seekers.

"What's so funny, Heinz?" It was Willi.

"Just thinking about last night."

"Oh."

He remembered at the last town, how they took over the town hall for the use of officers. They'd forced the spineless, crawling mayor to watch his chambers get turned into an orgy with his female staff. Willi had ordered the mayor to the middle of the floor to sing. The scared little Frenchie had complied, of course. Willi had hurled a waste-paper basket at him and yelled: "Encore! Encore!"

"Encore!" yelled Schrenk, laughing. Willi laughed too, in recognition.

"It was a good send off."

"I hope Villette will live up to it."

"I should think so. The mayor himself has a mistress."

"Dirty old swine. We'll have to requisition that," said Schrenk. His watch said 1.35pm. He tapped his driver on the shoulder.

"Move it up a gear."

SIXTEEN

"Y ou want to get us shot?"

Ed Barrow was feeling tense.

"Don't worry," said Mason, "the smoke'll mingle in with the chimneys."

"I wouldn't be too sure about that," Barrow said, wiping his face on his sleeve. They were exposed to the mid-day sun as they lay on their bellies on a rooftop patio, behind a low wall. They were concealed on all sides except the rear but had a good view of most of the square below. Behind them were the moss-covered steps that led through a three-storey house belonging to a baker. Marcel knew the man and had asked if his friends could use the patio to take a cine film of the parade. The busy man had been too harassed by an influx of customers grabbing bread and pastries before the arrival of the Germans. Mason and Barrow had pushed their way through the shop carrying their weapons wrapped in canvas, which could have passed as a tripod.

Mason felt the irony of spending two hours in the sun on the roof of a baker's. He looked again down into the square with its circular ornamental fountain gushing water.

Barrow looked at his watch: "Fuck it then, it's only 13.45, another forty-five minutes of this!" He took a cigarette and lit up. He was scared again. Not for himself as much for what would become of his wife.

Across the square, on the roof of the hotel, directly opposite Mason and Barrow's position, were Harry Tobey and Ray Miller. Neither of them smoked. They rarely spoke, which added to the impatience they felt. Tobey busied himself chewing a thumbnail. Miller kept checking his Sten gun, and looking at his watch.

Miller looked around at the other men's positions. He could see some of them, or where they were supposed to be. He knew once this action got started, he could concentrate on what he had to do.

Opposite were Mason and Barrow. He knew that because he could see their fucking cigarette smoke drifting away. He would see them about that later. Then, diagonally across from them, were Anderson and Armstrong, and in the fourth corner were the French Captain and one of his men, Marcel or Francois. He couldn't remember their names. Decker was a couple of roofs away to their left with another Frenchman, the one with the voice, he thought. Sterling Malone and Rob Thornton were each covering the east and west entrances to the square with Bren guns. Malone was in a room on the third floor of a guest house already pre-booked the night before and Thornton was under a layer of straw on a cart backed up at the side of the street. On ground level, he was possibly the most exposed but if they did their job right, he would be one of the most effective shooters. He also had all the narrow side streets to dodge down if things got too hot. He also had plenty of back up with another Frenchman, Jean, he thought, with Scalleni and Wheeler who waited further back. They would be the gate that would close behind the Nazis once they were in the trap. Yes, the square was covered from all angles.

"This is going to be one hell of a show," said Tobey.

"One hell of a show," Miller said, trying to picture how many dead bodies would be littering the place down below.

Decker took off his jacket. He was trying hard to hide his shaking hands from Francois.

"Won't be long now," he whispered to himself, his face twitching. The Frenchman lay on his back, eyes closed, passively sunbathing, his Schmeisser machine pistol cradled in his arms like a child. Decker looked at his bushy moustache, black with strands of grey. The lines on the Frenchman's face were relaxed, as if he was asleep, peaceful, at rest. Then Decker looked at his own hands gripping his Sten gun. They gripped hard and couldn't stop shaking.

He wished he could be an officer like Capitaine Lacloche, cool, professional, at ease in his own skin, sophisticated even. Lacloche had spent some time with him out in the farmyard near the well. He'd sensed Decker's nerves, he was sure, but had been too much of an officer and gentleman to mention it, despite his startling revelation that he was a communist. 'Breeding', his father would have called it.

It was so damned hot! The hottest he'd experienced since his time in the Middle East before the war. Before the war! It seemed a lifetime ago. Yes, he had helped Isadora's family to settle in one of the refugee camps, but he'd still been in deep shock concerning her death. Her family, all the refugees, the whole camp, reeked of death. He'd been relieved when his leave was over and he could return to his unit in Egypt. He was almost relieved, too, when the war in Europe broke out and, by January 1941, was returned to England away from the oppressive heat of the empty desert landscape that lingered with the memories of what he'd seen in Palestine. He hadn't relished fighting the Italians. He wanted to kill Germans - as many as he could before they killed him. He was among the first to volunteer for service in the commandos. In his first few missions, he was regarded as a brave, resourceful officer. That's how he won promotion to Captain. He didn't feel brave, just reckless, murderous. He had his wish granted. He killed Germans. Then, in 1942, last year, in August, Dieppe happened.

Capitaine Lacloche had told him the local legend of how the town of Villette was founded, back in Roman times, by a group of women who were camp followers who provided 'rest and recreation' for nearby legionnaires. Some of them gave birth to their bastards who then grew up and multiplied the small community and the village became a town. Decker remembered the Capitaine laughing, as he said: "You see, my friend, around here, it is not an insult but an honour to be called a 'bastard'."

"That bastard Solov," spat Phil Armstrong.

"What's that, Phil?" asked Joe Anderson, who was beginning to get sick of Armstrong's negative attitude to everything. Or maybe his own nerves were coming into play?

"How come he gets away with fucking murder, telling us he's a big soldier, telling us how to suck eggs? I don't see him here with us. He's back at the farm with that Frenchie woman."

"Well, when we get back, maybe you can tell him what for to his face?"

"What?"

"You're the fucking tough guy, Phil."

"What d'you mean?"

"I think the army made a big mistake taking your stripes off you. They should have fucking shot you. Would have been better for everyone in the long run."

"Fuck you."

Sterling Malone screwed his nose up in disgust.

The third floor room he was in was filled with the smell of a full chamber pot under the bed. Malone had positioned himself and his Bren at the window. The Bren rested on a small table out of sight. To escape the foul stench, he had to lean through the open window. Alternatively, he smoked to give him some relief.

The old crone who rented this room should have, at least, cleaned it up, he thought, but she probably couldn't even climb the stairs. Marcel had brought him here, with the Bren inside a holdall, its long barrel detached. Looking down into the square, he saw the bunting streaming from lamp post to lamp post, little flags of France mixed in with little swastikas, the French and

German banners hanging out of windows, the town hall steps festooned with more of the same and a microphone stand at the centre, near the front door. Quite a few people were beginning to gather. The brass band was playing practice pieces and tuning up. The French Capitaine had told them that, out of a population of eleven thousand, they expected about a hundred and fifty French civilians to turn out along the streets to wave flags at the Germans. All of them would be town council employees. They'd been ordered to attend by the mayor under threat of losing their jobs.

Malone wondered about Solov and what his plans were. Maybe he'd left the farmhouse by now? He wished he'd given the Russian his home address in Ireland, then he knew he'd be safe somewhere. Somehow, he wished Solov was with him now. He'd feel safer, and what a thing to tell the boys back home - Sterling Malone fought shoulder to shoulder with a real Bolshevik, a Russian Revolutionary!

Shortly after Decker and the others had left the farmhouse that morning, Nikolai Solov and Lucille had gone to bed.

It had been quite spontaneous. Solov, his nerves still taut from the last two days after the shootings in London, needed comfort and relief.

Lucille had left the chores of the day. She was nervous about what would happen in Villette and couldn't settle. She walked towards him where he was sitting in an armchair. She smiled, bent over and kissed him. He took hold of one of her wrists and responded without a word. Hurriedly, they sank to the threadbare carpet. Sex and death, so close together. Then they went to Lucille's room.

As soon as Schrenk's car reached the outskirts of the town, he ordered the driver to stop. He stood up, placed his hands on his hips, and took in what he saw of Villette.

It was larger than the other towns they'd visited so far. The narrow road ahead wound its way through to streets of shops and disappeared off to the left. He could just make out in the distance where the charming cobblestones began.

Behind, the troop carriers soon caught up. He signalled for all his men to dismount and form their ranks for the parade. The first carrier had the 1st company martial band, they'd follow directly behind his and the other officers' cars, then the main body after them. The troops' transport would remain here parked up at the roadside. His junior officer staff pulled up alongside his car then reversed in behind him.

"Let's see what this place has to offer, boys," he called to them. "Champagne anyone?" They all laughed and cheered.

"Forward, men! Sound the music!"

The crunch of jackboots broke out in unison, all down the line, as the voices of barking NCOs sounded above the din. And the music began to blare as Schrenk noticed some townspeople stop to passively stare, but not too closely. Some doors and windows opened, curtains were pulled back. Schrenk's car, once more, moved at marching pace. He hid his grin with the black leather gloves he clasped in one hand.

Willi looked at him.

"They're shitting themselves," said Schrenk.

"We're a little early, Heinz," said Willi.

"I know," he looked at his watch that said 14.15. "Fifteen minutes? So what? Catch them off guard and send them scurrying around like sheep."

He raised a hand to some civilian onlookers who nodded their heads and looked away. He faked a fatherly smile and wondered what the mayor's mistress was like.

"They're coming," said Lacloche, looking down from the rooftop, pulling himself up by gripping on to some tiles to get a better look. They were about a mile down the main street. He could make out three open cars, that would be the officers.

"Shit!" he said. "We should have arranged to knock out their transport. They've just left them parked."

He raised his arm with a red handkerchief waving. It was the signal to get ready.

"Christ, they're a little early," said Tobey. They hadn't needed the signal. They could hear the jackboots on their way, and the distant music.

"Just means the Krauts have shortened their lives by fifteen minutes," said Miller, checking his magazine and easing the safety catch off on his Sten. He guessed the others were getting ready. He tapped the barrel of his Sten in time to the music and the jackboots and caught Tobey's nervous grin.

"Okay, killer?" said Miller.

"The Germans are here!" yelled Mayor Cardogne, slamming down the phone in his outer office. He rallied his assistants, clerks and secretaries. "Everyone outside in the square. Is everybody ready?"

The office workers left their desks and began to filter out through the main doors.

"My speech, Claude, you have a copy of my speech? Good. Nadine, help me with my robe and chain."

Nadine left her colleagues who were adding the last touches of lipstick and face powder, saved sparingly for such occasions, and followed him back to his office. Behind the closed door,

Nadine found Cardogne and swiftly kneeled down to give his shoes a final wipe. He then took his mayor's robe and furled it around his shoulders. He fumbled with the buttons while Nadine brought the chain of office from his desk drawer. As she fastened it around his neck, Cardogne stopped and looked at her calm, beautiful face. He put his arms around her and pulled her to him.

"Listen, sweet. You are a beautiful girl. The Germans are dangerous people and we don't want to offend them in any way. If an officer wishes to sleep with you, I can live with it. It's politics."

"It's also called survival."

"Yes. I understand. But not the other ranks. If you're kind to an officer, the other ranks will leave you alone..."

"I know."

Cardogne wondered how she knew. The office door burst open and Nadine pulled away. The chain, caught in her blouse, snapped and fell to the floor.

"Idiot!" Cardogne screamed at the office boy who had been sent to watch for the Germans' arrival.

"Sorry, m'sieu. The Germans, they are coming."

"I know! Get out!"

Nadine picked up the chain.

"Put it in my desk drawer," he said, heading for the door. They reached the steps of the main entrance and joined the others outside overlooking the square. He looked up at the tricolour and swastika and tested the microphone. His office staff had barely a minute or so to assemble on either side of him, descending the steps in order of status and seniority. Around the square, council workers were lined up along three sides with their little flags. They could hear the approaching jackboots nearing the corner as the first Mercedes appeared and the martial music filled the square. The officers' cars slowly turned around the fountain. The first pulled up as the German band and the first ranks of soldiers marched in and the NCOs barked at them as they formed lines across the cobbled area, facing the town hall.

The square was a mass of black rows, the sun reflected off their weapons and their shiny, black helmets. Their boots flashed as each row stamped to a halt. The music stopped and the water from the fountain, for a few seconds, made the only sound before the opening and closing of car doors interrupted.

As Schrenk descended from his car with his second-in-command, his driver took his greatcoat from his shoulders for him and clicked his heels. The other officers milled about near the fountain. Schrenk alone mounted the steps to join Cardogne, and his council staff, next to the microphone.

"Welcome, sir, welcome to Villette. Firstly, let me introduce you to my staff..." Cardogne slowly waved a hand towards his people. "Before I accompany you inside for a tour of our municipal buildings and, perhaps, for some refreshments, maybe you, sir, would like to say a few words to the people of Villette..?"

Schrenk looked straight at him. His eyes then rested on Nadine over Cardogne's shoulder. She smiled and looked down.

"A beautiful town, M'sieu Le Mayor. Yes, I'm sure my officers would like some refreshments..."

Schrenk turned around to see where the sudden din was coming from and his instinct told him to move.

He pushed past the mayor and up the remainder of the steps. A hand pushed from behind, it was Willi.

"Heinz! They're shooting at us!" he yelled.

He caught sight of the square and his men breaking ranks. Some had fallen to the ground. Others ran or crouched for cover. Some threw themselves down. Schrenk, Willi and some other officers and the mayor's staff managed to get inside the building and slam the door shut. Some fell in the crush.

Somebody had an awful lot of firepower aimed their way.

SEVENTEEN

Sterling Malone couldn't have missed with his eyes shut. From behind the Bren, the Germans, in such a confined space, made things so easy.

His Bren hammered a path through the SS ranks assisted by Thornton on the other side of the square, on the top of the hay cart. Above him, he heard the sound of other weapons, the cries of the dying below him. Somewhere behind him, outside the door, he could hear the screams of the old landlady.

Armstrong was down on one knee to get a better aim once the Capitaine had fired the first shots. He'd aimed for the German officers. Killed two or three, the rest ducked behind the cars or ran into the town hall. Armstrong had hit some of the French staff. He sneered as he saw some of the women fall, then turned his gun on the SS troops.

Robert Thornton, from his position on the hay cart, joined in the firing with Sterling Malone from his guest house window. The nearest SS troops were only a matter of a few feet away. Some of them ran towards him, so he took them out first. A number managed to get a few shots off at him. He was in danger of being outflanked. The Bren was awkward to handle even with his strength. He had to change his position fast, rolling in the back of the cart. He regretted leaving his Sten behind now. This is where it would have been useful. He lost his footing in the hay. A bullet caught him in the head, killing him instantly.

French bystanders ran for cover and straight into panicking German soldiers. Mason and Barrow kept firing, not wondering whether it was their shots that were killing women and children.

"Go to Decker's position and get Francois," Lacloche yelled at Jean. "We're going after the transport."

Jean climbed down onto the patio, down the narrow steps and into the back alley. He heard the grenades going in. Decker's position was only a couple of houses along. He reached the top of the steps and waved Francois over. Decker was crouching behind the low wall. His face was pale, looking down into the square. The two Frenchmen left him.

Decker slumped down onto his haunches and was violently sick. He spat out a long string of saliva, got down on his knees, mumbling to himself.

Miller raked the square with fire while Tobey threw five grenades in quick succession. One of them landed in a staff car and set it ablaze. Miller saw Germans slipping past Thornton's position into the alleyways down there. He knew Scalleni and Wheeler and one of the Frenchmen would be waiting for them. Firing from down that way confirmed they'd clashed with them. Some Germans came back into the square and were caught by Tobey's Sten.

"That's Wheeler and Tony!" yelled Tobey.

"Where's Decker and the French captain?" said Miller. "Hold on here!" he ordered Tobey, "and I'll find out."

Miller ran low along the roof, keeping his head down. He reached the edge of the building. It was a six foot gap to the next roof. He looked down to the cobbled alleyway below and took a few paces back and cleared the gap. He was sprayed by shattered roof tiles as some Kraut took shots at him. He jumped down to Decker's position and found him on his hands and knees, whimpering like a child.

"Captain Decker! You okay? Are you hit?"

"Tell them to stop! Tell them..."

Miller seized Decker by the shoulders and shook him.

"Pull yourself together, you bastard!"

"Quiet over there. Do you think they've pulled out?" said Mason.

"Dunno," said Barrow, and he kept firing.

Mason looked to the left. Decker's position seemed quiet. He'd just seen Ray Miller make his way over there which meant Harry Tobey was on his own. He wished he knew what was going on. Especially when he could hear firing in the alley below.

"Think we should pull out, Ed?"

"Dunno…" Barrow's eyes looked past him…"Hey, watch it!"

Barrow moved to one side and fired his Sten at four Germans coming up the steps behind them. Two went down, a third was wounded, the other managed to get a couple of shots off before withdrawing. Barrow turned in time to see Mason falling backwards, sliding down the tiled roof. Barrow reached after him and grabbed one of his boots. Mason's head rested against a gutter.

"Mace! Mace! You alright?"

"Dunno…don't wanna go 'ere…not 'ere…"

Barrow pulled himself back up to the patio. He realised he was hit too. Felt like his collar bone was snapped. He could feel blood spreading under his shirt. He replaced the magazine in his Sten. He gave Mason another look. He'd definitely gone. He started down the steps, stepping over the Germans he'd just killed. He picked up one of the helmets by the straps and hurled it down into the alleyway. He heard it bounce all the way down. Nothing happened. Gaining street level, he crouched onto one knee and leaned out around the corner, in firing position. Nothing. Only dead bodies lay scattered. There were three SS troops and there was Tony Scalleni all laid out on the ground. Scalleni's legs were twisted, he'd been hit across the chest. He turned when he heard someone. It was Harry Tobey.

"You had the same idea, Ed, huh?" said the Canadian.

"Tony's caught it. We got jumped, and Mace caught it too. I got three of 'em. Tony got the other bastards by the looks."

Miller appeared, pushing Decker ahead of him.

"What's up, Ray?" said Tobey.

"His nerves're gone. The Frenchies have pulled out too," said Miller, watching Decker. "Take this," he said. Tobey took Decker's Sten gun.

"What d'you mean, the Frenchies have gone?"

"I mean the fucking French have run out on us!"

"What do we do then?" Barrow asked.

"We're getting out of here," said Miller.

"We're finished," said Decker

"Shut your fucking mouth." Miller prodded him with his gun.

"Here's Wheeler. He's got one of the French with him," said Tobey. Wheeler was followed by Marcel.

"Had any trouble with him, Wheeler?" Miller indicated the Frenchman.

"No, we've done well, haven't we, mate? It's a fucking massacre out there. It's still going on."

"His pals have run out on us," said Miller, "and if he's got similar ideas..."

"No, my friend," said Marcel.

"Well, get us out of here then."

"Ray, what about the others?" said Tobey.

"They'll have to find their own way back, as agreed. I can't risk losing any more men."

Miller pushed Decker ahead of him. The Frenchman took the lead. Wheeler followed behind. Tobey ran back down the alley towards the square.

"I'm gonna find the others," he called.

Miller called after him, but he disappeared.

The town square was littered with scattered bodies, some piled up on top of each other, either dying or dead. The stone fountain, chipped by flying lead, still bravely spluttered water, windows were smashed in almost every building and the walls were etched with pockmarks.

Sterling Malone looked down into the square from his window. There were still two main pockets of German resistance left. The larger group based around the remaining cars, and a smaller group behind the walls of the fountain. Without Thornton, he couldn't maintain the powerful crossfire he'd started with the two Brens between them. As the firing died down, it was becoming clear to Malone that only he and a couple of the others were still in position.

He was halfway through the last Bren magazine. He pulled his Sten from his shoulder. He knew there wasn't much chance of getting out alive if he stayed in this house. There were too many shots coming his way now, as the Germans left alive in the square were beginning to regain some confidence and regroup.

He couldn't recall any signal for the action to be broken off and to pull out. He looked out of the window for the last time. He'd better make a rear exit. He squeezed the Bren's trigger for the last time and caught two Nazis as they tried to make a break from the fountain. He then took the Bren and tossed it onto the bed. He was met at the door by the old landlady who started to scream at him and lash at him with a rolling pin. He took a blow on the forearm.

"You bitch!" and he struck her full in the face, flooring her. He stepped over her and ran downstairs. He inched the front door open. He could see firing from where Armstrong and Anderson were. He saw Armstrong stand up in full view on the roof and throw a grenade which landed amongst the abandoned staff cars. They went up in flames and the black smoke drifted across the square towards the guest house.

Malone saw four German officers move away from the burning vehicles through the smoke, Lugers in their hands. One of them was busy sliding another clip into his weapon. Armstrong and Anderson mowed them down.

This was a good time for Malone to make a break while the smoke helped to shield him. He ran, crouched forward, across the square, jumping over the dead and dying. Out of the smoke, he came face to face with several SS men and had to grapple with them immediately. He pushed two of them over, while another took a swing at him with his rifle. Malone stepped back and shot him down almost point blank. He turned his gun on the others. It jammed, so he took it by the barrel and hit another German staggering towards him as he struggled to cock his rifle. Malone beat him to the ground. A shot buzzed past his head. He turned and another German had taken a shot at him. Malone grabbed the dead German's rifle and charged with it, hitting the soldier with the butt. He went down. Malone found a Schmeisser machine pistol on the cobbles by a dead German. He picked it up in time to duck down and fire at five soldiers who ran towards him, some of them kneeling for cover. All of them hit, Malone turned to make his way out of the square but was immediately confronted by two soldiers coming at him. One held a rifle aimed at him, but his partner was already charging with a raised rifle and bayonet, screaming. Malone sidestepped and grabbed the rifle. He pushed the Nazi backwards into the other one who tried to get out of the way but they all went over onto the ground. Malone snatched the rifle and pounded them both. His way clear, he made a run for the alleyway, not before finding another Schmeisser machine pistol. As he ran, he scooped up a German grenade, unscrewed it and hurled it back towards the general direction of five SS men chasing him. They dived for cover, but three of them were hit. Another sent a volley after Malone that caught him in the legs. He dropped heavily, rolling over the dead bodies of more SS. Now, more firing came from the fountain area. Malone stayed still where he'd fallen. He was partly covered by two German corpses. He'd seriously miscalculated the situation. He heard the rush of jackboots approaching from behind. He gripped the machine pistol. At the corner of the square, he could make out the figure of Harry Tobey making his way through the smoke. He was walking into the Krauts behind him.

Malone made his move. He rolled over and raised the Schmeisser. There were three Germans making their way towards him. They all fired at the same time. The Germans fell to the ground, dead or seriously wounded. Malone rolled onto his back, his head resting on the chest of a dead SS man. He'd taken one in the head.

Tobey saw Anderson and Armstrong coming through the smoke.

"It's the fucking US cavalry, just in the nick of time," said Armstrong.

"Sterl's in there, somewhere," said Tobey.

"Harry, you can't do anything. We've gotta get out of here," said Anderson, gripping his arm.

"He's a big boy. He can look after himself." said Armstrong. "Let's go!"

"I'm going after him," Tobey said, walking into the square.

Anderson looked at Armstrong who shrugged and walked down the alleyway. Reluctantly, Anderson followed him.

Tobey walked past the hay cart where Thornton lay. Dried

blood covered the big man's face. He came across Malone's body, around him a lot of dead SS men.

Inside the town hall, Heinz Schrenk ordered one of the Frenchmen to see if it was all clear, as there hadn't been any shooting for a good few minutes. They began to wander out cautiously. Women began to cry.

"Bastards!" swore Schrenk, as he took in the damage. His second-in-command, Willi, leaned against a wall and began to retch.

"There'll be hell to pay for this!" Schrenk said, grimly, to no one in particular as two wounded troops helped each other towards the steps. He saw the scattered instruments of the band, a punctured bass drum on its side. He saw the riddled body of the mayor at the foot of the steps. His void eyes stared back at him. Nadine knelt beside him, weeping, her pretty face blood-stained.

He saw a dazed-looking French civilian walking towards him through the smoke. He was carrying a machine gun. Schrenk raised his Luger. Tobey went down on one knee and fired. He toppled Schrenk and a couple of others. People threw themselves to the ground again. A bare-headed SS man caught Tobey in the leg as he withdrew and he limped away into the smoke as quickly as he had appeared. Explosions filled the air from a distance. It was the sound of the troop carriers being destroyed.

There would be hell to pay.

EIGHTEEN

Solov took a cigarette, struck a match, inhaled deeply, walked across the room and put it between Decker's lips.

Decker was sitting in one of the kitchen chairs, staring down at the floor. He hardly acknowledged Solov. While he sat quietly, the room was in chaos.

Sergeant Miller was with Anderson, writing down a grid reference for an appropriate landing place for a plane to come and pluck them out of there. Lucille had told them of such a place some miles away, at the foothills of the mountains. A shirtless Barrow was getting his shoulder bandaged by Marcel. Miller had posted Armstrong and Wheeler outside on watch for any signs of pursuit. It was around 17.30 hours. They'd crammed into a car that Wheeler had managed to hijack from the town.

"Get on the radio, Anderson, right now," said Miller, "we're pulling out of here."

"I should have guessed," Solov said to Decker. "Your behaviour, the look on your face in the plane. You were frightened to death. Your nerve has gone. I should have had you replaced."

Decker took out the cigarette and exhaled.

"Why didn't you say something?" Solov said.

Decker started to shake as he sobbed quietly. "I've got...got a good record...I've just...just messed everything up...thought Miller was going to shoot me..."

Solov remembered how Miller had burst into the farmhouse and told him the operation was successful but they'd taken too many casualties. He was aborting any further action and calling for a pick-up plane. He told Solov he was only concerned about getting what was left of the men back, and getting Decker court-martialled. Miller had been close to finishing Decker off himself. The Sergeant walked over to them.

"Anderson's taking the radio upstairs and sorting out a pick-up. It's a little too busy down here. Marcel and Lucille's gonna guide us. It's a field near the mountains, the girl says. Thirty miles away."

"The sooner, the better," Solov said, "and this place could be swarming with Germans soon."

"We'll be sleeping out in the woods tonight," said Miller.

"And Decker?"

"He's coming with us." Miller snatched Decker's cigarette from his mouth and crushed it. "Nobody said you could smoke."

Decker stood up suddenly, but Miller pushed him back down, roughly.

"Stay down, Captain, and think about how many men you lost today," Miller said.

Solov pulled Miller aside: "Do you think any of the others will make it back?"

Miller shrugged.

"Those that aren't dead will find it hard finding this place without French escort, but they pulled out too, apart from Marcel here. Looks like they'll be on their own."

Corporal Harry Tobey was on his own, and wounded. After killing Schrenk, he'd made his escape through the maze of alleyways across the town. Nobody dared to challenge a man with a Sten gun. After a short while, he felt his leg beginning to throb. As he crossed a street, he saw a group of French civilians.

"Anyone speak English?" Most of them backed away, or just stared at him.

One of them spat at him, angry about the slaughter and what it would bring down on their heads. Tobey levelled his Sten at them. They followed him down the street at a safe distance, until he reached the edge of town. He climbed a wall into a meadow and hobbled into the woods. Out of sight, he rested, slouched against a tree. He had no idea which direction he needed to go to the farmhouse. Through the trees, he could see black smoke curling above Villette. He decided to wait for dark. He had to rest his leg and staunch the bleeding. He tore off a piece of his shirt and used it as a tourniquet.

As darkness drew in, the air was cooler. Tobey curled up for extra warmth. The longer he left it, he knew, the harder it would be to find the others.

"One of the best mates I've ever had," said Ed Barrow, sitting at the big table in the farmhouse. The radio was now on the table in front of him. They were waiting to receive confirmation of the pick-up point.

"It was a terrible way for a bloke like him to go...upside down, on his back, on a French rooftop." He massaged his bandaged shoulder. "He didn't deserve it," he said, looking over at Decker.

"Put a sock in it, Barrow," said Armstrong. "Could've been any of us. Talking like that is pointless."

"Alright, you two, it's half past eight," Miller broke in. "Anderson, take over from Solov. Armstrong, you take over from Wheeler."

"Me? Again?" Armstrong protested.

"Yeah, you. Again," Miller said.

Armstrong shuffled out.

Miller kept himself busy, compiling remaining ammunition clips, counting out grenades, checking weapons. He knew the shoot had gone well, would have been even better if they hadn't lost the mortar equipment, but any long campaign was out of the question.

Solov and Wheeler came back inside, relieved by the others from keeping watch.

"Wheeler, contact London again, see what's what," Miller ordered. "Then we're moving out. What are your plans, Major?"

"Obviously, I won't be coming back with you. I'll see you off at the pick-up point, though, if you don't mind?"

"Not at all, Major. Thanks. Got any further plans?"

"Got 'em, Ray!" said Wheeler.

Miller took up the headphones and microphone: "Come in, Fairground. Fairground. Dodgems to Fairground. Condition is winter. Repeat - winter."

Miller read out the grid reference for the landing zone. "Request Jackdaw," he said, "Jackdaw!" Miller signed off. It was dangerous to stay on air any longer.

"We're on, lads. Wheeler, take the radio outside, smash it up and throw the fucking thing down the well. We've gotta start moving. We've got to get to this field by 2300 hours tomorrow night."

"We taking the car, Ray?" Wheeler asked.

"No. There'll be roadblocks everywhere. We're going overland. Just fuck the car's engine." They began to clear their equipment away.

When they were ready, Lucille locked everywhere up. They set off through the woods, with Marcel leading them. Solov slung Thornton's Sten gun over his shoulder. He wore civilian clothes now. Lucille had fitted him out. He had several ammunition clips in his pockets. Before they set out, he'd burned his British uniform, along with the War Office ID, on the log fire.

Miller walked with Marcel, checking his compass, following his directions. Armstrong and Barrow walked in front and behind

Decker. Wheeler brought up the rear. Miller wanted to put a few miles between them and the farmhouse before they rested for the night. He wondered how his friend, Harry Tobey, had made out. He knew Thornton was dead, and Mason and Scalleni, according to Barrow. Maybe Harry had linked up with Malone? There was no chance they'd know where they were getting picked up, or even that they were getting picked up. They'd have to try and make it home themselves, or get to Spain or Switzerland. Surrender wasn't an option.

Tobey woke up with a start. He was cold, thirsty, hungry and tired. He was in pain. At least, the bleeding seemed to have stopped. He could hear small animal noises nearby. He pulled out a pack and decided to take a chance on a smoke. There wasn't much he could do until the morning. He could hardly see his hands in front of his face. His leg felt swollen and stiff. He needed to eat. Come the morning, he'd make that his first priority. He'd find a little farm. Steal a few chickens like he did in training. It made him think of the others, of Sterling Malone, young Scalleni, big Bob Thornton, and Barrow had said Mace was dead. End of a good squad, he thought, drawing on his cigarette.

He heard a noise. Some animal, maybe. His mind was playing tricks on him. He remembered the deserted farmhouse in England when Ray Miller said if there were any ghosts in there they'd have all been called up for the war.

"I'll bet," Tobey said aloud in the darkness, "knowing my luck, they'll be in this fucking forest."

NINETEEN

T obey finally got some sleep and woke up revived by the morning air. He felt better, that he could walk for miles, then he remembered his leg when he tried to move.

He pressed his back against the tree and used his Sten to push himself to his feet. His leg felt stiff and there was a dull ache through his thigh. It was a bloody mess where he'd torn his trouser leg to get at the wound.

He was hungry and his clothes felt damp. He knew he was only a mile or so away from Villette. He would have to be careful. He knew he had no chance of meeting up with the others. He just had to stay free, lie low. With any luck, he may be able to make some kind of contact with the resistance and rest up, get a doctor, then plan some way home. He could make for Paris, maybe, or Spain? Right now, though, basic needs. He had to find food. He made sure the safety catch was on the Sten, then started to limp his way through the woods.

Miller didn't let up on them. He pushed them hard through the night until visibility meant they had to rest as the dense woodlands shielded them from any light from the moon that dodged behind clouds. They'd made steady progress and the Sergeant hadn't allowed any obstacles like streams or hills to take them off course.

Decker found it hard going. He hadn't kept up with the training when Solov had arrived and he was paying for it now.

"On you go." Armstrong dug the muzzle of his Sten in his back with the kind of satisfaction only a soldier could get from pushing an officer around, a disgraced officer at that.

"No need for that," said Decker, sullenly.

"Is he giving you trouble, Phil?" said Miller.

"I'm still an officer and I demand the respect due to my

rank," said Decker.

"That's a fucking laugh," said Armstrong. "One more word out of you and I'll punch your fucking lights out."

"Move on," said Miller.

Solov moved on with the Sergeant.

"What are you going to do with him?" he asked.

"First off, we're going to get to this landing field, then we'll see what's what. If the Krauts turn up and things look nasty and we can't get away, Decker gets one in the head. If things turn out okay and we get back. I want him court-martialled."

"You sure?"

"Damn right. He should lead by example, the fucking coward. Snivelling while my men are getting torn apart, snivelling like a little kid."

They rested for the remainder of the night. They bedded down as best they could below the crest of a hill, below the tree line.

"If we'd have had more Brens, we could've got the lot of 'em, quicker," said Armstrong, firing an imaginary Bren, "and we should have used more grenades sooner."

"Nah," said Anderson, "the whole set up was wrong. It should have been out of town so no civilians would've got hurt. Bet they hate us as much as they hate the Germans now."

"Ah, well, only a bunch of Frenchies, anyhow. Which makes up for those Frenchies who pulled out on us when the going got tough."

"Wonder how Harry made out?"

"Dunno. The others had pulled out because some of the Krauts were getting down the alleyways, so I wasn't hanging around to be a hero."

"Like the Frenchies, eh, Phil? We're no better than them."

"What do you mean?"

"We could've given Harry some support in finding Malone."

"You saw what it was like."

"Yeah, well, they don't count either, I suppose, 'cos they're only Canadian and Irish."

"If you want to turn funny on me about it…yeah, okay then, yeah. What do I give a fuck for them?"

"Which probably explains why you don't deserve those stripes back you keep going on about…ever. Maybe you should never have had them in the first place?"

"Now, hold on a minute…"

"Fuck you!"

"Thought we were mates?"

"Mates? You're a shit, Phil. You're either bragging or whining. That's not good NCO material in my book, that's not leadership quality, y'know, like Ray or poor Harry? He didn't hesitate to go looking for Malone."

"What about you? You weren't breaking your fucking neck in following him in either…"

"That's 'cos I've been too busy listening to you, following your lead, like an idiot."

"Joe…"

"Would you have gone back for me, Phil?"

"What?"

"You heard."

"What?"

"I said, would you have gone back for me, your mate?"

Silence.

"Thanks, that's all I needed to know."

"Course I fucking would."

"So you differentiate between me and Harry Tobey, or Malone?"

"Well…"

"We're supposed to rely on each other as a team, Phil. I wish I had the time over again. Poor fucking Harry. We fucking let him down. I've let myself down because I fucking listened to you."

"Sometimes, it's every man for himself, Joe."

"It's all the time with you, though, Phil. When we get back, just fucking stay away from me in future…"

Franz Meckler was young to be a Feldwebel, a Sergeant in the Wehrmacht. But it was a rank he could handle well. When he was twenty-two, he'd been at the heels of the panzers when they broke through into France in 1940. He'd won promotion after a mopping up operation near Ypres. He and five of his comrades had taken nearly two hundred French prisoners without firing a shot. They were stragglers left behind and had virtually thrown themselves at their feet and a photographer had snapped them for the 'Völkischer Beobachter' newspaper back home. It had been his first moment of glory and he felt he could dine out on that story for years to come, with a few embellishments.

Since then, they'd been stationed in France, not that they complained. Feldwebel Meckler and his friends had a good war there. They even had their own business interests. There were lots of cottage farms all over the area where they had to patrol or had manoeuvres. He'd used army trucks to pick up foodstuffs at rock bottom prices and, through French retailers, re-sell them at market towns at a good profit. The farmers had to comply, they had no choice. Where could they complain?

But, yesterday, the call had gone out. There was some kind of resistance action over in Villette and HQ wanted a net thrown within a fifty kilometre radius. There'd been some kind of massacre at Villette town square. An SS outfit had been ambushed, more than a hundred and twenty deaths, and even more wounded. He knew Villette. Nice place. He didn't like the SS, arrogant bastards - thought they were a cut above, thought they were real soldiers. But, he thought, they were our bastards, and if they were being shot at, pretty soon, all Germans would be a target if this kind of thing was allowed to go unpunished.

It annoyed Meckler because this would be another disruption of his business. All leave was cancelled and they would have to man roadblocks and checkpoints, and HQ wanted the forests pulled apart.

Nevertheless, he and his closest friend, Kurt Waller, and a few others in his company, would make a detour with one of their trucks. Under the pretext of joining the search, they'd call in at one of their suppliers of poultry and vegetables, the Lancorde place. There were other motives too. Old man Lancorde had a beautiful wife and a pretty daughter. While the men loaded the crates of supplies, he and Kurt would dally with them both. Kurt and he vied with each other … who would get the mother, who would get the daughter. This time, they had it worked out.

"Okay, heads you're on diversion duty, tails it's me," said Meckler.

"Shit," muttered Waller. "You win, you bastard."

"You can't say I use my rank, Kurt." Meckler laughed.

The plan was to divert the old man out of the house while Franz tried to use his charms on the daughter, or the mother. He'd already made some progress with her, so he'd decided he would keep working on her.

The truck pulled into the farm's front yard. There was old man Lancorde sat on the porch, cleaning a shotgun.

"Bonjour, m'sieu!" called Waller.

The old man smiled, nodded and heaved himself to his feet.

"The chickens, they are ready, mein Herr," he said. "You are late?"

"Busy life today," said Meckler, winking at Waller as the rest of the men walked over to the barn where they already knew there would be bottles of beer stored. Lancorde always had them ready. He'd crated the chickens from the pens at the rear and had them stacked and ready at the front of the barn for easy access when the Germans called. It was a godsend for him as his own truck was no longer working. This way, the Germans transported them for him, at a price, of course, but without them, he wouldn't see much of an income.

"Kurt, why don't you take M'sieu Lancorde and sort out the prices?"

"Of course. M'sieu Lancorde, that's a fine weapon you have there. You think you're a good marksman?"

"Not bad, mein Herr, not bad at all," he said.

"Can I water myself?" Meckler asked him, indicating the house.

"But, of course. My girl will see to you."

Waller guided the old man towards his garden, looking back ruefully at Franz.

"Show me what you can do. Do you have any old tin cans? Maybe we could have a contest?" he said, drawing his Luger.

"France versus Germany?" said Lancorde. "Maybe, this time, we win?"

"Let's see about that." Waller looked around and Meckler

was already in the house. The other men stood grinning at the barn doors, handing the beer around. One of them raised a bottle to him, before knocking his head back, the cool beer dripping down his tunic.

The young woman, Celeste was her name, met Meckler as she was coming out of the kitchen. She wiped her hands on her skirt and smiled.

"Hello, Franz."

"Hello, Celeste, how are you today? Your papa said you were here. Is your mother in?"

"She's out the back. You want her?"

"No, it's fine. Papa said you would fix me a drink, maybe?"

"Of course." She turned to return to the kitchen, paused, then smiled. She darted a look out of the kitchen window then ran over to him quickly, embraced him and kissed him full on the mouth.

"When will you take me to town?" she said.

"At the moment, we're busy, did you hear about…?"

Two shots sounded out the front.

"Papa!" she said.

"It's the shooting contest with Kurt. You know, the ongoing contest?"

"Yes, Papa thinks he can re-fight the war…" She laughed.

They heard Kurt's voice calling.

"You know," said Celeste, "I think Kurt likes Papa. They always laugh together."

They heard more shots.

Celeste's mother came in the back way through the kitchen. She held her apron up to her face that read panic.

She embraced Celeste.

"Mama, what's the matter?"

"Oh, God, oh, God…" she pointed to the window.

Franz looked at Celeste. He pulled out his own Luger and went to the back door. He could see a half-finished washing line with a laundry basket on its side and clothes strewn across the garden. Beyond that were the poultry pens. He saw a man on his back, as if he was sunbathing.

Then, Lancorde came into view with his smoking shotgun, followed by Kurt with his Luger pointing down at the man.

"Intruder! Voleur!" shouted Lancorde.

"Franz! Over here!" Kurt yelled.

When he reached the entrance to the poultry pens, he saw the man Lancorde had shot. His chest was peppered with buckshot and a blood stain was rapidly spreading. The man had a chicken by its broken neck. His fingers trembled as he slowly released his hold. His legs were kicking, then stopped. He was already wounded in the leg, an old wound. A couple of feet away, Franz recognised a Sten gun, a British-made weapon.

Harry Tobey had been caught stealing a chicken again.

Solov saw them first. He called to Miller and halted everyone in their tracks. It was late afternoon and they were taking a risk passing through a thinly-wooded area. They took cover. Solov pulled Lucille behind him. She pulled her hand away: "It's okay. I'm not a child."

"Where are they?" Miller asked Solov.

The Russian pointed down the hill. Four German soldiers in forest green with steel-grey helmets, maybe the advance patrol of a bigger party.

"How many do you think are coming up behind?" said Miller. Solov shrugged.

"Sarge, more of 'em," called Wheeler, from behind. About two hundred metres, away over the rise, they'd been approaching slowly.

"Bad news," said Solov, taking the safety off his Sten. "Give me Wheeler, Armstrong and Anderson. You take the others. We'll follow on."

"Okay, Wheeler, Armstrong, Anderson, follow the Major's orders, delaying action. Keep your eyes on where we're going. We know the way."

Miller led them through into the darker, thicker woods with Marcel and Lucille, with Barrow pushing Decker forward.

Solov and his men spread themselves out amongst the bushes. The Russian crouched behind a fallen tree. The first German party was getting near. He heard one of them cough and spit. He looked at Armstrong. His cruel face was tense. Wheeler, just beyond Armstrong, was taking aim. Beyond Wheeler, Anderson was out of sight. Then Lucille joined him, gripping her Schmeisser.

"What are you doing here?"

"I can fight too," she whispered.

Solov saw a German officer only twenty paces away. He was tilting his head back, drinking from his water bottle. He was joined by others gathering around him.

Miller and the rest had vanished, but Solov knew they'd be waiting somewhere due west. The officer finished his drink and signalled his men forward. It looked like there were around ten to fifteen following on.

Solov stood up and began firing from the hip, joined by Lucille and the others. It was long and loud. The Germans fell where they stood. Some of them screaming, performing a crazed dance as they were hit. Some tried to run, but took it in the back.

"Jesus, look at that," Armstrong said.

Further down the hill, what looked like a full company of troops were swarming amongst the trees, taking cover, taking firing positions.

"Move out! Wheeler and I will cover! Fifty paces then turn and cover us. Go!"

Solov and Wheeler gave covering fire. They hit some of the Germans and sent the others back scattering for cover.

"Come on, let's go!" Solov called to Wheeler. They ran after Armstrong, Lucille and Anderson. They were in the woods behind another fallen tree.

"Over here, Major!" Armstrong called. Solov and Wheeler ran to them.

"We'll cover you fifty paces on," said Solov, and kept running on.

Armstrong, Lucille and Anderson immediately opened fire. The two German patrols were joined as one. But Armstrong and Anderson's fire kept them back. Lucille spotted some of them trying to outflank them, but she nailed them.

"Fall back!" Solov yelled. They ran and passed Solov and Wheeler's new position, and so it ran until they had covered a good distance. They were catching up with Miller and the others.

"We'd better stick together as a group now," said Solov, out of breath. "More fire power."

"We're keeping 'em on their toes, Major," said Wheeler, panting for his breath.

"How are we for ammo?" said Armstrong.

"Okay, here."

"I'm good."

"One clip left," said Anderson.

They each passed him one of their magazines.

"They'll probably try and spread out more. But that'll slow them down. Did any of you notice whether they had a radio? If they've got one, they're probably already calling for reinforcements to cut us off."

"That's right, Major," panted Armstrong, "tell us a few fucking jokes to cheer us up, why doncha?"

Miller's group had slowed down. He could hear the shooting behind them, and had even caught sight of Solov and Wheeler coming up from behind, taking fresh positions. Barrow's wound had re-opened and they had to stop to quickly re-dress it.

"Give me a weapon," Decker said.

"No chance," Miller said. "You wouldn't know what to do with it."

"At least, give me a chance to defend myself."

"Shut it, you coward."

"Don't worry, Sergeant, we're all going to die heroes now."

Miller shoved his Sten in Decker's face.

"Maybe we will, but you won't. I'll make sure of that." Decker stared at Miller's gun.

Solov led his group across a narrow lane that cut across the wood. They could hear a motor.

"Hang on a minute, Major!" called Armstrong. "There's something coming!"

Solov stopped. He'd heard that sound so many times before back in Russia.

"It's a half-track. Two of them. Maybe loaded with troops," he said.

"Reinforcements you were on about?" Wheeler said.

"Time to unload some of these," said Armstrong, taking three grenades out of his pockets. "Only slowing me down anyway."

"Okay, Armstrong," said Solov, "we'll cover you."

"No need. You and Wheeler and the girl catch up with the others. Me and Joe'll handle this. Right, Joe?"

Anderson nodded.

"That okay with you, Anderson?"

"Yes, Major."

"Okay, keep following this track. You'll be alright. We'll be waiting for you at fifty like before."

Solov, Lucille and Wheeler moved on as the half-tracks pulled into view, one behind the other. They were crammed with German troops.

Armstrong crouched beside Anderson and patted him on the shoulder: "Let's go," he said.

The vehicles moved cautiously along the lane until they were nearly alongside Armstrong who lobbed a grenade high into the second half-track, as Anderson, further along threw his into the lead vehicle. They flattened themselves to the ground as the voices of the Germans spelled panic. Some of them managed to jump down as the grenades exploded. Armstrong and Anderson got up and opened up on them. One of the trucks was on fire and careered into some trees, the other just ground to a halt. A few Germans, disoriented by the impact, staggered away from their vehicles and presented easy targets.

When they stopped firing, there was just the sound of one of the engines and two soldiers crying, obviously in severe pain.

The two commandos cautiously moved around the half-track that still blocked the roadway. If there were any Germans unscathed, they must have fled into the woods. But most of the bodies lay on the ground, or in the back of the half-tracks. Armstrong lifted a couple of Schmeisser machine pistols and slung them over his shoulder.

Somebody was crying in agony, lying on the grass verge where he'd crawled. The German's face was burned badly and he was bleeding from the top of his head.

"Shall I finish him off?" said Anderson.

"Nah," said Armstrong, spitting on him. "Let him die slow. Let's get the fuck out of here."

As they made to follow Solov, they saw more Germans coming up on their left flank.

"Fuck!" yelled Armstrong.

Anderson levelled his weapon at them but followed Armstrong instead. They could hear the Germans calling after them, their shots flew past them, hitting the trees around them.

Armstrong was way ahead of Anderson. Anderson could hear the Germans behind him, catching up.

"Phil! Hold on! I can't make it!" he screamed.

"Come on, you lazy bastard!" Armstrong yelled.

Anderson fell: "Fuck it! I've had it!"

Anderson knelt behind a tree, trembling as he heard the Germans calling to each other. He heard them on both sides now. He stood up and dropped his Sten, raised his hands as six German soldiers surrounded him. Two of them grabbed him roughly by the arms and started to drag him back towards the road: "Schwein! Arschloch!"

He gasped as he felt a rifle butt hit him a few times in his back. When they reached the roadside where the half-tracks were, some of the wounded there were being hurriedly attended by a couple of medics.

Anderson was thrown to the ground. One of the soldiers kicked him viciously in the stomach, repeatedly. He felt the pain, the tears streaming down his face, the taste of blood in his mouth, as everything began to turn black.

TWENTY

Darkness gave them no sanctuary. They marched on, slowly finding their way. Exhausted, hunted, but they put distance between themselves and the Germans who, as the night drew in, appeared to have called off the search until morning. Still, they avoided the roads which slowed their journey down. But, shortly after ten, that night, they found what appeared to be the landing zone as described by Lucille.

There was much to do before they could rest. Solov, Wheeler and Armstrong gathered wood and bits of broken fences. They made three separate piles, one at either side of the field and one at the far end, where the woods began, to signify the end of the makeshift runway. These bonfires would be started at the first identification of their plane.

It had been a long and dangerous day, running and fighting, getting lost, scared, cursing, running out of hope. But they'd stayed on the move. Miller had taken a hit in his left forearm, a mere graze, but it kept bleeding. Wheeler and Armstrong had been the rear guard, but nobody seemed to be giving chase any more, in the last hour or so. Solov had taken the lead with Marcel.

During the last skirmish, Decker had again begged to be given a weapon. Barrow and Miller, despite their wounds, had to restrain him.

They huddled together at the side of the field, out of sight. Barrow handed Solov a cigarette. Miller sat down on the grass, exhausted. The group rested in silence.

Only Decker sat off alone, leaning against a tree. He sat with his knees close to his chest and his arms wrapped around them. Solov looked at him, separated from the others. That had always been the case, he thought. He walked over, crouched down, and gave him the last of his cigarette.

"That's all I've got for you, apart from a friendly word."

"Thank you," said Decker, "but you can keep the friendly word."

"I was thinking how much you remind me of myself," Solov said.

"Really."

"We're both set apart. We're loners. We're both solitary people. But that's where the similarity ends..."

"You're a psychiatrist now."

"No, but if talking helps...? Very well. No more talking. I'm a soldier, not a doctor. I've got my own troubles. I just want to know what happened to you. You've got a brilliant service record."

"Not any more. I've lost it. Lost my nerve...everything..." He was weeping, quietly, his head in his hands.

"Dieppe saw me off," said Decker. "I lost it at Dieppe. I hid myself away and watched men die. I could have done something, but I didn't lift a finger. I didn't want to give myself away. I watched as I saw five men shot by the Germans. Somehow, I got back to the beach. We had some prisoners. Their hands were tied behind their backs. Twelve of them. I saw one of them. I couldn't take my eyes off him. You know when you think you've met someone before? But you can't place it. He looked up at me, then I knew. I thought I knew. In the end, I didn't know. He reminded me of a young German, a Hitler Youth, I met on the streets of Berlin before the war. They did some terrible things...anyway, this German soldier...it couldn't be him...but he had the same look. In Berlin, he was arrogant, cruel, but this soldier...his face was asking for pity, for mercy, much the same way his victim did...but were shown none. I told my men we weren't taking the prisoners with us, there was no room in the boat. I ordered them to be shot, laid down and shot. They were only young but..." Decker shook his head.

"Sometimes, such things are necessary in war."

"I don't know if I was doing it because we had no room or to wipe out my own guilt. I didn't feel like an officer any more, a leader. If I lost that, I lost everything. Then you came along..."

"That made it worse?"

"You were in command. You had authority. A supposed natural leader. You were taking over my command. You were a better man than I ever could be. It only reminded me of what I was, what I'd done, what I'd...become..."

"You've suffered some kind of trauma, maybe one too many…"

"Shell shock, you mean? That doesn't excuse me. They shot many a soldier in the last war for that. It's called cowardice in the face of the enemy. Look at that!" He held his hand out, the trembling hadn't stopped.

Solov took his hand and gripped it firmly.

"Major!" Miller called.

A low hum approached. It was an engine.

"Krauts?" said Miller.

Solov stood up.

"It's a plane for sure," said Solov.

They all stood up, it was most definitely a plane.

"Get ready to start the fires! Wheeler! Armstrong!" Miller called to them. Solov joined them in the run to light the bonfires. Within minutes, the plane's engines were getting nearer, but not yet in sight. First one, then two, then the third bonfire were up in flames as the silhouette of a plane was made out above the trees and began to circle the field. It disappeared over the hills, momentarily, to come around again.

"It's definitely one of ours," yelled Barrow. Armstrong, Wheeler and Solov re-joined them.

"Thank Christ for that. It's the RAF. They've sent us a Mosquito," said Armstrong.

The flames dangerously lit up the field and the plane hit the grass and skidded awkwardly, churning up the ground as its brakes were hit hard. The noise was deafening. It started to slowly turn and taxi along.

Lucille threw her arms around Solov's neck and kissed him. He swung her round and round. She looked over his shoulder at poor Decker, the officer he'd tried to support, but he was on his feet with a Sten gun in his hands. She stood back from Solov and the Russian saw her face and turned towards Decker.

The others also saw him. He'd grabbed the Major's Sten. Decker's face looked hard in the light of the fires from the field.

"I'm not going with you," said Decker, simply.

Behind Miller and the others, the plane was carefully taxiing away from the trees, one wing passing over the flames of the fire there.

Decker aimed his gun at Solov and began to back towards the woods.

"Down, Major!" Miller yelled.

Solov fell to the ground, taking Lucille with him, as Miller and Armstrong opened up and caught Decker across his legs and chest, knocking him over, backwards.

Solov ran over to where Decker was breathing his last, choking on blood.

He looked back at the plane and saw Barrow and Wheeler reach it as the hatch was flung open. Armstrong waved to Miller to come. Marcel climbed aboard.

Miller turned to Solov: "Are you coming?"

"You know I'm not," Solov said, his face red in the light of the flames. "I have less chance of survival back there than he had." He looked down at Decker's body.

Lucille came and stood by Solov, her arm around his waist and looked at the Sergeant.

"What about him?" Solov jerked a thumb at Decker's body.

"Fuck him. I don't deal with dead men," said Miller. He turned and signalled to Armstrong, still waiting at the hatch.

"What are you going to do now?" asked Miller.

"Head south to Spain, maybe head for South America, or Mexico. I might visit an old friend in Mexico City."

"One of your partisans?"

"He was something like that."

"I hope you both make it. Just goes to show, eh?" said Miller, turning towards the plane.

"What's that, Sergeant?"

Miller momentarily walked backwards to answer him. "Just like those old Western films you've seen. The hero always gets the girl in the end."

EPILOGUE

"Overall, the operation was a failure, in that, the enemy was to make political and propaganda capital from the loss of French civilians in the action at Villette - thirty-two French men, women and children were caught in the cross fire in the town square, fifteen deaths, the rest either lightly or severely wounded. The Germans laid emphasis on this in their press and on their radio broadcasts."

Colonel Lawler was making his report in a presentation to Combined Operations in London in early August, once he had all the facts to hand.

"It didn't sit very well with our French allies that so many civilians were caught up at the scene of the action. But we felt that, given the nature of the operation, little could be done to avoid some casualties. The Germans have also highlighted the use of British equipment, the remains of a British uniform found burned in a log fire at the farmhouse which our people used as a base of operations. We suspect that this was the one belonging to Major Solov, who forced his way on board the Dakota plane and went with them to France. Major Solov provided valuable training to our operations but, subsequently, we have learned that he is wanted in connection with the shootings and murders of three officials from his own embassy here in London. Our people reported back to us that Major Solov played a key role in their escape, directing a rear guard action as our men made their way to their evacuation point. However, I can only suggest the least said about this the better for our relations with the Soviets which, in part, this operation was devised to further in respect of diverting German troops from the Eastern Front in any way we could prior to our eventual return in force to the European mainland. It has been reported Major Solov died of his wounds while executing his rear guard action that enabled our men to make good their escape."

Colonel Lawler paused to take a drink of water before continuing.

"This, then, calls into question the conduct and behaviour of Captain John Decker who, according to Sergeant Miller's account, and the accounts of the other men, had to be arrested due to his unseemly conduct in the face of the enemy that further jeopardised the operation. He was escorted back to the pick-up point and placed under armed guard. He managed to gain possession of a weapon and attempted to escape. At which point, he was fatally wounded, his body abandoned in the field."

Lawler paused for another drink and shuffled the papers of his report.

"On a personal note, I find this incident quite depressing that a British officer of formerly excellent standing should fall in this manner. The impact of the ambush in Villette town square did not, to our knowledge, fulfil its requirements, that is, to invoke the Nazis to take reprisals thus acting as a spur to recruiting activists for a partisan war. The Nazis played this aspect very cannily, in contrast to what they did in Lidice, in Czechoslovakia, in 1942. They played up, as I've already said, the deaths of civilians, the aforementioned British equipment and uniform, and made a few arrests of suspects - one of them Andre Lacloche, known to us as a valuable contact in this, and previous, operations. At present, we believe he is in the so-called 'protective custody' of the Gestapo. Whether or not more drastic reprisals will be taken is anybody's guess. The French population reportedly see this as a bloodthirsty, terrorist action, of no military value. We have made nothing of this, as strong denials may make us look defensive. The only positive aspect was, of course, the deaths of around one hundred and seventy-five Waffen SS personnel. In that respect alone, the operation was a success..."

~ ~ ~

August 22, 1943. Mexico City. A hot, balmy day. A taxi pulled up to a cemetery gate. A man in a white cotton suit, wearing a panama hat, got out and walked along the long lines of white tombstones. He turned left at the bottom and, after some searching, he found the grave he wanted to see. A tall, white marble gravestone standing proud. He saw all the flowers, rosaries and beads, the red banners, the candles and the cards. These had been laid yesterday, on the anniversary of the death.

He placed a wreath amongst the others. On it was pinned a small card: 'A True Marxist Revolutionary'. He stepped back and looked up at the gravestone and read the name - 'Leon Trotsky'. Beneath it, the hammer and sickle was carved.

He stood there for only a few moments. The taxi was waiting.

THE END